Well Tended

Well Tended

a novel

By

Teddy Jones

NEW YORK, NEW YORK

Published by MidTown Publishing Inc.
1001 Avenue of Americas
12th Floor
New York, NY 10018

Library of Congress Control Number: 2014946157

ISBN 978-1-62677-010-2
ISBN 978-1-62677-011-9 (e-book)

In memory of Bill Overbey

Praise for *Well Tended*

In *Well Tended*, Teddy Jones gives us a love story with grit—an unsentimental, compassionate portrait of a nurse and rodeo cowboy as they struggle to tend, with humor and hard-won empathy, to each other in an unforgiving West Texas landscape. A moving novel that makes you care about both its place and its people.

—K. L. Cook, author of *Love Songs for the Quarantined, Last Call,* and *The Girl from Charnelle*

With grit and compassion, Teddy Jones's novel, *Well Tended*, tells not one love story, but several. It is the story of romantic love and familial love, yes—but it is also a love-song to the Western landscape and to a lifestyle that may be fading from American culture. The characters in *Well Tended* are sharp and real, seemingly chiseled out of the sandstone and rock of the place where they live. Teddy Jones may be one of the last true Western writers out there. She is certainly one of the best in the Western tradition.

—BK Loren, author of *Theft*: A Novel

Acknowledgments

Thanks and lasting gratitude to all whose criticism and support helped make *Well Tended* the story it is.

Generally, to family, friends, and strangers who keep me laughing and surprise me with kindnesses, thank you for all you do that keeps me hopeful and eager to write.

Specifically, thanks to John Dufresne, teacher and mentor, and the members of his 2013 Master Class at the Taos Summer Writers' Conference, Michael Hardesty, Peter Stravlo, Maureen Mullins, Ana Kolendo, and T.C. Porter. I also offer continuing gratitude to Martha Burns and Candace Simar, the two other members of our "gang of three." Their candid critiques and valuable suggestions prompted improvement with each successive revision of the manuscript.

Michael Zealy of MidTown Publishing has my gratitude for all he has done to make *Well Tended* a piece of work I am proud to offer to readers. And for reading the final work and lending it the weight of their public praise, I thank B.K. Loren, K. L. Cook, and John Dufresne. Coming from those three writers whose work I admire and who are excellent teachers, as well, those comments encourage me to continue."

Particularly, for reading the bits and pieces and for remembering things I don't and for all other support, thank you to my brother, Val Overbey.

And first, last, and always, I thank my husband, Jim Bob Jones. He knows why.

Teddy Jones
2014

Well Tended

a novel

By

Teddy Jones

Part I
1994

CHAPTER 1

January 15, 1994—Cheryl Magee
Price of Admission

All the way from Iris to Wichita Falls, close to seventy miles, Cheryl's mother didn't say a word to her. Drove with both hands on the steering wheel and eyes on the road, as if she were alone. And she didn't even have the radio playing that religious station on preset number one.

She did make one sound, somewhere between Electra and Iowa Park; she cleared her throat. The Lincoln, longer than any pickup on their farm and wide enough to double as a hearse, contained the sound, bounced it off the leather interior surfaces. Cheryl stiffened, stifled a sigh. Captive inside her mother's favorite possession, she knew that sound. Any minute now, her mother would launch into the entire speech again. And the punch line would be the same as it had been every time: confess your sins, repent, ask forgiveness, and you will still have a chance to go to heaven—don't, and you burn in hell. The price you pay. The throat clearing meant she'd finished her mental rehearsal.

Cheryl hid the smile she couldn't contain when just past the Wichita Falls city limit sign, before they passed the Sheppard Air Force Base exit, her mother said, "Cheryl LeeAnn, if just once you had paid attention to what I tried to teach you, you wouldn't be in this fix now—a sinner in the eyes of God and the world. Good parents and a good home, and yet you chose to behave like trash. Stopped attending services. And still the Lord will take you back if only you will confess…"

At that point, Cheryl quit pretending to pay attention. She'd heard it from her mother, every possible variation on the theme, since the day she'd finally told her she was pregnant. She watched Wichita Falls slide by, doing its best to pretend to be a big city.

The sound of her mother's voice changed, pitch higher, volume louder. Fence posts sped by at an accelerated rate. But even when not listening to the words, Cheryl knew to stay alert now, keep her peripheral vision open; her mother could surprise her, come up with a new play. Cheryl often thought of her as the point guard on an opposing team. Basketball, Cheryl understood, and breaking situations down the way Coach taught her to study plays made life seem orderly. Even if she knew it never would be.

"I'm giving you one last chance," her mother said.

Here it comes, she's going to try to throw a pass the full length of the court, catch me snoozing, Cheryl thought. "Tell me who got you pregnant. Your daddy will see to it he does the right thing."

Cheryl sat up straight, surprised herself as she did it. "Could be a lot of people. Forget it." No matter what, she'd never let her mother blame the one person who understood her.

Her only friends were other athletes, and most of them were boys. Ever since she'd been on the high school team, and other girls started dating, she didn't, she just hung out with the guys and a couple of other girls, a gang of pals. Mostly they shot baskets on the outdoor court at school, rode around on the county roads, talked, drank some beer, nothing dangerous.

On a Saturday night at the end of the summer, to celebrate the end of two-a-day football practice, one of the guys had brought a couple of bottles of tequila and the whole bunch of them met at the Mule Creek Bridge. They tuned the radios in all six pickups to KOMA and turned the volume up high. A cheer went up like someone had hit a three-pointer when the DJ said, "It's Saturday night and this is Coma-in-Oklahoma, 1520 on your dial. Let's party!" The bottles changed hands several times and by ten o'clock the other two girls had left, saying they had church early. No one at her house ever checked any more to see when she came in, so Cheryl stayed at the party, learning the taste of tequila.

Around eleven, the guys decided to go over to Frederick. One of the seniors yelled, "For twenty dollars apiece, we can all get a piece, I guarantee." She heard them all laughing and whooping while she was busy down the creek bank vomiting after her fifth straight shot. Getting home might be a problem.

"They're leaving. You need a ride?" It was Mark Thompson, the one she stared at when he wasn't watching. Sitting with her head in her hands, seeing the moon's reflection on the murky water, she hadn't heard him until he stood beside her. He tossed a stick at a frog on the opposite bank.

"Can't go home yet. You not going to Oklahoma?"

"No." He didn't explain. "Come on. We'll ride around, get a Coke." He took her hand and helped her up the bank.

After that night, he took her home several times. He never forced her; exactly the opposite. Even without the tequila that had made wrapping her arms around him that night at the top of the creek bank, kissing him open-mouthed and deep until she could feel his erection, and undressing herself in the moonlight seemed like the next correct thing to do, she led the way. If she tried to explain it, the only answer would be that she didn't care about consequences back then at the end of the summer.

Giving herself away to the experience felt free, and that was the only thing that mattered. And she never kidded herself about love having anything to do with the ache she felt each time he touched her. From that first time, she'd known without being able to explain it to herself, she had to learn about sex, and experience was her best teacher.

A month ago, she'd told him they were through—would still be friends—no harm, no foul. She thought he looked a little hurt, but relieved at the same time. He'd never know.

Her mother clicked the turn signal, moved into the passing lane. "There are tests. We could find out."

"You want a married high school dropout daughter and a grandchild?" Cheryl could just see herself dressed for a wedding, a tasteful beige suit—her mother would see to that, the ceremony in Vernon or somewhere at a neutral location, a J.P. officiating, her dad giving her away, carrying a shotgun. No, it would be her mother toting the weapon. "Do you, Cheryl LeeAnn Magee, take this poor sucker for your lawfully wedded husband?" She wanted to laugh, but didn't, not after she realized her mother was staring at her, not watching the road.

"I want you to be twelve again." Her mother sniffled; next she'd start sobbing. This is it, Cheryl thought, the long pass.

"I can hardly bear the thought of it, but if you don't confess your sins and repent, we will have no choice but to turn away from you."

"It's your choice. I'm not standing up in front that whole congregation and confessing, no matter what you do."

"You'll burn in hell!" Gravel sprayed as her mother drove off the road near Henrietta, slammed the brakes, and halted on the shoulder.

"I won't be alone there." She never talked to her mother this way, and certainly never raised her voice. She hardly talked to her at all.

"This is the last help you'll ever have from us."

"Daddy wouldn't do that."

"You'll never live in Iris again. I'll see to it."

"Who in their right mind wants to live there?" Her voice never gave her away. The thought of not being on the team next year almost made her want to make that trip to the front of her mother's church, blubber around in front of all those self-righteous people, ask forgiveness. Almost.

Her mother's sobbing didn't last long. She blew her nose and dabbed at her eyes without disturbing her mascara. Chin up, mouth set in a tight, thin line, her profile said she'd made up her mind that someone else would have to save her wayward daughter. Cheryl watched as her mother reapplied lipstick, and when she finished, twitched her nose as if smelling something vile, sulfur maybe. Her mother slammed the car into drive and sped back onto 287, headed for Ft. Worth and the Anson Gleason Home.

Cheryl gave a silent prayer of thanks to whoever was in charge—surely not that hateful God her mother knew—that her mother stopped talking and got on with the business of disposing of her.

She'd broken the news to her daddy December seventeenth, after the last game of the season, standing on the back porch at their house. She'd expected him to be disappointed, but his face, his shoulders' sudden sag, the slow shake of his head almost made her cry. She didn't. She'd already cried herself out three months before when the drugstore test she'd bought secretly on a team trip to Iowa Park confirmed what she'd guessed. Then sobbing again, her head covered by the blue plaid comforter on her bed, when she realized she couldn't make herself go to that abortion clinic in Lubbock. And a final time, after that night Coach told her dad, with her listening, that she'd be a cinch for All-district, maybe All-state next year if she kept playing like she did. He said she played tougher than any boy he'd ever coached.

Maybe if she had cried and begged him like her sisters would have, the way Mother always did to get her way, it would have turned out different. If he'd been the one who told Mother, maybe he could have made her understand that making Cheryl haul herself down to the front of the church while the congregation sang "Sinner Come Home" wouldn't solve anything. Maybe she'd already be in Ft. Worth, waiting out her sentence, instead of being locked in this tank of a car, sniffing the fumes of hell. She'd have been happy to ride the bus. Alone.

She watched in the side mirror as the road fell away behind the Lincoln. She considered a solution. Open the door, push off with her left foot, and end up next to one of the several piles of beer cans and plastic bags dotting the ditch. With her luck she'd only end up unconscious and still pregnant, not dead.

Daddy had said, "I can't tell her. It's up to you. But you should wait a little bit. No need to spoil her Christmas."

"If you say so."

He put his arm around her, hardly touching, really. "Your mother's had a hard life. Things you wouldn't understand. I hate to see it get harder."

She felt like she'd been apologizing since she was big enough to talk, for things that happened before she was born, for her mother's hard life. And sixteen years later, she still hadn't gotten the whole story about the baby boy who died and the miscarriages her mother had trying for another male child. But she had pieced together enough from her parents' anniversary date and the birth date on the baby boy's little headstone to know she wasn't the first in the family to miscalculate.

Staring straight ahead, she stepped away from him. "I didn't ask to be born." She kicked her ten year-old sister's pink bicycle. It fell sideways onto the sidewalk. "Sorry I'm not a boy."

"You know that's not what I mean." He patted his right leg to get their dog's attention. The big chow ran to him, positioned himself directly under his hand. "I can't tell her," he said. "You'll have to." He squatted and rubbed the dog's ears with both hands. "Don't let on you told me first."

She cried again that night, promised herself it would be the last time. Like Coach said, play through the pain. All-purpose advice, he'd said. She'd thought then, still did—what a crock of shit.

Her mother had refused to believe her. "Your periods have never been regular. All that running you do. I'm taking you to the clinic."

"Why would I tell you if there was a chance I was wrong?"

"You haven't had any morning sickness. I would have known."

She was right about the morning sickness. Cheryl felt great. The only difference she noticed was that her breasts felt tender and she peed more often. "I'm pregnant. The only reason I told is you'd know before long, from looking."

"You go get in the car this minute. We're going to Altus to the clinic." Cheryl hadn't moved. "I mean it. You have no idea what you're doing. If you are pregnant, we need to know how far along."

Altus. Just like her mother to think of that. Everyone from Iris went to the clinic in Vernon. But if they crossed the river to Oklahoma, no one from Iris would see them there. Apparently, in her mother's books, lying was a sin, but covering up wasn't.

After the doctor confirmed what Cheryl already knew and said her due date was June thirteen, her mother drove directly home, pushing the Lincoln's big engine to pass any vehicle in their path. Cheryl gripped the armrest and relaxed only after the car came to a stop in front of their house.

That same week, Cheryl had cut out the little ad in the personals section of the Wichita Falls paper, a tasteful item offering confidential information for the Anson Gleason Home. The woman who answered the 800 number asked her age and said she would need a parent to sign, unless she was an emancipated minor. Cheryl almost laughed. She wanted to say, "No one who lives in this house is free." But before she hung up, she got the important facts. Services provided without charge, including medical care, if you agreed to have the baby adopted. And she could live in Ft. Worth at the home.

   She put the ad on the kitchen table at her mother's place, went outside and shot free throws at the hoop on the garage for nearly two hours. Her official free throw average was 82%. That day she hit 68 of 100.

The sight of Decatur's old courthouse changed her mood. That meant they'd be in Ft. Worth soon. Some social worker would show her to her room, or maybe she'd only get a bed in a room full of other pregnant girls, or maybe it would be like a cell. Didn't matter. She could commit the rules to memory, learn all the plays, and live through the months alone until the birth.

   Cheryl closed her eyes. The parade of images of pregnant girls, babies, and rows of cells that flooded her mind made her open them again. She didn't dare get her book from her backpack; her mother would start in on her again. A person being taken away in disgrace should sit in misery, not spend their time reading *The Client*. She reached under her sweater and opened the top button on her jeans, took a deep breath. Her stomach growled. She knew it was imagination, but she tasted a hamburger with dill pickles and lots of mayonnaise. If she had that burger, she'd also need a chocolate milk shake, maybe some french fries.

"Are we going to eat?"

"I haven't been able to eat for two days." Her mother's voice sounded to Cheryl like some character on a soap opera. Strained, dramatic, high pitched. Her eyes never left the road ahead.

Cheryl said, "I'm hungry. And I need to use the bathroom." She pointed to the right. "There's a Dairy Queen."

No wonder her daddy catered to her mother—that sigh she let out sounded as if a huge weight bore on her chest at the very thought of eating, or stopping at the Dairy Queen. Cheryl ignored the sound and focused on the taste of a hamburger.

"You're supposed to check in by one-thirty." Her mother looked again at her watch, sighed again, and took the exit. She parked at the back of the Dairy Queen's lot. "You go use the restroom, and I'll get the food."

Checking in for admission at the Anson Gleason Home required nothing more of her mother than signing permission for Cheryl to be there. Then Cheryl signed a paper stating she accepted the assistance of the home based on her intention to place her newborn for adoption through their services. Procedure stated she would sign the papers to relinquish the baby within forty-eight hours after the birth.

The social worker showed her to a room holding two of everything—twin beds, small chests, closets, built-in desks, and chairs. But she had it all to herself because the last occupant had left the day before.

Her mother hesitated at the doorway, didn't enter. Cheryl

watched her face. It could have been molded from pale, hard plastic. She turned, chose the bed nearest the window, refrained from making a face at the flowery, ruffled bedspread, and unpacked her Duffel bag. The next time she looked toward the doorway, her mother had gone.

Once she folded the bedspread and put it on the closet shelf, the bed looked inviting. When you're alone and free to do as you please and don't have to keep any secrets, it's hard to know what you want to do—that was her thought, and then she went to sleep.

She didn't know what woke her, at first. But it happened again and she knew. A gentle tapping moved from the right side of her lower abdomen to the left, inside, a steady rhythm, an unseen drummer. When she'd read the "What to Expect When You're Pregnant" pamphlet she'd grabbed in Altus, she'd wondered if she would even know. She did. She wouldn't ever be home again, but she wasn't alone.

CHAPTER 2

January 15—June 15, 1994—Cheryl Magee
Separation

Later, that first afternoon, a knock on the door woke Cheryl. A woman, who said she was a case worker aide, apologized from the doorway, told Cheryl the other woman had brought her to the wrong place. She was supposed to be in a different room because two other new girls, arriving tomorrow, were assigned to this one. Cheryl rolled over, stood up, and trudged like a sleepwalker around the room, stuffing her things into the Duffel. She didn't ask any questions, just did as she was told.

Four doors down the hall, the aide tapped on the door and, as they waited for it to open, apologized to Cheryl again. She said, "I called from downstairs. She knows you're coming." With that, she left Cheryl standing outside the door, bag in hand, like someone waiting for a bus.

As soon as her roommate opened the door, Cheryl could see they were nothing alike. The girl offered a handshake and spilled out her name and hometown—Karla Rene Holder from Luling, Texas—as soon as Cheryl walked in. She spoke in a barely audible voice, gestured with her delicate hands, punctuated her sentences with rolls of surprised-looking brown eyes, and told Cheryl how glad she was to finally have a roommate after being at Anson Gleason two months. Cheryl mumbled a question about which dresser she should use and avoided staring at Karla's color coordinated maternity top and slacks. That delicate girl probably spent all her time curling her hair or experimenting with new eye shadow.

Cheryl stuffed her three pairs of sweatpants; a pair of shorts; one extra pair of Levi's; five Texas Tech Lady Raiders T-shirts, size XL; and two knit tops, one red, one black, into one of the drawers—her entire maternity wardrobe. So far she could still wear her 501s if she left the top two buttons open. Last week, just after she finished making arrangements for this place, her mother offered to take her to Wichita Falls to the maternity shop at the mall. Cheryl tried to sound polite when she said, "No thanks," but something in her attitude started her mother on another crying fit. Cheryl knew she should have tried harder to get along; soon nothing she had would fit, not even the sweats. Since she'd told her parents, it seemed like all she wanted to do was eat.

She turned her back to her cheerful roommate and cleared the socks, underwear and pajamas out of the bottom of her Duffel bag. She pointed at one of the closet doors and raised her eyebrows. Karla got it; she nodded. So Cheryl stowed her loafers and her second pair of Nikes on the floor of that tiny space and shoved her bag to the corner of the shelf above the clothes rod. Meanwhile, Karla retreated to her bed and picked up *People* magazine. After that little opening flurry of chatter, she didn't say anything else. Cheryl curled up on the empty bed, facing the window, and took deep breaths, three in a row, the way she always did before shooting a free throw. She let out the third and felt her back muscles loosen. She reminded herself, again, that she could and would make it through this. She turned to her other side, made herself smile at Karla and asked, "What time is supper?"

That first night they discovered that in all the important ways they were alike—each certain she had been born to the wrong family, wishing for a way out of her small town, impatient with rules, excelling easily in all she tried, sure she'd never get married, and fully aware she had made a huge mistake.

The social worker, her advocate, she called herself, found Cheryl at breakfast the next morning. She invited Cheryl to her office "as soon as it's convenient," which Cheryl understood meant as soon as she ate and helped clear away the dishes. She took several minutes to pace what seemed like a mile from the dining hall to the administrative offices, stopping every few feet to stare at pictures of gray-haired women and men. ENDOWING DONORS, a large brass-lettered sign declared over one cluster. SUSTAINING CONTRIBUTORS read another. She lingered in front of the portrait of a woman who could have been her mother's twin sister, if she'd had one. A large plaque told a little of the home's history—situated near downtown Ft. Worth, not far from the city's historic stockyards, Anson Gleason had provided a caring environment for more than seventy years—and so on. Cheryl wondered how many disgraced girls had left their homes in all those years, and what became of them afterward. Had they put on brave faces and gone back to their hometowns? Or had they managed to disappear? She looked away, as if she'd heard her name called, and hurried the rest of the way to Mrs. Carlson's office.

The social worker pointed to a chair. Cheryl took that as an invitation to sit. A small desk separated her from the woman who tidied a batch of papers, and inserted them into a manila folder. Cheryl focused on the clock on the wall above her advocate's left shoulder, watched 9:02 become 9:04 before the woman finally spoke. "I hope your first night with your roommate went well. We try to place our girls where they will be comfortable and compatible."

Cheryl nodded. She didn't mention they'd stayed up until four o'clock or that Karla already knew more about her than anyone else in the world.

Again, the woman said nothing for a long time. Cheryl tried to remember her name and found it engraved on a wooden block on the desk—Mrs. Carlson, M.S.W. She studied the photograph on the cabinet behind Mrs. Carlson's desk—her advocate with a man as pale and blond as she was, and two small dark-featured boys—and wondered if they were adopted. "If you want a change of roommate, this is the time to say so."

Cheryl straightened in the chair. "I like Karla. No need to change."

"Fine." She smiled. It changed her face, made her look young enough to have those two boys. Maybe she hadn't adopted them after all. "Today your job is getting to know people and the routine here. My job is to help you do that. So we'll take a tour."

Cheryl hurried to keep up with the social worker who moved faster than her matronly shape suggested she could. In less than an hour they had covered every space on the building's two floors. She met several of the other girls, most of them about her age—Mrs. Carlson told her there were twenty-four at the moment—the nurse, the counselor, and the chaplain.

She steered Cheryl first to the chapel and then to the fitness room, a large space with a two treadmills and two semi-recumbent exercise bicycles plus about seventy-five pounds of small free weights piled in a corner. The recreation room contained a television set, a boom box, two Ping-Pong tables, and several game tables. A jumble of jigsaw puzzle pieces covered one of them.

Next door, she ushered Cheryl into the study hall, a large room that housed several small desks and a library of textbooks. Mrs. Carlson nodded toward a woman sitting with a girl at a larger desk in the corner. "The tutor helps here from nine to five each day. I put a meeting with her on your schedule. You'll be able to keep up with your schoolwork by correspondence so you'll be ready for classes when you go home." She handed Cheryl a typed sheet—her schedule.

Cheryl held her breath. Mrs. Carlson didn't need to know she wasn't going back. She looked at the sheet. There were two headings: Day 1 and Weekly. Looked like they had planned the rest of Day 1 for her.

"That's the tour. I'm the person to find anytime you have a problem or a question. Do you have any now?"

Cheryl shook her head.

"I'll leave you on your own, then. But I'm here for you anytime you need help. And we'll have a brief meeting each week." She pointed to the schedule. "You're on for Wednesday mornings at ten-thirty. Please be on time." She started for the study hall door, then stopped and turned around. "I forgot. Basketball. Your mother said that's important to you. Follow me."

Cheryl frowned and followed her. What else had her mother told them?

She led Cheryl out a door to a half-court sized concrete pad with a regulation ten foot height goal at one end. The rest of the space surrounded by a tall hedge included a walking track encircling a lawn and a flower garden, bare except for four leafless rose bushes.

Cheryl stood under the goal, facing away from it, and then paced forward the fifteen feet to an imaginary free throw line. She turned, felt Mrs. Carlson watching. "Where do they keep the balls?"

"Closet in the fitness room." The social worker walked to Cheryl's side, joined her facing the goal. "You're free to use this anytime."

Cheryl woke five nights later to find Karla sitting beside her stroking her hair. "What?" she asked. But Cheryl knew. She had cried herself to sleep, silently, more than once. No one had caught her at it before.

"You were crying and talking." Karla kissed her cheek. "I did that every night for a month after I got here."

"I'm sorry." She wiped tears on a corner of the sheet. "I woke you."

"Don't be sorry. I'm glad you're here. So neither one of us has to be alone." She took the rubber band off one of Cheryl's braids, then nudged her to move aside. Karla sat against the headboard of the twin bed and placed a pillow across her own swollen abdomen. "Lean back against me." She freed the other braid and moved her small hands in gentle strokes from the crown of Cheryl's head through her hair. "I'll help you relax."

Strong kneading motions of Karla's fingers found and erased knots across Cheryl's shoulders that she hadn't known were there. She inhaled, closed her eyes, felt her mother's hands soothing her when she had the flu, a long time ago. The next morning, when she woke, she felt Karla lying behind her, belly against her back and right arm across her hip. From then on, one of them would slip into the other's bed after lights out every night, and they slept, all four of them, crowded into a single bed.

Cheryl spent time with the other girls only because Karla prodded her to leave her Walkman and the Eagles behind and join the giggling group in the recreation room after supper. But after a few minutes of the talk about hairdos and weight gain, she would manage a vague smile and pretend she needed to pee. To make her story believable, she would stop in the nearest bathroom on her way to the exercise equipment.

As her twenty-fourth week of pregnancy approached, she

abandoned trying to wear her Levi's. When not even the lowest button would close, she promised herself she would only gain twenty pounds before the birth. In place of filling her perpetually hungry stomach with popcorn, cookies and apples like most of the girls watching television each evening, she paced miles on a treadmill. When February became March, she slipped outside each afternoon after study hall and practiced free throws—she quit jumping for layups the day she felt a tiny stream of urine dribble onto the top of her right leg—for an hour or more.

Back in their room, she and Karla spent hours talking. They agreed the home treated them well, furnished everything pregnant girls needed, as far as they knew. And one night Karla said in her soft voice that no matter how nice it was, the place seemed like anything but home.

Cheryl said, "I wonder if any of the girls here now are daughters of girls who were here maybe sixteen years ago."

"That would be really odd," Karla said, sounding as if she were far away.

"If they were, they wouldn't know, unless the birth mother signed permission."

"Did you sign?" Karla sounded nearer now.

"No way. Can you imagine being thirty-one or something, having an important job and maybe a family, and out of the blue one day, some gangly fifteen-year-old boy turns up claiming to be your son? And worse, maybe he looks too familiar to deny?" She felt chilled thinking about the situation she'd described. "No way."

"I'm not certain. I mean, maybe if I was adopted I might want to know about my real mother, maybe see her someday."

Cheryl sat up to look at Karla, to see if she was joking. Lying on her back, still as a curly-haired statue, her roommate stared up at the ceiling fan. Maybe she'd been hypnotized by the slow rotation of the blades—surely she wasn't serious.

April Fools' Day gave several of the girls an excuse to play jokes on one another. As far as Cheryl was concerned, being at Anson Gleason qualified as one long bad joke, no matter what the month. She did her best to maintain a smile, sure it looked like a mask, as her tablemates cut up all through breakfast. She excused herself before the others finished eating and paced down the hall to wait at the door to the nurse's clinic to weigh. No matter what she did, how little she ate, at each of her required weekly weigh-ins, she had gained another pound.

Mrs. Turner, the nurse, looked up as Cheryl stepped on the scale in the alcove outside her office. "Concerned about your weight?"

Of all the people at AG, she liked Mrs. Turner best. She never wasted her breath preaching dos and don'ts, just listened if you wanted to talk, or if you asked for it, gave information. Cheryl stopped by more often than the once a week required for weight check. The nurse, who was old enough to be her mother but talked to Cheryl as if she were an adult, explained, in clear terms, all the concerns about normal changes of pregnancy—the stuffy nose, the itchy stretch marks, tender breasts, constipation.

Mrs. Turner wasn't like the counselor or her "advocate," who'd been after her for weeks about spending too much time working on her courses and not enough in "recreation." Cheryl didn't bother explaining to Mrs. Carlson that she intended to complete all her sophomore year courses and at least three of the junior year requirements before her due date. Karla did as much schoolwork as she did and the woman never badgered her, probably because Karla spent so much time pretending to be cheerful whenever any of the staff were in sight. Sometimes Cheryl didn't bother.

Cheryl said, "A little. I've been watching what I eat, but I still gain. Nearly thirty weeks and already twenty-eight pounds."

Mrs. Turner stood beside her as Cheryl moved the weights on the beam. "It's a good idea to focus on eating a healthy diet and less on the numbers. Never weigh more than once a week." Her hand on Cheryl's shoulder radiated warmth, made her want to close her eyes and lean on the nurse.

A genuine smile came to Cheryl without any effort at all. She said, "Thanks." Her next stop was the always-full fruit bowl in the recreation room. An apple in her hand, she stepped out the side door to the track to fast-walk twenty circuits that would make her first mile of the day. She usually did four; from now on, she intended to do five.

Karla's due date came and went on May fourteenth. Then the morning of the fifteenth, Cheryl woke when Karla said, her voice calm and low, "My water just broke. My back aches."

Cheryl sat up, and fought the sheet to get out of her side of the bed. She pulled back the rest of the cover. "I don't see blood, just wet." She stared at the large damp spot, imagined it becoming a wave. "Are you afraid?"

"A little. But I'm ready for this to be over." Karla grabbed Cheryl's hand. "It's starting." She frowned and squeezed her eyes shut. Cheryl counted silently to forty-five before Karla took a breath and said, "That was the first one."

"We're supposed to time them," Cheryl said. She jerked open her bedside drawer, pushed aside Kleenex, opened her eyes wide when camphor vapor from an open jar of Carmex hit her nose, and finally found her watch. "Shouldn't we call downstairs?"

"Not yet. I'll get dressed." Karla's short trip to the bathroom reminded Cheryl of someone walking on ice. She watched as Karla brushed her teeth and applied mascara and lipstick, then gripped the doorjamb through another contraction.

How could she seem so calm? Cheryl said, "You're supposed to focus on your breathing and try to relax when the pains come. Like we practiced in class."

Karla smiled, tight, thin-lipped, briefly. "It was easier when it didn't hurt." She sat on the foot of the bed, hands open in her lap, back straight, alert, like a child waits for a surprise.

Cheryl didn't sit. She paced and hovered near her friend, timing the length of the contractions and the spaces between. In the next twenty minutes, three times, Karla stopped whatever she was saying and reached for Cheryl's hand. Together they breathed and pretended they knew what they were doing, that they were in charge.

The third contraction, which followed the second by eight minutes, gripped Karla for fifty-five seconds, according to Cheryl's watch. As soon as it passed, Karla got up and walked to the dresser, moving as if she were in foreign territory. She lifted sweats and a shirt from the drawer. Cheryl wondered why her friend's movements looked like a slow motion video playback, jerky and uncoordinated. Karla dropped the shirt and folded forward, wrapping her arms around her abdomen. She groaned, the loudest sound Cheryl had ever heard her make.

She guided Karla back to the bed. "The last one came only six minutes ago. Isn't it supposed to start slow? I'm calling downstairs." Cheryl couldn't keep her hands from shaking as she dialed.

The AG staff had done this all before. Like a well-practiced team, Mrs. Turner, Mrs. Carlson, two aides, and a van driver deposited Karla and Cheryl at the hospital emergency entrance in less than fifteen minutes—three more hard contractions. From there, hospital transport took over. Cheryl rushed to keep up with Karla's wheelchair driver on the way to Labor and Delivery two floors above. Another contraction interrupted the transfer to the labor bed. Karla never made a sound after leaving Gleason, but she gripped Cheryl's fingers until they hurt.

Then everything came to a halt. Contractions stopped. Karla asked, "What's wrong? Why did they stop?"

Cheryl shrugged. She wouldn't guess because the only possibility she could think of involved a dead baby. Mrs. Turner and Mrs. Carlson came to the door, and a hospital nurse followed. The nurse said, "I have to do an admission assessment, so I'll need everyone to wait outside a few minutes."

Mrs. Turner explained, when Cheryl told her about the sudden lack of contractions, that first labors sometimes progressed erratically. "As soon as the nurse checks her, if everything's okay, I'll go back to Anson Gleason and Mrs. Carlson will stay here, in the waiting room. You're coaching, right?"

"Yes. I promised."

"You'll do fine and so will she. If you need Mrs. Carlson, she'll be here." It didn't matter what she said, it was the hug she surrounded Cheryl with that made her feel hopeful and a little calmer.

The labor and delivery nurse beckoned from the door to Karla's room. "She's fine. Having another contraction. She needs her coach." She pointed to Cheryl. "That's you, right?"

Having a job to do made the waiting easier. But when she wasn't reminding Karla to pant and breathe, or rubbing her back between contractions, Cheryl imagined herself in the same position. Her own due date was in less than a month away. Some nurse would coach her. But it would be different. Instead of calmly laboring, working to finish the delivery, she saw herself screaming with every contraction and fighting against any advice to pant.

The other thing she thought about in Karla's brief intervals of rest was that as soon as Karla's baby was handed to the new parents, the best friend she'd ever had would go back to the small town she had briefly escaped. The two of them had promised to write and later to go the same college, be roommates. They hadn't decided which college. But even when they swore it would all work out, Cheryl knew they were pretending. Karla never said it, but the look on her face after her parents visited a month ago told the story. She'd be back in Luling as soon as the baby came. Cheryl knew she'd have to do the rest all alone.

The baby girl arrived after a seventeen-hour labor. Karla came back from the hospital two days later. Mrs. Carlson brought Karla's bag, and when she left their room, Cheryl hugged her friend carefully. Karla gave Cheryl a weak smile. She hadn't bothered with makeup that morning, and dark circles emphasized her eyes, huge and brown like a frightened fawn. That smile gave way to silent tears, which turned to loud sobs. Cheryl gathered her close again, stroked her hair. She knew she would need to remember all of this. She asked, "Is there something I can do? You look like everything hurts."

With her shirt sleeve, Karla wiped the tears and snot from her face and drew a ragged breath. "No, just let me get it over with." Then she fell over and buried her face in a pillow. Cheryl sat beside her and wished she knew what to do.

They had promised each other they wouldn't say goodbye; they were friends forever no matter how long they had to be apart. So the next morning, Cheryl stayed downstairs, went to the study hall after breakfast, and didn't come back to their room until after lunch. The only thing left of Karla was a red, loose-woven cotton scarf, the one she'd shown Cheryl how to drape around the neckline of her black knit top, saying it flattered her, telling her she could borrow it anytime. Cheryl folded it into a triangle, held it to her face. It smelled like Karla's soap and shampoo—lavender, clean and fresh.

Cheryl's dad had called her each week the whole time she was there and sent her a money order for $75.00 at the end of each month. She wondered how he settled on the amount. He would help her, wherever she wanted to go, she knew. Even though she wrote her mother because Karla convinced her that parents wanted what's best for their children—she never heard from her. After that, she knew she could never go home. Her dad said it would take time, just be patient.

The day after Karla left, Cheryl already knew what she'd do. It came to her in the night, a solution. Aunt Jean, Daddy's older sister, lived outside of Borger on a ranch with her husband. Their only son, already grown, lived in Dalhart. If Aunt Jean and Uncle Skip would let her, she'd live with them and get the rest of high school behind her as quickly as possible. That would give her time to figure out what to do about college.

She didn't wait for her dad's next weekly call. After breakfast, after rehearsing what she'd say, she went back to her room and called home, collect. Her mother answered and told the operator she wouldn't accept charges. Cheryl slammed the receiver down. "Hypocrite."

She tried taking deep breaths to settle the baby's kicking. She couldn't help uttering, "Hateful bitch," when she exhaled. On her way out of the room, she slammed the door hard, then stopped absolutely still. The baby moved so violently, nausea lurched upward. She leaned against the wall, rubbing her abdomen gently, whispering, "I'm so sorry. Please don't be upset. I promise to be calm." When the movement subsided, she returned to her room and lowered herself carefully to the bed.

Late that afternoon her dad called. "I'm sorry I wasn't here to answer when you called."

"I won't keep you long. I know what I want to do when I leave here. Go to Aunt Jean's. Will you talk to her?"

She wondered if he'd heard her. It seemed like a long time before he said anything. "That might be a good idea. At least for a while." He spoke softly, like an old man without enough wind. "She knows about the baby and all. I told her. She knows how to keep her mouth shut."

"I can finish school there."

"Count on me taking care of it. I'll call back tomorrow."

"How are the girls?"

"Fine. They ask me about you."

"Tell them I said hi."

"Okay. I'll call tomorrow. Honey, I love you. In case you don't know it." Then he kind of laughed like he'd made a joke.

He hadn't told her he loved her in a long time. She hung up and cried a while, wishing she could stand next to him on the back porch again, smell that mix of sweat and tobacco and tractor grease that hung on his clothes when he worked. Then she went downstairs to watch television—her celebration, a reward to herself—all her correspondence courses were finished—four As. Now all she had to do was deliver the big baby boy the doctor said she was carrying and sign him over to the people waiting to give him a home. Nearly finished.

Daddy always kept his promises. He called after breakfast the next day. Like he might be in a hurry, he said, "Jean understands. I knew she would. Judging people isn't her way."

She heard herself sounding like a five-year-old when she

said, "Thank you, Daddy." But she didn't feel too grown up, having to ask for help and not knowing who else she could count on. "Tell her I'll be there soon as it's over with." She stopped and wiped her eyes on the back of her hand, sniffed a little. "Tell her I won't be any trouble."

"You're no trouble." She heard him breathe in and sigh. Then he said, "When you get out of the hospital, you call me. I'll come and take you to Jean's."

"I have the money you sent. I'll ride the bus." She closed her eyes and saw herself, sad and pale, dragging her Duffel bag, loading it onto the bus. "I'll let you know when I get there."

It was as if she could hear him thinking in the silence, maybe relieved he wouldn't have to tell her mother before it was a fact. "If that's what you want to do."

"It's the easiest way."

"You feel okay?"

"Now I do." A mockingbird trilled from his perch on a tree outside her window. "The social worker showed me a picture of the people who are adopting the baby. They look nice, young." The bird whistled a four-note tune. "Doctor says the baby's a boy, a big one."

"I better go now."

"Daddy, I love you."

She stood at the window a long time, holding the phone and hearing a recorded voice say if she wanted to make a call, hang up. The bird cocked its head, watching her. Then it flew.

After a long nap, she woke with a dull ache that covered her entire head. The baby moved and she shifted to give them both more room. Then she slept again. When she woke the second time, the headache had disappeared. For the first time in two weeks, she went to the equipment room to find the basketball. For thirty minutes, she shot free throws, one after another. After hitting twenty-nine in a row, she made herself stop. No sense continuing until she missed. Tomorrow she could try for thirty—have patience, like Daddy said.

That night, after she brushed her teeth and stared in the mirror at the profile of her distended abdomen, she straightened the books and papers on the desk. Her due date, June thirteenth, shone bright red on her calendar; she enlarged the date with an indelible marker. Before she turned out the light, she marked off May twentieth.

Without Karla there, every step she took in their room echoed. More than one evening the next three and a half weeks, she started to the door, to go to someone else's room just to hear other people talk, then didn't. She'd have to explain why she wouldn't stay and gossip. And several times she took her pillow to the TV room, but left soon after the first commercial, regardless of the program—*Seinfeld* or *ER*, it didn't matter.

Nothing tasted as good as it had earlier. Her appetite all but disappeared. But she still gained four pounds in two weeks. Everyone saw the doctor each week in their last month; her next visit was scheduled for June eleventh. But two days before, on the ninth, she went to the nurse's office and told her she had to pee every hour. Mrs. Turner asked several questions about other symptoms, felt Cheryl's belly, listened with a stethoscope at several places on her abdomen, checked her blood pressure, looked at her swollen feet, tested her urine, and told her she didn't have an infection. Said the baby was engaged and pressing against her bladder.

Then she said, "Your blood pressure's up a little, too. I want you to go in tomorrow to the doctor instead of waiting until the end of the week. Meanwhile, you have to rest in bed." She put a hand on Cheryl's shoulder. "You're frowning. Do you have any pain?"

"Nothing hurts." Mrs. Turner held out a hand to help, and Cheryl pulled up to a sitting position on the exam table. Then she scooted to the end of the table and stood. Every movement required concentration. Being with Mrs. Turner usually left her calm and smiling. Today the muscles in her face had forgotten how to arrange themselves as anything more than haunted vacancy.

"Are you worried?"

"A little." She aimed for a smile, again, and failed.

"I'll come up and check on you later. This baby may want to come early."

In her room, in bed, Cheryl imagined all that could go wrong, and listened to her pulse pound in her ears. If it wouldn't hurt the baby, she would be happy for it to come today. She knew for sure if this didn't end soon, she would lose her mind.

Muscle twitching, the kind that happens in a dream about falling, woke Cheryl. She often jerked herself awake that way on nights after a ball game, when she'd run so far and fast that her legs ached. "Cheryl?"

"Yes?" she answered. Her tongue felt thick. How long had she slept?

Mrs. Turner was standing just inside the door, holding a blood pressure cuff and stethoscope. "How do you feel?"

Cheryl shrugged. "I need to pee." She rolled to her side and sat up, then moved to stand. Nausea pushed her down.

Mrs. Turner said, "Stay still." Almost before Cheryl's head found the pillow, the blood pressure cuff squeezed her arm. The nurse listened, then repeated the measurement. With the stethoscope still in her ears, she asked, "Have you felt the baby move?"

"Asleep." She shrugged again, feeling stupid as she did.

Mrs. Turner listened low on Cheryl's abdomen in three places. "You're going to the hospital." She tossed the stethoscope on the bed. She dialed 911 from Cheryl's phone, told them immediate transport to Harris Hospital ER was required for OB emergency and gave the location. The next call she made got the doctor. "He'll meet us at the hospital."

Cheryl tried again to sit up.

"Don't move. The baby's in distress and you're in danger."

Cheryl gripped the nurse's hand. "Please, don't leave."

"I'll stay with you all the way."

She remembered being lifted onto the ambulance cart, then feeling her legs twitch, small movements at first, then she couldn't control them. Warm liquid flooded beneath her. Someone said, "Meconium stain." After that, spinning, siren shouting, then nothing until lights blinded her and she heard the words, "Mag sulfate."

"Cheryl, can you hear me?" When Cheryl looked toward the voice, she only saw a blurred figure she didn't recognize. Her mother's face appeared, but then disappeared. She worked to focus—Mrs. Turner. She smoothed Cheryl's hair back from her face. "You're okay now."

"The baby?"

"I'm sorry, sweetie, he died. You had seizures, went into hard labor, and then a precipitate birth before they could do a section. You had to have a lot of stitches for tears. The cord was wrapped three times around his neck."

Cheryl rolled toward the nurse, gripped her hand. Crying so hard she could barely catch her breath, she gulped back a sob. "What did I do wrong?"

"Nothing. Eclampsia can be sudden." Mrs. Turner leaned over her, held her to her chest. "We'll talk more later. You rest now. You'll be here a few days."

"Tell them I'm sorry." She closed her eyes again, continued holding onto the nurse's hand.

"I called your family."

"Does my mother know?"

"I talked to your dad. He'll come when you call him."

Cheryl shook her head. Her brain sloshed inside her skull, shooting pain to her eyes. "The light's so bright."

Mrs. Turner closed the blinds and turned off the light over the bed. "I'll be back in the morning." She kissed Cheryl on the forehead.

"What day is this?" she asked the nurse's aide who brought her fresh water and helped her to the shower. "It seems like I've been here a long time, and I've slept through most of it."

"June thirteenth. They said in report you might go home today."

"My birthday."

Minutes after the aide left, the phone rang. Her dad said, "Happy birthday, honey. I hope you're feeling better." His voice sounded odd, like he had a cold or someone had tried to strangle him. "Mrs. Carlson said you'll probably get out of the hospital soon. When you do, call me and I'll come take you to Jean's. I'm not having my daughter take a bus."

She forced herself to smile when she talked so he'd believe she meant what she said. She told him she felt fine and wouldn't leave Ft. Worth until she was plenty strong for a bus ride. "Here's a nurse with some medicine. I'll call you before I leave for Borger."

She heard him breathing. He hadn't hung up. She

pictured him sitting, shaking his head, staring at the phone. "Daddy, I love you. Bye now."

Mrs. Carlson and Mrs. Turner came together that afternoon to take her back to AG. Mrs. Turner winked at her when the social worker talked non-stop on the short trip. Her final words were the only ones Cheryl actually paid any attention to. "I understand you plan to travel home alone, by bus. If that's what you intend, let me know when you need a ride to the bus station."

For some reason that she couldn't quite name, Cheryl didn't want Mrs. Carlson to be the person telling her goodbye and good luck at the Trailways station. Mrs. Turner must have known. She said, "Oh, I forgot to tell you. It's already taken care of. I promised to give Cheryl a ride."

The nurse followed Cheryl to her room. "This must seem unreal to you right now. It's been hard, physically and emotionally. Don't be surprised if you feel depressed for a while."

Cheryl felt as if all the words she knew had deserted her. She nodded and sat down on the bed.

"Let me know when you need that ride."

Cheryl did the only thing she had the strength to do, lie down and close her eyes.

Although she'd intended to call for the bus schedule, Cheryl went to sleep and didn't wake up until the next day. Out of place didn't half describe how she felt that morning when she went to the dining room. The only thing she ever had in common with the other girls, pregnancy, was now gone. Disappeared, nothing left behind. After eating scrambled eggs and toast, as quickly as she could, she took two apples and three bananas to her room so she wouldn't have to sit among those pregnant girls again before she left.

Back in her room, she called the bus station. The best connection to Borger had already left by then. She reserved a seat for the following day—Borger, Texas, departing 7:22 a.m., June 15, 1994.

Lying on the bed, she tried to see herself as she'd be in six months or a year. No image appeared. Even the plans she and Karla had made for college seemed impossible and foolish. They had actually talked about having fun, as if they would ever be like other girls their age again.

The next morning Mrs. Turner came early, as she had promised. All the way to the station, they didn't talk. That pleased Cheryl. And when Mrs. Turner handed Cheryl a package of peanut butter crackers and a Snickers bar, it even made her smile.

The nurse said, "Road food. In case you're hungry before there's a stop." She took a card from her pocket, and handed it to Cheryl. "I hope you'll write. I promise to write back. And if you want to talk, call."

When the boarding announcement echoed in the big, almost empty, waiting room, she hugged Cheryl, a tight embrace that made her wish she could sit on the nurse's lap all the way to Borger. As the bus pulled out of the station, Cheryl allowed herself to remember how her mother's lap had felt, back when she was a child.

CHAPTER 3

January 15—May 27, 1994—Ryder Sheldon
Luck or Lack of It

"I don't give a goddam what the coach says, you're not dragging a horse and trailer across Texas and New Mexico all summer and fall with that rodeo team." He looked at his wife, as if she might have something to say and shouldn't. "I'm not made out of money."

Ryder's dad had started in just after his mother put the noon meal on the table and bowed her head to give silent thanks. He always seemed to enjoy making mealtime misery—liked spoiling everyone's digestion while never missing a forkful of mashed potatoes himself, never slowing between bites of fried chicken. Now he held a drumstick in his left hand and a slice of white bread in the right.

The fact that Uncle Butch had driven up for Saturday dinner from down at his place had set his mother to preparing the meal early. She probably thought this time would be different if she cooked all the right things. Uncle Butch concentrated on getting gravy on his potatoes, a half smile on his face, the expression of a man who'd heard his younger brother carry on plenty of times before.

Ryder pushed his plate back, half a thigh the only thing missing. Didn't matter now, even though it all smelled so good. Bad timing. He shouldn't have mentioned it this morning, should have brought it up last night. He did his best to keep his voice even, reasonable. "The college pays for gas and horse feed for the rodeo team. And you'll get a refund for part of my tuition."

His father waved the bread, now half gone, and upped his volume. "You may think you're a cowboy, but I raised you to be a farmer. You mess with me and you'll not finish another semester at that college. I can teach you everything you need to know."

Hell yes, Ryder knew what the man had taught him—how to say "Yessir" and do every dirty job on the place; how to keep his mouth shut when his old man took out a loan and bought another half section; how to work like a hired hand, but without the wages.

Ryder cut his eyes toward his mother. He could see her starting in on another prayer under her breath. Next thing, she'd be pulling out her rosary. He didn't dare smile when he noticed Uncle Butch raise his eyebrows.

How his dad and Butch came from the same parents never failed to amaze Ryder. But ten years could make a difference. So could eight, like him and his only, older sister. She and her herd of kids and her banker/farmer husband fit right in with the old man's plan, his mother's too, for that matter.

The way it worked, women had kids, went to church, kept their eyes on glory in the hereafter, and fooled themselves into believing they had any effect on men in the here and now. The men owned and farmed as much land as they could get their hands on, planted every square inch, used all the water available, and put something in the ground every season. Except Mary Margaret's husband never drove a tractor or hauled a bale of hay. He hired his work done.

Ryder figured it was bad luck put him in this family, the only son, and born late to a forty-year-old father to boot.

"I'm not likely to forget anything you taught me. I'll graduate soon enough. Rodeoing some till then won't hurt. I'm the best roper they've got."

"Useless. Might as well be the best knitter they got, for all the good it does anyone. World needs more smart farmers, not cowboys." He raised his glass—not a toast; a signal for his wife to scurry to his end of the table to refill his iced tea. "I'm right, huh, Butch? When's the last time anyone called on you to do any fancy roping?"

Uncle Butch's grin suggested he had a reply he intended to keep to himself. He shrugged and reached for the green bean casserole. "This is really good, Mary Frances. Nobody cooks like you do."

Ryder's mother had gone all out. She'd ironed the good white linen table cloth and napkins, and made it look like company dinner with her mother's china and silverware. A fancy chocolate meringue pie sat on the buffet behind the dining room table. A smile of the sort reserved for grandchildren and men who complimented her cooking lit her face. Butch had that effect on women.

His dad took another breath and started again, "Like I said, you tell that coach you have work to do here this summer. No roping until the wheat's harvested and the milo's planted." His plate stood empty. He pointed toward the pie. As if a magnetic force transported her, Ryder's mother left her place at the table and appeared at her husband's right elbow in less than a minute, offering a large piece of pie on a china dessert plate, a clean fork, and the same patiently resigned look she usually wore.

"And another thing. You may not be going back at all. Haven't seen your grades, yet."

Ryder pointed toward the den. "They've been on your desk right in there since I got here. All A's. Momma looked at them." She nodded, even if she didn't say anything. Ryder gave her credit. He pushed back his chair, trying to decide whether to eat pie or get the hell out of there.

"Everybody gets A's at that junior college. A glorified high school, if you ask me."

"Your choice, not mine." He could have gone to Texas Tech, but the old man said it was too big a place for a small town kid, said everyone knew that. Ryder watched as the chocolate pie disappeared off the china plate in four huge bites. He decided he wouldn't have any.

As soon as his dad shoveled the last bit of meringue into his mouth, Ryder said, "Momma, that was real good. Thanks." He pushed his chair back and picked up his plate and glass. "I have to get packed."

"You heard what I said." His dad would choke if he didn't get to have the last word.

Ryder had it on the tip of his tongue to say, "Okay with me. Talk all you want. Turn red in the face. Eat another piece of pie. Get fatter." Instead, he said, "Yessir." Just the way he'd been answering his dad since the day the old man first stuck him on a cabless tractor at nine years old, handed him a can of Off and said he'd be back to get him at dark.

"Just plow it straight and don't forget to drink water. It's gonna be hot today," the old man had said. Ryder still remembered how scared he'd been and how he'd stood crying after he hooked the disk in the fence on his last pass around the field. There'd been hell to pay after that. Lots of *yessirs* and *no sirs* and plowing after school and on weekends followed until he learned to do it right. And here he was nearly twenty, still repeating those words like a trained parrot.

In the kitchen, he scraped the rest of his dinner into the trash and set his plate and fork in the sink. He walked quietly into his room, hoping to get packed before his dad thought of some other piece of wisdom to impart. The little room invited him to stay; it hadn't changed since he was twelve and started papering the walls with rodeo posters. Donnie Gay, Jim Shoulders, Roy Cooper, Leo Camarillo—all the old guys. And above his dresser hung a picture of Uncle Butch with a bunch of his pals at some rodeo when he got back from the war. Well, one thing had changed. His mother had added a big jar of some kind of stuff that smelled like apples and cloves. Must be what she thought a happy home smelled like.

He heard Uncle Butch in the dining room saying something about hating to eat and run. Ryder jammed the underwear his mother had laundered into his Duffel bag. If he hurried, he figured he'd start down the road about the same time as his uncle.

At the intersection five miles from the house, where Ryder would turn east to get back to school and Butch would continue south toward his place near Muleshoe, his uncle waited for him, the window on his driver's side rolled down. Ryder pulled off the road and stopped his pickup and crawled climbed into Butch's cab. He breathed in the combined aroma of horse feed, tobacco, and stale coffee, a familiar, comfortable smell. "I was glad to see you today, Uncle Butch. Sorry about dinner."

"Pie was good. Everything was. Your momma knows her way around the kitchen." He removed the toothpick from his mouth and inserted a Camel. Ryder watched him light it with a gofer match, going through all the motions—separate one match from the rest, bend it forward without breaking it off, close the flap, scratch the match head on the emery strip, hold the pasteboard package like a handle—moves he hadn't yet quite perfected himself. After a long drag on the unfiltered cigarette,

Butch said, "Guess he got you told." He seemed to be studying a bug smeared on the windshield.

"He tried." He took a long breath and shook his head, then shrugged. "It's okay. I don't have to be on the team to rodeo. Besides, if I do stick with the team, I'll have to stay amateur. You saw me rope over at Portales. I think I could do okay on the circuit, get into PRCA before long."

"Gonna stay in school?"

"I started. I'll finish." They both studied the Chevy's front glass a while, each raised an index finger at a passing cattle truck driver. "Maybe I'll just go ahead and sign on with the team and then tell him next May I did it. Get in some good practice between now and then."

"May's nice weather for a shit storm, I guess."

Ryder snorted a little laugh. "Yeah, ain't that the truth. Better weather than today." He pointed at four tumbleweeds hurrying like a pack of coyotes running from the cold southwest wind. "Need some moisture out here."

Butch nodded. "That's a fact." He rolled up his window. "You know, your dad wants what he thinks is best for you. Reminds me of our daddy. That's who he acts like."

"That why you're a cowboy? Your old man wanted you to be a farmer?"

"I'm not much of a cowboy these days. But yeah, that's what he intended me to do. Turned out to be a big disappointment to him. Oldest son, a worthless cowhand. Worked out okay for your dad, though. He wouldn't have had a pot or a window if he hadn't heired the home place."

"He thinks if he yells loud enough, I'll get it, turn out just the way he thinks I should. He thinks I'll go through life needing his supervision every step of the way."

"That's the way our daddy operated. Your dad never had a chance to take a step he wasn't told until the old man died. He's had his own hard row."

"He could have left. You did."

His uncle shrugged. "Well, he didn't."

If he could do exactly what he wanted to, he'd rather just go home with Uncle Butch, listen to all his seventy-one years worth of collected stories, drink a few beers, prowl around on horseback out at his place, load up and go to a roping on the weekend, watch the sun go down as the sandhill cranes flew in. Didn't matter if they'd have to batch it without chocolate pie. "I guess I better go," Ryder said.

"Well, you come on out any time. You know where to find me." Butch turned the ignition, shifted into drive. "Let me know if you need anything. At all." He was looking down the road, south, when he said that.

Keeping his grades up and rodeoing, not necessarily in that order, kept Ryder fully occupied at school until late spring. At the rodeo in Vernon in early May, he'd decided since he'd already won a buckle in the roping, he'd also try some saddle bronc riding. How tough could it be? Just crawl up there, get a good grip, keep one hand in the air and work your spurs. And damned if he didn't have a high point ride. Everyone spent a lot of wind congratulating him, saying how he should change his event, any cowboy worth his beans could rope, not everyone could or would ride bucking horses. Stuff like that.

So the next night, in the final go round, he felt pretty good as he climbed aboard. And he still didn't feel too bad when he ended up on the ground, because he was pretty sure the buzzer sounded before he took flight. You couldn't blame the horse, and he sure didn't blame himself. Just bad luck.

One of the hazers yelled at him, "Can you hear me?"

He knew he nodded, but he didn't have enough air to talk yet. The ground had met him pretty fast.

"Can you stand up?" Two guys were pulling him up, and he tried his best to help.

"Did I make a ride?"

One of them nodded, said, "Yeah, good points, too. But right after the buzzer you were outbound."

"Damn." Just then the numbness in his left arm disappeared and a pain shot down to his hand and up to the middle of his back. Nausea welled up and his legs weakened.

The cowboy on his right probably figured it out when Ryder sagged and stumbled, then pitched forward and puked on his own boots. The cowboy on his left said, "Whoa! Hold on a minute. Something wrong?"

If he stood there smelling vomit and dirt and horse piss thirty seconds longer he knew he'd empty out entirely. "Get me on out of here. I'll be okay."

He heard the announcer asking the crowd for a round of applause. Supposed to encourage you if you'd gotten a mouthful of dirt.

"Fractured ulna," the rodeo doc said. He'd taken an x-ray and offered Ryder a shot for pain while they waited for the film to dry. The diagnosis the man pronounced wasn't news to Ryder. No one needed to tell him the reason for that grating sensation when he moved his forearm.

"How long will it take to heal?"

"Four to six weeks, depending. You're fortunate." Ryder failed to see any good luck in this deal.

"Clean break. I'll cast it. You go in tomorrow for follow up." The doctor fiddled around in a cabinet, pulling out packages of whatever it took to make a cast. "You might as well take the pain med. You won't be leaving for a while yet."

"I'll drink a beer and take an ibuprofen or two later on. Go ahead and do what you need to."

"Cowboys," the doctor muttered.

Ryder's main concern was how he was going to get back to school. He'd come to Vernon by himself. Since he wasn't rodeoing for the school, he'd done most of his traveling alone, finding someone with a good horse who'd let him use it to rope, mainly to keep in practice and maybe get some people to notice him. Later on he'd need some name recognition. Plus he didn't want to go home on the weekends while his friends were gone making the college rodeos. Didn't seem like there was much else to do. Now here he was with his first fracture. It had to happen sometime.

He left the medical tent sporting a bright red cast and carrying a headache that took his mind off his arm. Two ibuprofen later, after dozing in the pickup, he decided he could drive right-handed. Five hours after that he parked in his dorm lot and dragged himself inside. Only two more weeks until school was out. That should have been good news, but the main thing it meant was going home. And he knew what that meant.

"You're late," his father yelled from the porch when Ryder drove up. He'd left school an hour and a half earlier, just before sun up. "You were supposed to be here yesterday. We started cutting first thing. Don't bother unloading. Get to the south section and drive the grain truck to the elevator. When you get back, get on the tractor and pull the grain cart. And don't stop until the combine does. I'll deal with you this evening."

Apparently the old man hadn't noticed the cast. Just as well. Ryder could drive anything he had to one-armed. All he needed was for nothing to break and need fixing. As his father's main hand, repairs fell to him to do. With supervision and lots of loud instruction, of course. Well, maybe nothing would break. But he couldn't expect it wouldn't before harvest was over. Something always broke or wore out. And even if he was nowhere in sight, it somehow ended up being his fault. The old man worked on the principle that someone always had to take blame.

Ryder made it all the way to dark without having to talk to anyone or seeing his father. He drove the truck four trips to the elevator, pulled the grain cart around the field beside the combine, and kept his head down.

Just when Ryder returned to the field after his last trip to the elevator, his dad drove his pickup next to the grain truck. "Get to the house. Your mother's got food ready." Not a word about how good the wheat looked or how nice it was everything stayed running with no breakdowns. The man had not a grateful bone in his body.

Ryder knew his dad was watching from the porch as he unloaded his pickup. Carrying his bag and wearing his backpack on one shoulder, Ryder trudged toward him. He also knew the first thing his dad would say. Sure enough he did, "What's that about?" He pointed at the cast.

"Broke a bone in my arm. Nothing bad."

"Better not be. You'll have plowing to do soon as the wheat's cut." He eyed Ryder like he might be waiting for a smart-ass reply. Ryder ducked his head and walked toward his mother who waited behind the screen door.

As soon as she started asking a question about the cast, he hugged her with his good arm and whispered, "Shhh. I'll tell you later." Then in a louder voice, "Hi, Momma. Smells like beans and cornbread in here."

She said, "Your favorites. And chicken fried steak."

His dad stepped between Ryder and his mother. He said, "I don't want any damn beans. Fry me some potatoes."

As soon as they got to the table, right after he filled his own plate, he started again, not waiting for anyone else. "Break that arm falling off a horse, I suppose?"

"Something like that." Ryder wasn't going to miss this meal no matter what. He hadn't eaten since before the sun came up.

"Guess that broke you of being a cowboy. Good enough for you. Now maybe you'll concentrate on what you need to. Working this place. I've a mind not to let you go back to college in September."

"I'll finish college." Ryder said it flat. He noticed his mother looking at her lap, working her mouth, no sound coming out.

"Only way you will is if I say so."

"Pass the beans, please."

His dad looked at him. Ryder stared back, not blinking.

"As soon as this wheat's in, you're going to plant milo on every acre we've got. Price is up and I need the income. Note's due end of October."

Ryder didn't say anything, didn't mention that letting some acres lie fallow, rotating crops, would benefit the land, or that the cost of irrigating all their acres would eat into the net gain. Saved his breath.

"I know what you're thinking. Had the idea I'd let you off on the weekends. Not gonna happen, mister."

"This is a real good supper, Momma. I was ready for a

home cooked meal."

"Are you paying any attention to me, boy? You intend to inherit this place, you have to contribute." He forked a second piece of steak from the serving plate. "It's time you worked like a man."

Ryder ate two more mouthfuls of steak and beans. Took his time, chewed it all very well. Then he laid his fork across his plate. His cast bumped against the table as he moved his chair back. He stood, walked to his mother and patted her on the back. "Thanks again, Momma."

"Don't you leave when I'm talking. Put your butt in that chair."

"Got to get to bed. Lots of work tomorrow."

The only way out of the room passed by his dad's chair. When Ryder came within reach, without standing, his father grabbed Ryder's casted left arm with both hands and jerked downward, hard. Ryder fell to his knees. "When I say sit down, I mean it."

On his knees, his eyes level with the old man's, he made himself a silent promise, planned his entire future before either of them blinked. He stood, backed to his chair, sat down, waited.

"You understand how it's gonna be now, boy?"

"Yessir." He smiled at his mother. "Can I be excused?"

CHAPTER 4

June 15, 1994—Ryder Sheldon
Tied Down

Ryder heard his dad talking. Hell, people in the next county could hear him. It was the way he started every morning, before the sun came up, like his loud voice was required to officially start the day. With his eyes still closed, Ryder pictured the scene in the kitchen—his father, in overalls and long-sleeved khaki shirt, no matter what the weather, seated at the table, a plate smeared with bits of fried egg and congealing yolk in front of him—his mother, in sandals, a white blouse, and plaid skirt, covered by an apron, facing the stove.

The smell of frying bacon eased into the bedroom, nudged his eyes open. In between his father's comments on the weather and the food, little bits of KPAN's market reports intruded, each time prompting another blast of braying from the man of the house. This morning the price of wheat had him worked up. And the occasional silences, Ryder knew, were when his mother would offer some bland response in a voice no bigger than a whisper, the only voice she ever spoke with there at the house. Maybe she was protecting the real one, the steady alto she used when she sang harmony in the St. Jude's choir.

If he covered his head with his pillow, he might be able to go back to sleep. Nope, he'd smother. He tossed the pillow toward yesterday's dirty clothes piled in the corner to his right. Might as well get up and face it. Another day as an unpaid hand on Richard Sheldon's idea of the perfect farm—mortgaged to the hilt. He'd get through this summer, and after school started he'd never come back. If he had to drive a manure truck, smelling it would be better than listening to non-stop bullshit all day long every day. If it wasn't about what he'd done wrong or might have if his dad hadn't been right there supervising, then it was what someone else was doing to try to cheat his dad out of everything he'd worked to make. To hear that man tell it, he was on the minds of a lot of people all bent on his ruin.

Ryder took an abnormal psychology class as an elective last semester. Since then, when he managed not to take personally every nasty comment that began with "Listen here, boy," he found himself matching up his dad's attitudes and actions with some of the descriptions in the book. So far, paranoid personality fit best. But then he wasn't a psych major, so maybe he missed something.

He rolled to his side and sat up, banging that short arm cast against his knee in the process. No matter what the doctor said, he was getting that off next week, if he had to saw it off himself. In just three weeks of disuse, his forearm had shrunk and the cast jiggled around loose. No telling how long it would take to get back in shape to rope again. Even if he were right-handed, he'd never win any prizes operating one-armed.

His Wranglers waited on a chair near the window. Without making a sound he got them on and straightened up his bed, patting the pillow fondly, like a friend he hoped to see soon. He pulled a T-shirt on, so as not to have to wrestle the cast into a long-sleeved shirt. Carrying his boots and socks, he tiptoed to the bathroom. When he came out a minute later, he wore a smile he hoped his mother would see before something erased it.

"Took your time getting up." His father pointed to bacon and toast on a plate in the middle of the table. "Eggs are gone. You'll have to eat what's left. There's plowing to do today."

"Morning, Momma. Yes, sir. I'll be out on the tractor in three minutes." Ryder took the large glass of milk his mother poured as soon as he walked in. "Where do you want me to start?"

"The Schmucker. I expect you to get a hundred acres done before dark or don't bother to come in."

If he'd said what he thought, Ryder would have popped off about how he could get that done fine if he didn't stop to pee or eat any dinner, and if that old sweep plow held together, but he just nodded. No sense making little waves. Save it up for the big one in August. He ate a piece of toast in four bites and winked at his mother over the rim of his glass when he gulped the milk.

He gathered his sunglasses and cap and Red Man from the cabinet top next to the back door. "I'll see y'all this evening."

His mother followed him to the back door where she handed him a thermos of iced tea, a bottle of water, and a paper bag. It would have two ham sandwiches, some Fritos, sliced carrots, a Snickers, and a handful of cookies in it, as it always did. She saw to it he never went hungry.

The John Deere 4640 stood in the equipment yard taking on a glow from the rising sun. He crawled into the cab and met yesterday's dust that hadn't fully settled. Once he got all his stuff arranged—lunch bag and thermos stowed behind the seat, water bottle next to the armrest, Red Man in his pocket, spit can up next to the right hand window—he turned the key marked with the deer. Diesel smoke puffed out the exhaust stack, just one gust, and the engine chugged its familiar bass rumble. The air conditioner spat out a whiff of dirt, then hummed and blew. He turned it off, intending to wait until he needed it. In June, a High Plains morning would reward him with a cool little breeze coming in the push-out window.

He stepped out of the cab and walked to the back to check whether all the connections looked right, not covered by a greasy coat of leaked hydraulic fluid and dirt. Satisfied the green machine would handle the day, he hauled himself back into the cab. As he pulled slowly out of the equipment yard, he stuck an ancient Maines Brothers cassette in the dash-mounted player and hummed along with "Flatland Farmer."

Two songs later, he'd made it the three miles south to the field. Once he chose the angle he'd plow on and aimed for a spot on the horizon, he could almost put himself and his tractor on autopilot. Like the Maines sang, "Four rows up, four rows back," except the twenty-one foot sweep rig he pulled cut a slightly wider path. It'd be a long day. Might as well plan to find something to enjoy about it.

For a while he thought about Darla Hanson, whether to keep taking her out. He'd dated her a few times at school after he broke his arm and couldn't rodeo on the weekends, mainly to have company. She didn't talk too much and liked going to movies. She hinted a couple of times about going dancing, but he figured that compared to a movie, you doubled your cost going to a dance hall. Even if they only drank beer, there would still be the cover to pay. Not that he hoarded cash, but his dad paid tuition and room and board and sent a hundred dollars a month for gas and walking around money. His way of keeping him on a short leash. Anything else came from money he'd saved raising show animals in high school. And he wasn't inclined to piss off much of that taking girls out, not right now. Besides, as long as there were rodeos, there would always be girls.

Two hours into the morning, the sun hitting him in the eye every time he made a round going east, he sat up straighter and popped out the cassette. Something told him to get serious. There was a lot to take care of if he intended to get registered at West Texas A &M University, get a job close to Canyon, and figure out a cheap place to live, all before the end of August. No matter what, he would be gone from this farm before this summer was over and on track to finish college in two years or less.

Maybe it wasn't wishful thinking, but he got to looking for his dad. He usually came around at some point and always had something to say—Is that all you've gotten done? Set that plow deeper!—stuff you tell a hand too ignorant to think on his own. Coming to pester him gave his dad a reason to get off the tractor he was driving. A fat man's seldom comfortable anywhere for long. Picking at Ryder was just an excuse. Today he hadn't seen hide nor hair of him. Not that he was eager or that he needed any direction. Maybe it was wishful.

Around two o'clock, he stopped the tractor, took his lunch and sat in a spot of shade next to a tractor wheel to eat. For once, he took his time. He wadded his napkin and stowed it in the paper bag, and then walked around the entire rig, checking that nothing had fallen off or broken. A hawk watched from a fence post close enough for him to hit if he threw a clod. He didn't. That bird had kept him company all morning, swooping down after rabbits and mice scurrying out of the wheat stalks as he plowed through them.

After taking a leak and drinking half the thermos of tea, he mounted the steps to the cab and fired up the engine. He just might finish a hundred acres today. Not a cloud showing and the wind hadn't picked up, so he wasn't troubled with dust going either direction. It wouldn't be dark until after eight. As he lifted and dropped the plow, satisfied everything worked, he and the rabbit hunter started another round.

At six-fifteen, his mother's car pulled onto the turnrow next to the field. She often came out during harvest to deliver dinner, but this wasn't harvest. She drove to the spot where he'd end his next round. By the time he got there, she stood outside the Chevrolet, clutching the bottom of her apron, wearing a frown. He jumped down. "What's wrong, Momma?" He felt like running.

"It's your dad. He didn't come in for supper. I'm afraid to go find him by myself."

"Did you try to get him on the phone in his pickup?"

"No answer. He usually doesn't bother to put it on the tractor, too much noise."

They walked fast to the car. She pointed to the driver's side. "He said he was going back to the south field after dinner. Barely ate."

"Let's don't go buying trouble. He may have had a breakdown."

"On that new tractor?" She leaned forward, holding onto the dash. He drove too fast down the turnrow, bouncing them both against the doors, then headed south on the county road.

He skidded onto the turnrow on the south field, raising a plume of dust. He knew he'd catch hell if his dad saw him driving like that. The red Case-IH tractor's exhaust flap jittered; it was stopped, running, with no driver in sight. His mother pointed toward the far end of the field at the white pickup, parked on the fence line. Ryder sped toward it. She pulled a rosary from her apron pocket. A little way down the turnrow toward the pickup, he braked to a halt. "Momma, can you drive?"

She nodded but didn't look too certain. He said, "I see Daddy on the ground on the other side of the tractor. I'm going out there." He jerked open the door, got out. His mother didn't move. He pointed to the driver's seat. "You go to the pickup and call for the ambulance and call your cousin William to come help, too." He stopped briefly as he hoisted a leg over the fence, and turned back to her. "Do it now, Momma. Pretty sure he needs help."

Ryder ran toward the tractor, stumbling on plowed ground twice before he got there. His dad lay on the ground just below the last step, his left fist on his chest, his right flat on the ground and flung open skyward, like he might be waiting for rain. For a second that seemed longer, Ryder felt completely disconnected, useless and free as a tumbleweed. He fell to his knees, yelling, hoping his dad's eyelids would flicker and close against the sun's glare. No pulse beat in the folds of his thick neck; none at his wrist. Ryder slammed his fist against his dad's unmoving chest, once, twice. Still no pulse. "Daddy, wake up!" He knew how useless his words were as he shouted them again. He grabbed his father's left fist, whispered, "I'm sorry, Daddy."

The ambulance moaned its way to the pickup, then crept across the plowed ground out to where he huddled beside his dad. By the time the EMTs jumped out with their equipment in tow, smears of dirt tracked Ryder's dried tears down both cheeks. He'd stopped bawling like a calf, but he couldn't control his voice. So he stood mute and shook his head, watching them go through the motions, confirming what he already knew.

He saw William's pickup tear down the county road and thump its way to his mother's car, saw her rush to her cousin and lean against him. All this, he saw like the view through the wrong end of binoculars, small and distant, not connected to him. He refused the offer of a ride in the ambulance. Instead he followed it on foot, trudging slowly across the stubble-dotted furrows to the field's edge.

His mother's people, their speech peppered with German phrases, gathered to help her get the funeral arranged. It took three days, but seemed a lot longer. The whole time folks came and went. Some stayed, too long as far a Ryder was concerned. Women toted in casseroles, bowls of noodles, and cakes; men stood around asking questions about the land and equipment Ryder knew his mother couldn't answer and he wouldn't; and the old priest shuffled around the living room doing a lot of nodding and hand-patting. So many crowded the small space that Ryder couldn't get a breath.

As soon as his sister came in the back door the morning after their dad died, Ryder told her he had work to do, used the old man's intention to plant milo right away as a reason. Then he got the hell out of there. He drove his dad's pickup to the west field, parked on the turnrow, and hiked out to his dad's tractor. It seemed like a long walk. He couldn't make himself step on the footprints or the spot where his dad lay yesterday. When he hauled himself to the top step and opened the cab door, looking down at the depression the body had made, he saw it was a lot smaller than he'd thought—deeper maybe, but not as big.

Uncle Butch drove up as Ryder pulled the red tractor out of the field. It wouldn't do to leave equipment sitting in the middle, so he'd plowed his way out, driving slowly, trying to figure how he could get all the acres ready and planted in time.

"Ryder."

"Uncle Butch."

"I'm sorry, son."

Ryder kicked at a clump of weeds balled on one of the sweeps. "Heart attack, they said. We were too late. Nothing we could do for him."

Butch lit a cigarette. "Never has been." He took a short drag and then blew smoke through his nose. He pointed toward the field and the one next to it across the fence. "This isn't all of it, is it? I know he'd bought more."

"Bought but not paid for. He worried full time about the note payment in October. Said we were going to plant every acre to milo next, and that might make enough, with what the wheat did, to make this year's."

"Runnin' pretty close to the margins. A bad year or two in a row and the bank gets it all—right?"

"Far as I know." Ryder took a deep breath, like that might relieve the feeling he'd been closed into a cage.

"Any hired hands?

"You're looking at him."

Butch shook his head. He dropped his half-smoked cigarette and stepped on it. "Got another tractor? Might as well help out, since I'm here."

His dad and Butch were all there was to the Sheldon clan, but his mother's people took up the slack. St. Jude's in Bethel held a crowd the morning of the funeral. After the service and the burial, the women of the church fed everyone in the fellowship hall. After what he considered a decent interval following the meal, Ryder edged toward his mother to tell her he was going to plow. She left the group of women surrounding her and walked with him toward the kitchen's back door. "I know you need to leave." She held his hand, spoke in a voice stronger than he knew she owned. "We have to talk, just the two of us. Things to decide."

"Yes, ma'am." She kissed his cheek, patted him on the back. She felt sturdy, able, when he hugged her.

When Ryder got home, Butch wasn't far behind him. He pulled his pickup in behind Ryder's and walked with him to where they parked the tractors the night before. Butch said, "Don't think too ill of your dad. He wasn't the only one bull-headed, wasn't always that way. Our old man kept on him till he knuckled under. I could have offered to help. Maybe he'd have let me. If I hadn't been too busy doing everything I wanted to. He worked hard.

Tried to do right. Probably wanted to leave you something."

"Maybe so." Ryder shrugged. "Guess we'll never know now." He'd been looking at his boots a long time before he said anything else. "I'll plow the south field if you'll do the west."

By dark that evening, between the two of them, he and Butch had plowed all but three quarter sections. At the diesel tank, filling both tractors, they agreed they should be finished in two days, three at the most. "When you intend to plant?" Butch asked.

"Got to buy seed, first. Unless he hid it somewhere, there's not any here." He lifted the nozzle and peered inside the tank. He talked as he moved the nozzle to the red tractor. "And I'll have to see if anything needs replacing on the planter."

Butch sighed. "This is the most hours I've put in on a tractor since I left this place fifty years ago."

"You hate driving tractor as much as I do?"

"No, it's kind of hypnotizing. That's not what I minded. It was being tied in place." He slapped his gloves against his leg. "Want any help when you start planting?"

Ryder busied himself fooling with the nozzle. He wondered if he'd know what to do, working alongside a man who didn't spend his time yelling at him. "Could sure use it."

"We finish this, I'll go check on things at home and wait till you call." He reached for the cap to the fuel tank while Ryder locked the elevated diesel tank and redid the baling wire holding the hose off the ground. "You think your mother's going to be okay?"

"I think so. Trouble is he never told her anything about the business. I know that for sure. Don't even know if he left a will. I heard her tell Mary Margaret yesterday he didn't have any life insurance."

"Hell of a mess. A man never thinks he's gonna die…"

Butch didn't finish whatever he thought. "You going to be all right?"

"If I don't get trapped."

They left the tractors and walked side by side toward the pickup, Ryder with his head down, noticing his boots felt heavy. About halfway there, Butch put an arm across Ryder's shoulders, and he felt like he ought to stand up straight.

Part II
1996-1998

CHAPTER 5

October 5, 1996—Ryder Sheldon and Cheryl Magee
First Dance

Ryder could see it in the near distance, graduation. Come December, he'd finish what he'd said he would. And he didn't have a clue what he'd do next. A bachelor's degree in Animal Science might get him a job selling cattle feed or teaching ag and sponsoring a Future Farmers of America club in a high school somewhere. But neither one of those required his real skills—roping and riding. At least that's how it looked to him. There'd be some recruiters coming to campus. Maybe someone needed a college graduate to manage a small ranch raising rough stock for rodeos. He heard his old man's voice saying, "Maybe you'll shit if you eat regular—more chance of that."

He told himself to quit staring down the road and get dressed. At least he didn't have to go back home and drive a tractor. The Rodeo Club always welcomed the football team onto the field at home games. The seniors in chaps and spurs, all wearing black hats, led the way, with one of them on horseback right out front. Tonight was his night. Out front.

The dorm room mirror didn't lie. If he did say so himself, he cut a pretty fine figure. Wouldn't have to look far for partners at the dance after the game. Girls loved cowboys; lots even favored them over the football jocks. He'd wondered about why and decided it had to do with most of those girls never actually knowing any cowboys. Romance of the unknown, he'd labeled it.

He tied a black silk wild rag at his throat three different times before it satisfied him. Cowboys seldom actually wore one except when it was cold enough to freeze snot, but being out front tonight, he thought qualified as a wild rag occasion. That and his birthday hat. He brushed the 20X Stetson one more time.

That hat was the biggest birthday surprise he could remember ever getting. His mother, whose presents usually ran to a new pair of Wranglers or one good shirt or such, had made him close his eyes before she brought it out.

His sister and her husband and their troop of kids weren't there—maybe they weren't invited. His mother took him to dinner for his twenty-first, July 24th last year, at a steakhouse in Canyon. When they got back to the house, she made him hold the fancy box while she took out the hat. Before he could even thank her, she said, "I have something to tell you. Not even your sister knows." Her words burst out in a rush, like calves penned up a long time. "Now that you took care of getting me out from under your father's debts …You're going to finish college next December…Be on your own…" She stopped talking and stared at the hat she was holding in her hands, treating it like one of those altar cloths she embroidered.

He waited. She'd say whatever was on her mind eventually. All those years of keeping quiet, she could be out of practice.

She handed him the hat and let out a deep breath, like she'd just paid off on a bet. "I'm going to ask you to do one more thing for me. Sell this house and the five acres that's left."

"You want to move to town, live near Mary Margaret?

She shook her head. "I'm going to move to Fredericksburg. Get married. Next year." She halted. Maybe she expected him to argue.

He said the first thing he thought. "Why?"

She laughed, a gentle, happy sound that made him glad.

"Being married is what I know. It's been more than a year."

"Who?" He could probably count on his fingers all the men she ever spoke to, including the parish priest and her cousin William.

"Someone I loved when I was a girl. Before my family moved here. Albert Friedrichs."

He looked at her closely. In the lamplit living room, her face seemed too young to be his mother's. Happier than he'd seen in years, maybe ever. He sat down on the couch, holding the hat. He leaned forward, elbows on his knees, and fit the hat on, cocked at a go-to-hell angle. He looked up at her, saw her smile. He said, "This is an expensive hat. I promise I'll never wear it on a bucking horse."

She sat down, close, put an arm around him. "A grown man. Hard to believe. My baby."

"Guess I better get to work on selling this place." He stood, looked around the room. "It'll sell better if we paint the outside. Brighten it up. I'll take care of it, Momma."

Killing time until the game, he sat down on his dorm room bed. He took the soft bristled brush from his hatbox and whisked at invisible specks. That hat always made him remember his mother's face that night. Together, as well as separately, they'd accomplished a lot in the past two years.

Getting the farm business settled after his dad died had taken nearly a year. They couldn't find any will, so the judge said his mother inherited everything, debt included. If they had defaulted on the loan, anyone could have scooped up those acres at bargain prices. Ryder told her they couldn't do that to his father.

His brother-in-law said he could get a month's extension on the loan, until December first. Ryder planted milo and harvested, worked the rest of the summer and into the fall, all the while talking to himself about how a good son would have appreciated what his father was trying to do. How he had only wanted to leave something behind for his only son. But Ryder never was able to convince himself he had to want the same thing.

The milo crop put enough in the bank to make one payment. That, plus an auction of all the equipment, left his mother with enough equity to come out a little more than even when the land sold. No surprise to Ryder, the buyer turned out to be his brother-in-law's younger brother. Seems he had no trouble getting financing.

Soon after that birthday night, his mother had Mary Frances come out, and she went through the official version about the man she intended to marry. He never let on she'd told him earlier. The story was that they had been childhood friends, he had been married, his wife died years ago, they had no children. He had retired from the military and moved back home to the Hill Country a few years ago. Her cousin Hilda had told him about his mother's being a widow.

Then one evening this past August, Ryder'd just gotten inside the front screen door when she came out of the kitchen carrying two glasses of iced tea. "I thought maybe we could sit out on the porch and visit before we eat," she said. "We're having a cold supper tonight, salad and sandwiches, so there's no rush."

He sat in one of the wooden rockers, the porch chairs, she called them. Sometime in the past year she had changed their positions. Instead of side by side, facing forward, the way they'd been ever since he could remember, now they faced toward each other at an angle. She sat in the other one. She asked if he needed new Wranglers before he left for his last semester at school; they talked about a couple of the details of the sale of the house. The wind settled from a strong breeze down to a whisper. He wondered out loud if she was sure she was ready to leave West Texas. She was, she said. Then they both drank tea and rocked.

The sun going down in the west turned the wispy clouds they faced on the east a shade of coral that belonged on jewelry. She halted her rocker and said, "When I was in town the other day I bought a six-pack of beer. I thought I'd like one. Would you?"

He nodded, made himself not smile at the thought of her buying a six-pack. Maybe she and Albert lived it up when she went to Fredericksburg to visit. The things he didn't know about his mother, his father, too, for that matter, made him sad. He'd grown up watching them through a peephole, it seemed, only able to make out their shapes and the main features of their faces. Little bits of their actions showed if he turned at just the right angle.

As soon as he nodded, before he could ask if they were celebrating something, she went inside. Soon she was back, carrying an old Anthony and Cleopatra cigar box with two gold and brown labeled, brown bottles resting on top. She handed him one and returned to her chair.

He said, "Shiner. A good beer."

She raised her bottle toward his; they clinked a salute. "Central Texas beer. Albert recommends it."

Ryder leaned back against the chair's horizontal slats, rocked gently. If he let himself, he could fall asleep right there, beer in his hand.

After a few minutes, with him quiet and his mother rocking, occasionally sipping her beer, she leaned forward. "Maybe you wondered about me taking up with Albert so soon."

He shrugged. If he told the truth, he really hadn't given it any thought at all. She seemed happy. That's all that mattered.

As if he had asked, she said, "Packing things, I stopped to

look through that." She pointed to the cigar box. "I thought you might want to know."

She leaned back, but didn't rock. "When I was a girl, before we moved out here, he and I were serious sweethearts. Had talked about marriage." Ryder stopped rocking and leaned toward her. "But I was too young. He's four years older. I knew the first time he asked me out—I was fourteen—we were meant for each other." She cocked the neck of her beer bottle toward Ryder. "I saw you raise your eyebrow just then. Yes, I was fourteen. Not allowed to go out."

"Did you sneak out?"

She rolled her eyes. "Had to go to confession right away. Lying, dishonoring my parents. Yes. Snuck out to meet him."

"Just once?"

She shook her head. "Every chance we could. Then daddy moved us to West Texas. His uncle and cousins knew about cheap land out here. One day you can read the letters Albert sent. Wrote at least once a week. He was at A & M." She glanced at the cigar box. "Right up until I met your father. Now, your father, he was determined. He did the smart thing—talked to Papa before he ever spoke to me about marriage. So, it was settled. Albert joined the Air Force after college. No more weekly letters." Her chair squeaked when she leaned back, then rocked gently.

"After you were married, did you ever wonder, wish things had been different?"

"I wondered a few times. But I never wished things different." She looked him in the eyes. "Son, if we hadn't moved here, and I hadn't married your father, I'd never have had you. I never have wished that."

"There was only one secret I ever kept from your father. All those years, once a year, Albert sent me a letter—sent it inside a Christmas card to Cousin Gertrude. Trudy would bring it to me; she never opened any or threatened to tell."

"Did you burn those?" He imagined his father raging if he'd ever found one. There would have been hell to pay.

"Saved them all. They're in there too. He loved me all those years. You have no idea how important that has been for me, always." She took a final drink from her bottle and reached for his empty. As she opened the screen to go inside, she said, "Let's not tell your sister. It would only upset her."

"Okay, Momma. I won't."

Even without hearing anything about the letters, his sister still had a fit about their mother remarrying. She harped on it for the whole year. But it didn't stop their mother from packing and making plans. The day the new owner signed the contract for the house, his mother told Ryder half of the money would be in the bank in Amarillo, in his name. She'd arranged for the other half to be in a C.D. for his sister's children. "I won't need it," she said. "Albert's done very well."

The morning the new owner took possession of the house, Albert Friedrichs arrived in his black Suburban, pulling a matching sixteen-foot utility trailer. Two days later, Ryder waved goodbye to his mother. Every time he thought about her having a secret love all those years, a hopeful feeling swelled up in his chest.

His sister tried to get him to be upset about their mother's leaving, saying she was behaving like an adolescent, improper for a woman of her age; they should stop her from making this mistake. He thought about arguing with her, about asking her if she had any idea about who their parents really were, why they married, why they stayed together, whether they were ever in love, whatever that was. Instead, he said, "She's happy. I'm happy for her."

And for the first time since he could remember, Ryder had felt entirely free.

He had to admit, tonight, right now, free was a pretty confusing way to be. The mirror wasn't going to cure that. He situated his hat, tipped just a hint to the right, and headed for his horse trailer.

Her roommate, Julie, pulled Cheryl to her feet so they were standing along with all the other fans on the home side of the field. As the Rodeo Club entered, led by a cowboy on horseback, followed by the buffalo wrangled by four of the club members, and then by the football team, the crowd all around her cheered. Cheryl could tell from the looks on the faces of the faithful that homecoming at West Texas A & M was a very big deal.

She watched the people around her more than the ones on the field, mainly because the seats they got were near the top of the stands, making the distant buffalo look like a shaggy stuffed toy. She cheered as if she had years of loyalty built up, which she didn't. She was the new girl on campus. Fit in. That's what she intended to do. Start over, fresh.

"That's the one I'm going to marry," Julie said. She was a junior and never missed a game.

"How can you tell who's who with their helmets and face masks on?"

"Not a football player. The cowboy on the horse. His name's Ryder Sheldon, a senior. As God is my witness, tonight I'm going to meet him if it's the last thing I ever do."

Cheryl had to smile. Julie's dramatic speeches entertained her, even if she never took them seriously. Life was one continuing rehearsal for theater majors, if Julie was any example. Since Cheryl had arrived, Julie had seen to it she seldom stayed in her room when not in class or the library. "That's the only reason to come to college, other than the degree, I mean. It's your chance to experience as much as possible, as quickly as possible. Live every moment as if it's your last, my dear!" Cheryl could have told her a lot about the results of living like that, but didn't.

The first night in her dorm, Cheryl hadn't slept. Instead, she watched lights from the street below playing across the ceiling and allowed the feeling of "new" to take hold. The past two years at her aunt and uncle's house, she'd worked hard. Not that they treated her like hired help—more like a daughter—but because she drove herself. She set out to complete as many dual credit courses as she could to graduate from high school without delay and with at least thirty college credits. The result, just the way she planned, was that she had no time for anything other than schoolwork and the job at the convenience store the past two summers. Nothing except daily exercise—running, riding the old bicycle her uncle repaired for her, and shooting fifty free throws every evening on the goal he installed above the garage door.

As if they all laughed on cue, the crowd's noise changed. Cheryl stopped watching the old man and woman next to her situate their stadium cushions and thermos bottles and peered where Julie pointed. The entire home team clumped together around the buffalo; the band switched from "Fight On, Buffs" to "I'm An Old Cowhand." Julie's future husband had roped the opposing team's mascot. The giant pig's papier mâché head stood nose down, one tusk drilled into the turf. The pale blond boy wearing the rest of the red porker's body struggled against the loop holding his arms against his chest.

"Definitely, he's the one," Julie clasped her hands over her heart, melodrama style.

Cheryl shook her head and rolled her eyes. From the looks

of it, he might be as inclined to jump on stage as her roommate. "Just your type, for sure."

After the team's homecoming win over the visiting Javelinas, as the crowd filed out of the stadium, Julie said, "You simply must go with me to the dance. Don't worry, lots of girls go without dates. Just pretend you're waiting for one of the players." Cheryl argued she had to study for a test scheduled on Monday. Julie said, "That's for tomorrow. I need your help. Tonight's the night I meet Ryder Sheldon." Then she added, "Seriously. I can't possibly go alone."

Julie said they shouldn't arrive at the Student Union's ballroom until after the team did. Cheryl knew her well enough already to know that making an entrance was part of the plan. She had an idea that Julie had cast her as a supporting player, the slightly mysterious new girl on campus, attractive enough to draw glances, but not enough to upstage the star. Well, why not? She'd promised herself a fresh beginning and some fun. Tonight was as good a time as any to start.

She also guessed that the football team's presence held less interest than the group of black-hatted guys in boots clustered in the far left corner of the room. She paused at the doorway, doing her best to keep a smile on her face as Julie waved at someone near the cowboys. Cheryl followed her roommate as she headed toward the girls she'd waved to halfway across the room. Better that than be left standing in the doorway. The night felt like early fall, cool, but most of the girls had turned out in short summery floral print dresses and chunky high-heeled shoes. One wore black Doc Martens with a skirt and a tight sweater.

Julie had vetoed Cheryl's choice of Levi's and a paisley print shirt plus a purple sweater. "No way," she said. After a look in Cheryl's closet, she jerked a long black jersey skirt and a purple, long-sleeved leotard from a pile on her own bed. "No fair hiding that great figure. Wear your boots if you want to, and throw that around your neck." "That" was a long, ruffled, purple flowered scarf.

Cheryl hardly recognized herself when she stood next to Julie in front of their mirror. Instead of a slim, five-foot seven, dark-haired eighteen-year-old with long legs and sexy curves, she saw the sad, overweight, too-old-for-her-age girl who'd spent the past two years literally running away from those pounds and the sadness that had only recently lifted. As she continued considering her image, she saw that different girl, the one her roommate saw, emerge from a shadow.

She noticed Julie watching, and busied herself fussing with the scarf, finally twining it twice around her neck. "I feel like I'm in costume."

Julie laughed. "Isn't everyone? All the time?"

Now, here she was at a dance, dressed in someone else's clothes, acting a part. Trouble was, she didn't know the lines. She stood on the edge of the group, eight of them in all, and hoped no one would ask her any questions, or God forbid, ask her to dance.

Her face felt stiff from holding her smile in place. If she knew how, she'd relax, try to enjoy the music, join the chatter that surrounded her. One of the girls asked her name.

Yes, that's what she could do, introduce herself, tell them all she graduated from high school in Stinnett and planned to major in nursing. For a second her smile felt genuine. And then that second lasted. Cheryl felt her shoulders loosen; she reminded herself to breathe.

The band struck up its first number, "We Are the Champions," and she felt the people in the room take up the business of the evening. She and the group she'd become a part of stood not far from the clutch of cowboys who clustered around one of their own. She had no doubt it was the roper. All around her, the girls chattered—clothes, their courses, recent dates—as she continued smiling. She had that part mastered. Maybe the rest would come to her eventually.

The crowd encouraged the band with loud applause. Without much of a pause, they switched to country mode. After only a few chords, laughter infected the room. "Mommas, Don't Let Your Babies Grow Up to Be Cowboys," bounced from the walls and ceiling. The black-hatted group cheered and pushed Ryder Sheldon toward the dance floor. A baby spotlight found him there alone, shaking his head, grinning, and finally raising his hands in surrender. Another of the cowboys yelled, "He needs a partner!"

Several voices joined, yelling, "Dance, dance."

Cheryl pushed Julie forward. She whispered, "Now's your chance."

The band shifted into a two-step and Julie and Ryder danced as if they'd rehearsed.

The rest of the cowboys ignored the couple and penned Cheryl and the others behind a ring of rodeo rowdies. She heard at least two proposals of marriage and several requests to dance addressed to no one in particular. Cheryl's carefully maintained smile fell away in a spasm of laughter when one of the girls balked at going onto the dance floor until the guy who'd claimed her removed his spurs. The rest of his club immediately started clapping and chanting, "Take 'em off, take 'em off." By the time he managed to remove his hardware, the band finished the song. Ryder and Julie elbowed their way into the laughing crowd until they stood next to Cheryl. One of his friends, the one who'd put an arm around Cheryl and breathed a beery, "Hi there, sugar," at her earlier, slapped Ryder on the back and pulled him close to whisper to him.

Julie hugged Cheryl and whispered, "Thank you! My future is determined, as of this night! He dances like a dream." She fanned herself with her right hand. "I'm going to the restroom to redo my makeup. Be right back."

As Julie left the group, Ryder turned from the other cowboy and stared directly at Cheryl. Then he grasped her right hand. She looked at it as if it weren't connected to her; she felt her smile slip. He said so softly that no one else could hear, "Dance with me. It's an emergency." Before she could answer, if she could have thought of anything to say, he'd pulled her away toward the dance floor.

Some song she didn't recognize, a waltz beat, set dancers circling counterclockwise around the floor. She let Ryder lead her onto the floor and relaxed a little when he winked at her. With a gentle pressure on her right hand, that he'd never yet let go of, he twirled her once, into an old-fashioned dancers' embrace, touching only at her waist and the right hand. She rested her left hand lightly on his shoulder. He was easy to follow.

Ryder wanted to see her smile again, to erase that sad, distant look that had come into her eyes. "I'm Ryder Sheldon. What's your name?"

"Cheryl Magee."

"Thanks for rescuing me."

He knew she didn't understand. "If I don't get away from them, the guys will carry me high all night long. You're stuck with me."

"Why me?"

"Don't know. I heard a voice. It said, 'She'll rescue you.'"

She laughed, just once, like he'd hoped she would. He hadn't told her she looked as skittish as he felt, like she might just go over the fence any minute, like she'd have to be treated with great caution, like a fresh colt.

The waltz ended and without a pause the band played into "Dance With Who Brung You." He pulled her a fraction closer and felt her take a deep breath.

As they moved into a two-step rhythm, Cheryl couldn't control quivering in both her legs. It started when Ryder drew her toward him and a familiar fragrance met her—English Leather, the favorite of all the boys in Iris, Texas. She missed the beat and stumbled, her boot colliding with his. He apologized. She said, "Not your fault. I need to sit this out. Haven't danced in too long."

He didn't let go of her hand, thought he might never catch her again. "I'm ready to leave if you are. Let me take you home."

"I came with Julie. She'll be upset."

"See her hanging around waiting?"

He pointed across the room at Julie dancing, flirting with a tall boy wearing a football jersey. "I'll tell her. Wait for me at the door." He took a step away and turned back. "Please."

She estimated the distance to the door, knew she could be gone and back to the dorm in minutes. He'd never know where and probably not bother to look. She avoided couples as she crossed to the exit where she stopped. He'd said please. So she waited.

CHAPTER 6

December 14, 1996—Ryder Sheldon and Cheryl Magee
Commencement

Ryder took one last look in the closet and the built-in dresser. Killing time. He knew he'd cleared out everything from his dorm room except for what now filled the canvas bag he'd hoisted onto the bare mattress. Wearing the disposable black graduation gown he'd been issued over his Wranglers and starched white shirt, he was certain he looked as stupid as he felt. He also knew that as soon as he tore off that gown and traded the mortarboard for his good hat, he'd pass for a taller version of George Strait.

He hauled the bag down a flight of stairs and locked it in his pickup. Mrs. Albert Friedrich and her doting husband would be waiting to see him walk across the stage and smile for the photographer when he received his degree. With any luck, Cheryl Magee would be, too. He knew she admired George Strait, and when Ryder had asked her to be there, she'd said probably.

He fidgeted in line behind a girl whose last name was Sawyer—he read that on the card she was holding—everyone had been issued one to hand to the reader before they walked across the stage. He stretched and peered over her, searching the auditorium for his mother and Cheryl. They wouldn't be sitting together. He hadn't introduced them yet. Cheryl was the first girl he ever even thought of mentioning to his mother, let alone having them meet. Even for this mid-year ceremony, people packed the front half of the auditorium. Faculty in their academic regalia, lined up in front of the graduating students, blocked his view. He gave up. They would find him soon enough.

If it hadn't been for his mother, he wouldn't even have bothered with this ceremony. The real diploma came in the mail anyway. But she would have been crushed if she hadn't been able to be there to take pictures of him in his cap and gown. She'd show everyone who'd hold still and then she'd add them to the scrapbooks she'd been assembling since his first Little Britches rodeo.

A recording of "Pomp and Circumstance" blared into the auditorium. The procession of faculty followed by soon-to-be-graduates marched at a stately pace to their assigned seats. Following a speech he half-listened to about how the graduates must follow their dreams, he strode across the stage, gripped the President's hand, said "Thank you, sir," and grinned for the official photographer. Back in his assigned seat, he thought briefly about following a dream.

His mother found him as soon as he walked out into the pale winter sunshine. She was wearing a bright blue coat he'd never seen, with a plaid scarf. He hugged her and said, "Momma, you look beautiful."

Albert stood beside her, nodding when she said, "I'm so proud of you, Ryder." Then she stood on tiptoe and whispered, "Your father would be, too."

The three of them asked and answered the questions people trade about how their trip was and was he happy to be finished, and so forth. Then Albert took an envelope from his pocket and said, "Here's something to help you get started. You made your mother very happy. And that makes me happy." Ryder looked inside and saw five one hundred dollar bills, crisp new ones all facing the same direction. It took him a few seconds to get the sense to shake Albert's hand and thank him.

They continued standing, the older two looking pleased, Ryder feeling like he was supposed to do something but didn't know what. And all the time they talked, he scanned the little wads of people strewn around the lawn taking pictures and hugging, looking for Cheryl. When he saw her, he interrupted Albert who had just begun a comment about how much colder it was up here than in Central Texas. "Excuse me," Ryder said, "there's someone I want you to meet."

Before they could ask who, he hurried to Cheryl. "Come with me. You have to meet my mother and stepfather." He caught her hand, felt her hesitate. "It'll be fine. Come on." He knew better than to push or pull. In the several weeks they had dated, he'd seen that head up, widened eyes look that meant "Don't try to make me, I'll balk," enough times to know. Like a nervous filly who knows she might be prey, she never missed an opportunity to protect herself. He spoke softly, "Thanks for coming."

She took a deep breath and walked in the direction Ryder led her. She would have had to be locked in her room to keep her from coming. Since their first real date the next night after homecoming, they had seen one another every day. At first, she thought he turned up in her vicinity by coincidence.

Julie said, "Oh, please. You know he's stalking you. And you like it." Her roommate had stayed huffy, or pretended to, for maybe thirty minutes after she came in from the homecoming dance. Then she admitted she had fallen for the star fullback as soon as they danced and he told her she was the most beautiful woman he'd ever seen. "He's so strong, so masterful. I love being swept off my feet and I know he's the one who will do it, literally." She made that declaration and fell back on her bed. "We danced every dance until the band quit playing. He didn't want to let me go."

Cheryl thought the jock also might have been too flattered to look for anyone else when he already had a pretty blond adoring him. Julie had "adoring" down, all the way. Something she did with her eyelashes and making herself seem a little helpless. Julie said, "So you're free to take Ryder Sheldon."

She hurried to keep up with Ryder's long strides. The graduation gown didn't seem to slow him down. Ryder stumbled on the words, "my stepfather," as he raced through introductions. He and his mother had the same blue, almost turquoise, eyes and the same gentle way of speaking. Cheryl told them she was so glad they had been able to be there and that she hoped they had a good trip. She said to Ryder, "I'll go now so you three can celebrate."

All three of them started talking at once. Ryder won. "No, don't go. They promised me a steak dinner if I made it across the stage. You're invited, too."

Mr. Freidrichs said, "Yes, it's my treat. I would be honored if you would come with us." His speech sounded a little formal, as if he had planned it before he opened his mouth. She watched Ryder's mother watching her husband. She had adoring down also, it seemed.

When Ryder's mother produced a camera, Cheryl volunteered to be the photographer. She took several shots of Ryder alone; he couldn't resist mugging, it seemed; a couple with his mother; and one with his mother and stepfather. She handed the camera back to Mrs. Friedrich who said, "Now I want a few shots of the two of you together." Cheryl didn't know why that should have made her want the woman to adopt her, take her home right then.

She didn't have time to think much about it because Ryder stepped behind her and put a hand on her shoulder. He said, "Make it a good one, Momma. I want a copy." They both smiled and stood together, still as people waiting for a tintype to stop time.

On the way to Albert's Suburban, he whispered to Cheryl that he wanted to talk to her after supper. She nodded and he set to thinking about what he would say later. They'd only been dating a few weeks, but he wasn't ready to call it quits, not by a long sight.

He knew his mother wouldn't be happy unless she saw him eat a big meal. So he ordered a rib eye and finished the entire thing. He and Albert talked about deer hunting. He wanted to know when Ryder would come to visit and would it be before turkey and quail seasons were over. Ryder didn't have the heart to tell Albert he had more important things on his mind.

The four of them lingered, Ryder doing his best to make it worth his mother and Albert's nearly five hundred mile drive getting there. He told them about some of the classes he'd liked and jobs he'd interviewed for, and neither of them frowned when he said he hoped (he chose that word) to sharpen up his roping and compete in several rodeos in the spring. "I haven't given up on getting in the PRCA, making the circuit, while I'm still young enough to do it."

"This is the time, if you're going to, while you're young and single," Albert said. Sounded definite, like he meant it.

His mother's smile said whatever he wanted was okay with her. "Just as long as you try not to break any more bones. I want you to be happy, most of all."

Ryder watched Cheryl's face. She focused on her steak and looked up after she'd cut a nice-sized piece. With it on her fork, she said, "I haven't seen him rope yet. Not a calf anyway." He enjoyed the sound of her laugh that followed.

Full of steak, sitting back in their chairs, glancing at the rest of the post-graduation crowd in the dining area, they had coffee all around, Cheryl drank hers and listened to them talk about his family—sister, nieces and nephews, his mother's cousins. More than once, he'd mentioned his father to her and how hard he'd been to please. She watched his mother chatting and laughing now—not the quiet, dutiful woman he had described to her. Cheryl hadn't asked any questions when he'd talked about them before, and wouldn't tonight. She would listen, but families were something she didn't talk about.

Ryder told them he had rented a house near Hereford with two guys from the rodeo club and that he'd probably take the job he'd been offered with a veterinary medicine company, selling supplies to feedlots in the area. "I might not stay with it long. I'd rather be on horseback if I could." It was the first time she'd heard about the house. She had already concluded the movie last weekend had been their last date. Probably for the best. She didn't need any distractions if she was going to get the grades for admission to the nursing major.

When a spell of silence surprised her, she saw his mother and Albert both nodding, as if Ryder's preference for horseback wasn't a surprise. Cheryl leaned forward and asked his mother if they were staying overnight. They were, at Ryder's sister's, having their Christmas with the grandchildren tomorrow morning because they would be home in Fredericksburg on the actual day. "And it's time we got on the road. They'll be expecting us," his mother said.

Albert drank the last of his coffee immediately, signaled for the check, and paid for the meal in short order. Meanwhile Ryder's mother got in a plea for a weekly phone call or letter from him, and made certain Cheryl knew she was happy he had such a nice friend. "If he ever comes to visit us, we'd be pleased to have you come with him."

Hugging and shaking hands and waving goodbye took a few minutes after they arrived in Ryder's dormitory parking lot. Then Ryder and Cheryl got in his pickup, which he'd left out on the far edge of the lot, parked tail in, ready to leave. He turned on the ignition to run the heater. The radio came on with the Eagles doing "Desperado." He tapped in time on the steering wheel and she hummed along softly until it finished, then he turned off the radio. He asked, "Do you need to be at your dorm right away?"

"Aunt Jean's picking me up in the morning, early."

Another silence made him think of turning the radio back on. He didn't, because he had something to say. As soon as he figured out what, exactly, he'd say it.

"Thanks for going with us. My mother liked you. I could tell."

He looked across the cab, thought she might be holding her breath she was so still. He could see only half her face. The early evening December near-dark surrounded her with a shadow. Her silver hoop earrings caught a light from the moon. He shifted in his seat to see her better.

"I enjoyed it." Her voice got very soft. "Thanks for wanting me to go." She seemed fully occupied by something on the windshield.

Her left hand lay on the between-seat console just close enough for him to touch. When he did, she didn't twitch or move away. He touched the back of her fingers with his fingertips, slid them to her wrist, then held her hand, barely touching. Warmth passed to him, slid up his arm. It happened every time he touched her and surprised him every time. She looked at him, a look that could have been sad or tender. After a deep breath she squeezed his hand and said, "I should go pack."

"When will you be back in the dorm?"

"Day before classes start."

"I want to call you before then."

"When?"

"Maybe tomorrow afternoon." He wanted her to laugh.

She said, "You have a piece of paper?"

Her hand disappeared from his. The small emptiness in his palm went cold.

He found a scrap of paper in the console. When she handed it back, he folded it, placed it in his billfold. "I know it's only three weeks, but I want to see you sooner."

"You shouldn't."

"You don't know that."

"There's lots you don't know."

"That's why people date."

She leaned back and stretched, shaking her head, answering some question he knew he hadn't even asked. "You're too old for me anyway. Graduated." She smiled when she said it; maybe she was joking.

"I am. Everyone knows girls mature faster though, younger."

Her face changed before he finished the sentence. As surely as two fingers on a wick snuff a candle, words extinguished her essence. He'd done it in an instant but had no idea how. He said, "Let go somewhere now. Get coffee. You can pack later." He turned to face her, wanted her to see he was serious, hoped she'd see he was sorry he'd stolen something from her.

Now the shadow nearly covered her face. She didn't answer, looking again toward the windshield. He said almost in a whisper, "My graduation day. Shouldn't you humor me? Just one cup?" He turned the key on again, to let the heater chase the chill. "Please."

Cheryl opened the pickup door. She said, "I really have to go. I'll walk from here. Thanks for inviting me." She heard herself talking faster than usual, but couldn't stop. Before she closed the door, she waved goodbye.

Her hands in her coat pockets, head down, she walked in the direction of her dormitory, watching her feet. When the growl of his truck motor told her he was leaving, she ran.

CHAPTER 7

September 20—September 26, 1997
Cheryl Magee and Ryder Sheldon

First Rodeo

Just like Julie had promised, Ryder Sheldon found her after the rodeo. "As if by a magnetic force, he'll be drawn to you." When Julie said that, Cheryl had laughed at her perpetually dramatic roommate. She suspected Julie read paperback romance novels late at night and hid them in her lingerie drawer.

"And music will play and sparks will erupt; waves will part?"

"Laugh if you will. But don't forget your perfume. And wear something sexy."

As if he'd sworn to meet her exactly in that spot by the door, he walked directly to where she stood. He ignored the people passing on both sides, greeting him, slapping him on the back, and said to her, "Dance with me?" No greeting, no small talk. Like they might have planned it yesterday, not parted abruptly last December.

A lot could happen in nine months. Cheryl thought that just before she said yes when Ryder asked her to dance. The sensation she felt when he touched her hand was the same as the first time they danced. Same as the last time nine months ago, the day he graduated. Something between a thrill and a shiver, between excitement and alarm; it affected her whole body. But tonight she managed not to go rigid, to miss the beat. Not like his graduation night when she ran back to her dorm, feeling that if she didn't run she'd be caught, whirled in a boiling cloud back to that bridge in Iris.

"You've been practicing," he said.

She wasn't about to admit how many times she had two-stepped last summer in her room at Aunt Jean's, alone with the country radio station.

"Nursing students can do anything. Even dance without tripping their partners."

It was true as far as it went. The nursing course she was in now, her first one, had convinced her already; she was meant for it. Every new piece of information she learned, every clinical day, left her standing tall, certain she could be the best, and sure she could control any cloud that threatened her. She'd left Iris for good.

"You're in the dorm again?"

She nodded. "Same roommate, too." It was Julie who had made her promise, one day last week, to come tonight. Julie often operated as if she were in charge of the rest of Cheryl's life. Most of the time, Cheryl didn't mind. Without her prodding, she'd probably study too much and laugh too little.

"I see she's here," Ryder said. He nodded toward Julie and her fullback, several couples away from them, dancing as if they were alone in the crowded, barnlike hall. They'd been dating since last year and to hear Julie tell it, there would be a proposal and a ring before graduation.

"They dragged me along. I'd never been to a rodeo before." She looked up, caught him staring at her. She concentrated on the music. "I can see why you love it. All the excitement." For some reason she didn't understand that made him pull her close. She didn't resist. "And you won."

"A belt buckle. A little money. Not much." He couldn't

keep the excitement out of his voice, didn't try too hard. He'd finally won enough at sanctioned rodeos to fill his PRCA card. Now he'd be a full member. That and finally seeing Cheryl after looking over all the girls at every rodeo dance since last December, made this the best night in a long time.

They stayed on the floor and danced several dances. Sat out, no, actually stood near the floor during one, and then moved smoothly into the mass of couples when a waltz began. After they made several turns around the large hall, the old fashioned music ended. But instead of taking a break, the band picked up the pace, and hit the opening bars of "Cotton-Eyed Joe." Laughter rippled across the floor as couples shifted into lines, stumbling into the first schottische steps. He winked at Cheryl and twirled her into position next to him, his arm around her waist. Before long, as they and the lines of dancers spun like spokes around the floor, he felt sweat creeping below his hatband. By the time the last chorus played and the crowd shouted "bullshit" a final time, he needed to catch his breath.

    Milling dancers made getting off the floor a slow process. He and Cheryl had only taken a few steps when a bull rider whose name Ryder couldn't remember tapped him on the shoulder and asked, "How about sharing your partner?"

    Before he could answer, Cheryl said, "Sorry. Maybe later. He promised to buy me a Coke."

    Ryder shrugged. "Sorry." The bull rider swaggered away like beered-up cowboys do when it's still too early in the evening to start a fistfight. Ryder said, "Guess I better get us something to drink. Be right back." He took two steps toward the bar, then turned back and said, "Don't you leave."

    Waiting for their Cokes, he thought if he'd been eighteen

instead of twenty-two and a grown man, he'd probably have taken the smartass bull rider on—if it had been past midnight. Cheryl was worth the trouble, but he didn't know for sure why.

Three different guys stopped and asked her to dance while they stood near the edge of the dance floor drinking their Cokes. He didn't say a word when she turned them down. They finished their drinks and danced again, another fast one. Walking off the floor when the band took a break, she said, "Didn't you bring someone to the dance? You probably need to mingle or something, being the champion roper and all." That last sounded like a question when she said it.

"I came here looking for you."

"You came here looking for a beer, and you haven't even gotten to have one. Seriously, don't let me slow you down."

He studied her face; she didn't look upset. He laughed, more a chuckle. "Okay, a beer would be nice. I'll get us one; we'll talk."

"Another Coke for me, please."

When he returned, a long-necked beer in one hand, a Coke in the other, she and Julie were standing close, talking. They stopped when he edged up.

"Interrupting something important? I can stand over here to the side."

Julie said, "No, it's just that we have to go. Dustin has to study. Got to make his grades. Eligibility rules, you know."

Grades and studying already seemed like a long time ago, to Ryder. He nodded, said to Cheryl, "We need to stay a while. Let me take you home."

He knew before she said it. "I'd better go." She put a hand on his arm and leaned close. "I'm glad you were here. Maybe I'll see you somewhere again."

"I'll call. Give me your number."

"I don't have anything to write with."

"Tell me. I won't forget."

She leaned closer to tell him and a faint scent rose from her that made him think of his mother's kitchen—bananas, so ripe they must be used today, and cinnamon. He considered touching her hair. Instead, he repeated her number.

He left the dance soon after she did. No sense staying; he'd already had the best night he'd had in a long time. Driving from Amarillo, pulling his horse trailer, with Clint, his roping horse, on board, Ryder took the country route back toward Hereford. He and his two friends had lived in the renovated farmhouse since graduation. Mostly it felt like camping out. They each sort of stuck to their own bedroom, and in the evening, whoever was home watched television in the living room. They all avoided the kitchen, except for the refrigerator, where the beer resided. The only improvement they had made to the old stuccoed frame house involved adding the television dish. Tonight Ryder believed he'd have the place to himself.

He tried to figure out why he couldn't get Cheryl off his mind. He'd gone out with three girls since graduation. And before that, several, but most of them were the sort of girls a guy could meet without making any effort, take out just to have a little company, and then stop calling when she started getting sure enough of him to ask about plans for the next weekend. He'd even made the mistake of taking one of them to a motel for the night after a rodeo. But he'd never been a skirt chaser interested in racking up a "babes I've bedded" list. And he'd never brought any of them out to the house.

More times than he could count, he'd gotten up in the morning and found some blonde in the kitchen searching for coffee, wearing one of his housemates' shirts and nothing else. After the first time that happened, not a week after they moved in, he'd gotten the guys to agree that the bathroom at the back of the house was off limits to visitors. At least there was one place in the house he could be sure not to run into someone's last night date. What if one of them turned out to be his own date from the weekend before?

The steering wheel vibrated as he drifted onto the shoulder. A person had to pay attention full time pulling a trailer. He slowed and gently corrected back onto the roadway. What did he need with a girlfriend anyway? He had plenty else on his mind. Top of the list was the money his mother gave him when he sold her house. He'd stowed it in a CD, $47,000 and planned to save all he could to go with that until he had enough to buy some acres and start a little place raising stock. He'd have to decide whether roping calves or horses made the best investment. So far, in nine months, he'd added nearly $10,000. His buddies called him a tightwad. He called himself a long way from having enough.

The house sat dark, a quarter mile off a county road twelve miles north of Hereford. Someone's old home place, redone several times since it was built in the 40s, it looked best in the dark. In the daylight, a person could see it needed another facelift. A paint job would help a lot, and a new swamp cooler would have made summer more tolerable. But it did have a serviceable barn and horse fencing around thirty acres, plus corrals. The rent, split three ways, came out cheap. So it was okay for now, for three cowboys with jobs in town and roping to do on the weekends.

He flipped on the porch light and the lamp in the living room, and made a beeline for the refrigerator. With a beer in his hand, he called the number Cheryl gave him two hours before.

Legs aimed sideways, doing her best to fit into the back seat of Dustin's Camaro, Cheryl tried not to eavesdrop on Julie and the fullback; some sort of disagreement was in progress. It had begun before they left the dance and had continued at low volume as they sped from Amarillo toward Canyon.

She closed her eyes and replayed the best parts of the evening, scanning fast like avoiding the credits on a rented movie, stopping to slo-mo her favorite parts. As far as she was concerned, the best scene in the drama showing inside her eyelids was when the hero and the female star first began dancing. The second best showed him, his black hat pulled low over his eyes, roping from the back of his galloping horse, halting abruptly, leaping from the saddle, running to the calf, tying three of its legs, and flinging up his hands. Never a wasted move, strong and gentle simultaneously, and all in less than eight seconds. The announcer proclaimed it a championship ride.

Maybe he'd never call again, but tonight she'd been happy, and she could make that last for a while.

"What are you smiling about?" Julie asked. Cheryl opened her eyes, rolled them and shook her head. She closed her eyes again. She didn't intend to give Julie even a bit part in her movie tonight. Cheryl's roommate tended to spread gloom on all in the vicinity if anything little displeased her. Poor Dustin had been tonight's first target. Now Julie wanted to darken the night for her, too. Cheryl thought of Karla; she would have understood and been happy for her.

The sodium vapor lights of the dorm parking lot surprised her. Somehow she'd fallen asleep. Dustin opened his door and leaned forward for her to get out. Julie stayed busy acting put out. Cheryl patted Dustin's shoulder and said, "Thanks for the ride." She ran to the dorm door and took the stairs to her second floor room two at a time.

All last spring semester and during the summer, Cheryl had focused on her coursework. The effort paid off. She made the Dean's List and by the end of the summer earned credits enough to be classified a Junior. Plus the most important part, she'd been admitted to the upper-division nursing program. All that work, plus the hour of exercise she fit in every day, kept her busy, almost busy enough to forget about Ryder. She'd told herself they'd only had a few dates and he was too old for her anyway. In July, back near Borger, she'd even gone to the movie a couple of times with a boy visiting relatives for the summer, people Aunt Jean knew.

As she stood in the dorm bathroom, washing her face, watching in the mirror, she saw her smile turn wistful, then disappear. Who was she kidding? Her original plan had been right. No serious dating until she finished school and had a job far from the Panhandle of Texas, somewhere she could start fresh, be the new person she had already started becoming. Something about the way she felt when Ryder Sheldon arrived on the scene told her they could turn too serious, too fast. She dried her face and hands, then brushed her teeth with a slow, steady intentness the job didn't require.

As she opened the door to their room, Julie handed her the phone, its receiver off the hook, long cord dangling. Cheryl covered the mouthpiece and whispered, "Who is it?"

"I didn't ask." Julie had progressed from put out to snotty.

Cheryl carried the phone to her bed and turned her back to Julie. A voice, Ryder's voice, said, "She said you were awake, out of the room. You have a minute to talk?

"Sure. I was brushing my teeth."

"I wanted to tell you. Well, just to say I'm glad I saw you tonight and we danced."

"Me, too."

"I thought maybe you were still mad. From last December."

"I never was mad at *you*."

"Well, never mind, then. Can we go out next weekend, Friday?" He sounded like he'd been running. Then she heard him swallow, thought he must be drinking a beer.

She wished for the sort of background music that plays when you're on hold with a bank or a doctor's office, something snappy and bright to fill the silence. Now, she couldn't even hear him breathing.

She'd just formed a sentence and inhaled when he said, "Remember, I told you once, people date so they can get to know each other. We'll have fun, the way we did before. That's it."

She exhaled; heard herself saying the opposite of what she'd intended. "Okay, what time?"

They agreed on seven o'clock, for supper and a movie or whatever she wanted. She waited again, another silence connected them. Maybe he had nosy roommates too, and didn't want to talk any more than she did.

She said, "Guess I'll go now. Lots of studying to do tomorrow."

"See you Friday."

From her bed, Julie said, "You can thank me now or thank me later. I told you it was *imperative that you attend* the rodeo."

Cheryl laughed. Julie could make a pronouncement out of the simplest thought, and deliver it as if an audience waited eagerly for every line. She said, "Thank you. Now, go to sleep. *I refuse to respond to any queries tonight.*"

Driving from one feed yard to the next; stopping at every large-animal vet clinic in Deaf Smith, Parmer, Bailey, Castro and Lamb counties; going through his canned speech about the latest in vaccine to prevent BVD, Ryder managed to get through until Wednesday before he gave in. He needed to talk to Cheryl. The sensation affected him like a hotshot must feel to a calf—surprising, aggravating, a little frightening, definitely requiring action. She couldn't talk but a minute, she said, had to get in her run for the day. But hearing her voice, sounding happy and relaxed, was enough.

Friday evening, he rushed through all the calls his Vet Industries job required. He made his last scheduled stop at a feed yard near Dimmitt. Ordinarily he would have been tickled to death at the size of the order they gave him because it meant a big commission, but mostly, impatience gouged him as he wrote the invoice and then said his thank-yous and goodbyes to everyone. Careful to stay under the speed limit, he took the shortest route to the house, watching the fall sun cast long shadows across plowed fields awaiting planting of winter wheat.

He parked his pickup and went straight to the barn to feed his horse. The horse listened patiently as he told him about how he planned to make Cheryl laugh and how she deserved special care and treatment the same way a good horse did. He'd have sworn Clint rolled his eyes at that.

When he got near the front door, Ryder knew he wouldn't need the key he held in his hand. The door stood open about two inches. He yelled his housemates' names and got no answer. He walked off the porch and looked around both sides of the house, saw no one. He went around the back. The screen door drooped at a sad angle from one hinge and the back door moved farther open with each gust of the wind.

An old snake gun he carried under his pickup seat would put a scare in anyone still inside. He crept to the pickup and opened the driver's side door without a sound, found the little shotgun, and walked to the porch again. "This is your last chance to get out," he yelled as he pushed the front door wide open.

Whoever had been there had known they had plenty of time; they'd taken everything, including clothes, television set, and all the beer from the refrigerator. The closets in the three bedrooms gaped open, like so many startled mouths. Not a stitch hung in any of them. They'd even taken the underwear.

The telephone on the kitchen wall probably held no attraction for thieves. So it still worked. The other one, from the living room, seemed to have joined everything else in a trip to who knows where. He called the Deaf Smith County Sheriff's number, explained the problem.

The only thing he knew to do, cuss at the top of his voice, wouldn't do a bit of good. So he sat at the dining room table with the snake gun across his lap. Like that would help. The living room echoed without the couch and chairs and television set. "Guess we could have a benefit dance in here," he said, and listened to his words bounce around the room.

About twenty minutes later, which was sooner than he expected, two deputies arrived and made the same circuit he had. One said, "Damn, looks like they cleaned you out." Ryder wanted to compliment him on his powers of observation, but told himself being a smart ass might not pay.

They questioned him about the usual habits of the three of them who lived there, recent visitors, any suspicious people in the vicinity, and a whole of lot other things. Finally, the one who seemed to be in charge said, "This is the fourth one of these in the county this month. We have some leads, but no suspects yet. We'll try to get some fingerprints here and see if there's any tire tracks."

Ryder smiled when he said that, first because he pronounced tire like "tar," and then because all three of them who lived there drove pickups and they'd probably made enough tire tracks around there to keep a deputy busy for a day or two. He said, "Anything you need me to do, let me know."

The in-charge deputy pulled a three-page form off the clipboard he toted around. "You'll need to list as many things as you can remember that are missing."

"Think you might recover any of it?"

"Not usually, but you never know. You'll need the list for insurance, anyway."

Ryder asked for a form for each of his housemates. Then he went to see what he could do to repair the back door, which looked as if a battering ram had served as a key. The jamb had been splintered, leaving the lock free, and a dent about eight inches in diameter centered like a target in the door's middle, with fractures radiating outward.

"Whatever they used to ruin that door, it's the same as at the other three places." The second deputy stood ready to dust for prints. Ryder backed away, thinking a big piece of plywood might have to do on there for the night.

Before long, just after dark, first one, then the other of his housemates got home. He explained, in as few words as possible, and left them talking to the deputies.

He sat on the front porch and tried to fill in the list of stolen items. What would anybody want with his old Wranglers? The beer he understood, and the television set, but they'd even taken the bedspreads off the beds. Why didn't they want the dining room table and chairs?

After the deputies left, he went inside and found his housemates sitting in the dining room like a matched pair of bookends, elbows on the table, heads in hands. He sat down, too. Nobody said anything for a while. Then one of them said, "Hell, boys, I think we need some beer. I'll make a run to the liquor store. At least we still have the refrigerator." The two of them left, saying they'd be back soon.

Ryder started again on the list. Then he stopped, just as he wrote "assorted underwear." He stood so fast that his chair toppled. He ran the several steps to his bedroom where he jerked open the dresser drawers, all four of them, starting at the top, left hand side. All completely empty. "Shit! They even got my paycheck!" He'd picked it up the day before and intended to deposit it tomorrow. "If that doesn't just rip it. Son of a bitch. I'd like to catch those bastards." He stopped mid-rave. Cussing seemed useless with no one to hear it.

He lay across his mattress with his eyes closed, his mind as empty as the dresser drawers. That didn't last long. He went to the kitchen again, scrambled around in the junk drawer, found the landlord's number and called him. For some reason, the man didn't seem too upset, just said something about how it had been a long time since anything like that happened, and told Ryder he'd bring out his tools tomorrow and fix the door.

His housemates surprised him by coming back not long after he hung up. The three of them each drank a beer quickly, in silence. With the second one, they all three began talking, not really making much sense, just cussing and wondering what to do about getting a television set and some new clothes. One of them said, "I had a date tonight. But I don't think she'd like me turning up smelling like the manure truck I drove all day."

Ryder stood up again, nearly tripped on the table leg as he headed to the kitchen phone. "Goddamn, I have a date!"

The other two laughed. One of them popped open another Miller. "Don't worry, there's girls around every corner."

"Not this one. Y'all be quiet." He punched the phone's

numbers as if they were to blame.

As soon as he heard a hello, he said, "Let me speak to Cheryl, please. She's not? Do you know where? This is Ryder." He listened to her roommate explain that she'd come upstairs and changed into her running clothes after she'd waited for him downstairs an hour.

"When she gets back, tell her I'll explain everything. There was a burglary." He stopped Julie when she started asking questions. "Just tell her not to leave. I'll be there in thirty minutes."

He hung up before Julie could ask any more questions. He had plenty of his own tonight.

Ryder pulled into the dorm parking lot in just under twenty-five minutes after he left his near-empty house. He worried all the way there about how to make Cheryl believe he hadn't pulled some slimy payback trick standing her up. That, and a lot of other things—could the thieves cash his paycheck before he could get in touch with Vet Industries, what was he going to wear to work next week until he could buy some new clothes, and who in the hell steals bedspreads? And just as he passed through Umbarger, when he quit feeling sorry for himself for about two minutes, he noticed his gas gauge move into the red space just above empty.

He made it, barely, and now he had to find Cheryl and try to explain. Damn, he wished he'd had something to eat. He probably still smelled like Shiner. Only a few cars waited in the parking lot, all casting long shadows in the glow of the tall safety lights spaced around the perimeter. Standing by his pickup door, he scanned the vehicles for signs of life. Only one, a dark blue Toyota in the far corner showed a glimmer. Someone smoking. Trudging toward the dorm lobby, he told himself she'd understand, hoped she wasn't the type who'd blame him for something he had no control over.

Julie answered the phone when he called from the lobby, said she hadn't seen or talked to Cheryl since he'd called earlier. She sounded peeved, like she'd been the one stood up. He heard her draw a breath, knew she'd make a speech if he gave her a chance. He told her he'd wait for Cheryl in the lobby and hung up before she could say anything else. He felt a second's pity for that football jock she had buffaloed. Then he went back to feeling sorry for himself.

He stared out at the parking lot, and past, into the shadows between buildings, not moving from his post just inside the double glass doors. Three plump girls wearing loose T-shirts, too-tight shorts, and athletic shoes ignored him as they giggled past. Each wore a towel draped around her neck and carried a bottle of water—girls without dates working at having fun. Guys would just go drink beer.

Ryder told himself he could stand there and comment on the dorm lobby traffic or get outside and try to find Cheryl. She ought to know better than to run in the dark.

When the clock in the dorm lobby showed seven forty-five, Cheryl walked slowly up the stairs to her second floor room. She shrugged when Julie asked why she was still there. "I'm going for a run."

"Any message for Ryder?"

Cheryl shook her head. She left her skirt and sweater in a heap on her closet floor and pulled on loose fitting track shorts, tied on her running shoes. She dug in her top drawer, found a sweatshirt, pulled it over her head, and added earphones which she plugged into her Walkman. Without a word, she quietly closed the door on her way out. The sound of ZZ Top's "Sharp

Dressed Man" pushed aside her urge to cry. In seconds she stood in the parking lot. A minute later, she shifted from a fast jog to a full run, headed east, into the shadows hugging the campus buildings. The dark had never frightened her.

She found her pace, steady, rapid, not a strain. After crossing the campus, instead of retracing her route, she jogged in place, watching date night traffic pass the south entry to campus. She switched the cassette off, left the earphones in place, and heard her breathing grow shallow, bordering on erratic. She swallowed the lump of disappointment that could turn to tears. A pickup braked to a screech as she ran in front of it, across the street and onto a street of small, weary, rental houses. She counted twelve blocks on the residential streets and then doubled, then quadrupled it, by passing the same houses first heading south, then north, and so forth. And with each circuit she pushed her pace faster.

Maybe she deserved being stood up. She had left without any explanation after his graduation. But couldn't he have just ignored her at the rodeo, or not called that night, or never asked her out again? She'd thought three years of self-imposed weekend nights alone in her room had formed a callus over all the tender spots she'd had at sixteen. He'd showed her some were still exposed. She ran on, noticed some houses standing vacant, a few yards obscured by trash and rusting appliances. Broken street lights left long stretches of street completely dark.

She flipped the earphones down to rest around the back of her neck, and heard footsteps behind her, distant, but as rapid as her own. Not changing her speed, she glanced left and right, intending to run toward any bright light she saw. If she turned back the way she had come, she'd have to face her follower. She continued forward, accelerating gradually, telling herself silently she could outrun most men.

The steps behind her quickened and came closer. Cheryl heard panting. She remembered an algebra question that ended, "How many miles before B overtakes A?" but didn't recall the rest of the problem. Six blocks more and the footsteps behind her still seemed to match hers exactly. Those together with her heartbeat deafened her.

At the next intersection, without slackening her stride, she turned abruptly to her right, in the middle of the street, and ran west, staying near the center of the pavement. A few more blocks and she'd be on Twenty-third.

On a controlled track, a final lap, all-out burst could shock an opponent, shave critical seconds, make the difference between first place and also-ran. But she'd already run all-out for more than a mile. She'd spent what she had. Each successive breath hung higher in her chest. With the lights on Twenty-third in sight, she stopped dead still and turned around, hands on her hips and what she hoped passed for a fierce scowl masking her face.

A skinny guy, holding a leash attached to a panting pit bull, ran toward her. He yelled, "Thanks for pacing me! Bozo needed the exercise." With a block between them, he tugged the leash and reversed direction. She bent forward from the waist and sucked in a breath that filled her chest, then two more. After that she stood erect and walked the rest of the way to the dorm, listening to the little old band from Texas.

Ryder knew he'd never forgive himself if someone had hurt Cheryl. It was bad enough that he probably had, but running in the dark, she'd be an easy target for anyone. He sat in his pickup alternately watching the borders of the parking lot and scanning the dorm doorway. Nine o'clock and still no sight of her. He leaned toward the glove compartment, opened it, and found a nearly empty package of Red Man. He sniffed the stringy contents, getting a whiff of moist tobacco. Then he saw a girl in shorts, showing great legs, walk slowly from the edge of the lot on his right toward the building. In hurry to get out of the pickup, he flung tobacco in the seat, but he managed to get to the dorm door before her.

He called her name, and didn't wait for her to answer. He said, "I'm so sorry. Will you let me explain?"

He couldn't read her expression; disappointed, sad, and relieved each registered for an instant. And all the while, she never looked away. She seemed to study him for a long time. Then she smiled. He relaxed. She said, "I need to sit down. I ran a long way."

He put an arm around her shoulders, loosely, carefully. She leaned against him. He told himself it was probably for warmth. He said, "Come with me. I have a sad story to tell you."

CHAPTER 8

June 12-June 13, 1998—Cheryl Magee and Ryder Sheldon
Happy Birthday

Early Friday morning, Cheryl had answered the phone in the kitchen. The connection crackled, but she clearly heard Beth say, "I'm coming to Stinnett for your birthday."

Cheryl said, "My birthday's not until tomorrow."

"I know. That's why I'm calling today. So you can meet me." The voice belonged to her middle sister, but its cheerful sound made her words a foreign dialect. For the past three months, Beth had called at least every other week—a new upset she had to talk about, no one else would understand—and always her voice came muffled and damp, hurrying ahead of dammed up tears. So far, she had always settled down after telling Cheryl about her latest thirteen-year-old misery—girlfriends who gossiped about her, a teacher who gave her an F, arguments with their mother about clothes, about going to a dance, about almost anything you could name.

Cheryl always listened because she remembered being thirteen, and how one word, or a snub—real or imagined—could spark an outburst and ruin a day that had been "the very best day ever." For her at thirteen, nothing—no event, not any person, and never her mother—had ever been just okay. The only emotions she had recognized then were the extremes. And still, some days she found herself either near the edge of a pit or on the threshold of paradise. Listening to Beth, she always made certain she didn't offer any advice beyond "Don't make any decisions when you're very sad or very happy." She'd learned a lot since thirteen, and that was a big part of it.

Cheryl asked, "Does Daddy know, and Mother?"

"I'll be on the bus that gets to Borger at ten in the morning. It's been so long. I can't wait. Bye!"

Ryder was coming up tomorrow, to meet Uncle Skip and Aunt Jean. He'd be there by eleven. Cheryl planned to show him the Canadian River and Borger's points of interest; she'd laughed when she said that. Although Borger wasn't a bad town. Certainly better than Iris. Now, with Beth turning up, she wondered if she should tell him not to come. There was sure to be some kind of drama.

She didn't allow herself to think long about how often she'd found herself smiling since he called Wednesday night. Not that the call surprised her; the past two semesters, he'd called often and they'd been together almost every weekend since September—seventeen rodeos and assorted other good times. But now, back in Stinnett, she was two and a half hours away from him, not thirty minutes down the road. And she would be all summer—geographically inconvenient, someone labeled it.

He'd asked to take her out to dinner for her birthday, even invited her aunt and uncle. Aunt Jean had said, "He must be a very nice young man, inviting us to dinner and all. But we'll be happy just celebrating with you here for dessert." Then this morning, just before Beth called, Aunt Jean told Cheryl to place her cake order. She would make any kind she wanted. "Your twentieth should be extra special."

Cheryl watched her aunt assemble ingredients for the devil's food cake she chose, moving from cabinet to refrigerator to kitchen drawer without a wasted step. Her aunt asked, "Everything okay?" She said it without looking up.

Cheryl relayed Beth's announcement. "I doubt she's asked permission. Mother wouldn't allow her to come alone." She dangled the phone receiver to loosen the coils that had twisted themselves into knots. "Maybe I should call Daddy."

Aunt Jean dusted three cake pans with flour and wiped her hands, leaving a white print on each rear pocket of her Wranglers. She said, "Or I could, and just invite all of them to come up tomorrow. How would you feel about that?"

Her mother probably wouldn't come anyway, but her dad and both her sisters might. "That's a lot of trouble for you."

"Not really." Aunt Jean measured shortening into the bowl of the standing mixer that lived on the kitchen counter. "You might have to have dinner here unless they'll stay overnight." She looked at the recipe propped against the toaster. "Has your daddy met Ryder yet?"

"No."

"Do you want him to?"

Cheryl said, "We could make something easy for dinner, maybe ham and potato salad and slaw, sort of a picnic. Less trouble." She watched her aunt add sugar to the shortening, the grains spilling smoothly from the metal cup. She stopped herself before asking if she could lick the bowl—thought a person one day short of twenty years should probably be past such things.

Aunt Jean ran a rubber spatula around the inside of the bowl, then pushed the power lever on the mixer head forward. She raised an eyebrow at Cheryl, and said, "Well…"

The sound of the mixer filled the space between them. Her aunt added eggs, one at a time, then the mixture of flour, cocoa, soda and salt alternately with buttermilk, each slowly, as if nothing about the process could be hurried. The mixer hum pitched slightly higher.

Cheryl's dad called her at least once a week, Wednesday evening, when her mother went to church. When she first got to school, Cheryl thought he worried about her. But now it seemed more like he needed someone to listen, same as Beth. He'd talk about the weather, about cotton prices, machinery he'd repaired, something about her sisters. And usually, just before he hung up, he'd say, "Your mother's okay, I guess. Just about the same."

She didn't know what that meant. Her mother hadn't answered any of the letters Cheryl had written. Beth's occasional notes always included some mention of an argument they'd had or how "She's gotten even stricter and if it wasn't for Daddy and volleyball, she'd have me in church all day Sunday and every Wednesday night plus going out door to door, witnessing." Because it was Beth, she didn't count on the absolute truth of every word. Exaggeration seemed to go along with being thirteen.

Cheryl watched the beaters spin. She said, "I don't mind if he meets him. He's not likely to jump to conclusions like some people would." So far, she and Ryder had been too busy having a good time for either of them to talk much about family details. It was bound to happen sometime.

The mixer noise stopped. Aunt Jean said, "I'll call your dad as soon as the cake's in the oven."

Driving between sales calls to close out his work week, Ryder couldn't focus on the details of the newest animal remedies he should be pushing for thinking about what to tell his landlord. His housemates had both moved out, one just after the first of the month, and the other two days ago. There hadn't been any more break-ins or other trouble. Both of them left because of love, or at least because of girls, and if they told the truth about it, because they were too lazy to cook or clean up behind themselves. To

Ryder, that kind of move seemed awfully close to a permanent commitment.

Until yesterday, he'd thought finding new housemates to split the rent or packing up and finding a new place were his only choices. It was one of those choices Uncle Butch would have called "shit or go blind." Then last night the owner came by and offered to sell him the place and the twenty acres it sat on, plus he'd finance it. Five percent interest. "Contract of sale. No down payment. You keep paying what you three have been paying and in a few years, it's all yours," he'd said. Made it sound simple. Ryder knew better. Meant he wouldn't have any equity until the whole $86,300 was paid off, and a big part of the payment would go to interest every month. He still had the money his mother had given him from selling their land, but that was for later, to get his stock operation started. On the other hand, if he did take the owner's deal, he could walk away from it any time.

He still hadn't come up with an answer by the time he got back to the house after work. And he didn't have a birthday present for Cheryl. He doubted she expected one, but he wanted to surprise her. Rushing through his work had left him enough time do a little shopping, if he hurried.

The mailbox at the gate offered a handful of junk and an envelope from his mother. She didn't usually write, just called. He tore it open, leaving the pickup idling. The last lines of the letter, after a half a page of "everything here is fine" told him what she wanted. Would he take flowers out to his father's grave—artificial would be fine, would last longer. She had done it every year on the fifteenth of June since he died, but couldn't make the trip this year.

He slammed the flap on the mailbox closed, and drove to the barn where he fed and watered his horse. Then he raised dust getting to the county road. In fifteen minutes he parked in front of Walmart in Hereford. When he left, he carried a large artificial flower arrangement, a birthday card, and a giant bag of Cheetos. On his way out of town, he stopped at Allsup's for a Big Gulp size Dr Pepper.

The Catholic cemetery outside Bethel showed the results of its caretakers' efforts. The congregation's women did that and every other tedious job in the parish. Until she moved to Central Texas, his mother had been one of the most diligent members of that group. If any people belonged in heaven, they did. Ryder figured out as he drove from Hereford that his mother had a reason for sending him, instead of his sister, on this errand. Otherwise she would have made the trip from Fredericksburg herself, no matter what. He hadn't been back to the cemetery since the funeral four years earlier.

The spindly legs of the easel holding the arrangement didn't want to hold in the hard ground. After some grappling, Ryder dropped to his knees and managed to jam each of the four wires deep enough to withstand a stiff wind. Still kneeling, he offered an "Our Father." At the end of the prayer, he crossed himself, and then he stood.

Well, he thought, that's done, as he dusted his hands on his pants. He leaned down once more to straighten the flowers, jiggled the arrangement to see it would hold, straightened up, and couldn't make himself move. Finally, he squatted, the way cowboys do, and, for the first time he could recall, he talked to his dad. He told him about his job, rodeoing on the weekends, about the nice girl he was seeing, how he had to decide about where to live, how sorry he was they never got along—talked until he ran out of things to say. Off to his right, a jackrabbit sprinted between headstones and then stopped and watched him. Ryder stood, dusted his hands again. "Bye, Dad."

He took his time on the trip back to the empty house. By the time he got there, the burglar light the landlord installed lit the place. And he knew he wasn't ready to buy a house and land. Owning a place was something you did when you were ready to settle down. No need to rush that. Tonight he had to get ready to go to Borger tomorrow.

Lynette, their ten-year-old sister, elbowed past Beth as they got out of the car. And she flung herself into a hug around Cheryl's waist. Beth pouted her way up the sidewalk to the porch, but couldn't keep up the bad humor long after Uncle Skip told her how pretty she'd gotten since he saw her last. Cheryl's dad moved more slowly than either of the girls, as he carried a large bag in one hand and a covered baking dish in the other. "Your mother sent some rolls to go with dinner." He lifted the baking dish.

Then he raised the bag. "And this is your birthday present from her." He nodded and raised an eyebrow. Cheryl didn't know what that meant.

Soon after her dad and sisters arrived, Ryder pulled slowly into the driveway. Cheryl waited for him on the porch. She hugged him briefly and whispered, "Plans changed. I hope you won't mind."

He shrugged. "It's your birthday. You get to do whatever you want."

"I'm so glad you came." She led him toward the door. "My dad and sisters drove up from Iris. So we're eating here, middle of the afternoon. They'll leave before dark. Come meet them."

Cheryl introduced Ryder to everyone, starting with Aunt Jean. She watched her dad squint at him and then seem to relax after Ryder took off his summer straw Stetson before he shook hands with her aunt. Uncle Skip made things easy by asking Ryder how rodeoing was going. And when Ryder told about how the last calf he roped managed to get out of his tie down, and him losing his hat to boot, they all laughed. Then her uncle asked if he'd come out to the barn and tell him what he thought about the horse he'd gotten in trade for two steers last week. Her dad and uncle and Ryder headed outside. Cheryl took a deep breath and smiled at Aunt Jean.

Her aunt said, "Don't worry. They'll like him. He has manners." She put an arm around Lynette and said, "Come tell me about school while I work on dinner."

Beth pulled at Cheryl's elbow. "Why did you tell? I have to talk to you. Alone."

"Daddy would worry himself sick if you took off on the bus. And mother would have a fit. What's so important?" She steered her sister to the front bedroom.

Beth closed the door. She sounded breathless when she said, "I think Mother's losing her mind."

Cheryl waited. Better to let her tell it her own way.

Her sister paced from the door to the window and back before she spoke again. She sat on the bed. "You'll probably think I'm making this up. I know Daddy would so I haven't told him. She thinks people are watching the house. Makes me lock all the doors whenever we're there, won't let me or Lynette go outside unless she can see us. And now she's planning to put some kind of dummy in the window anytime we leave so *they* will think we're still there."

"Who does she think *they* are?" A raft of questions came to Cheryl; she'd just finished her psych-mental health course.

"I don't know. I'm afraid to ask. First time she said those

things was last week." Beth started crying. "Don't you think that's crazy?"

"She could be sick, not necessarily crazy."

"She made us start going to a different church. A new church. The preacher is a plumber during the week. Everybody shouts, speaks in tongues. Her, too. Scares me. But she makes me and Lynette go with her." She stood up and paced the same path she made earlier.

"You have to tell Daddy."

"You think he'll believe me? She acts normal around him. Well, normal for her."

"Yes, you have to tell him." She patted the bed, pulled Beth down to sit beside her. "She may need help. He'll see she gets it."

"If you'll come home, he might."

"He'll help her." She kept her voice calm, even though the thought of going back to Iris made her swallow to settle the knot in her throat.

Beth fell over on the bedspread. She cried the same way she had when she was six and her puppy died, sounding as if her heart would never be whole again. Cheryl rubbed her back. She wondered if she would ever have it in her to be a good mother, to be able to help a child go through all the normal misery and not be the cause of anything worse.

Gradually Beth's sobs slowed to whimpers and sniffling. Then she sat up and blew her nose and dried her eyes. She said, "Thanks." After a couple of deep breaths, she said, "You never told me you had a boyfriend. He's so good-looking."

"Are you okay now? Aunt Jean probably needs help with dinner."

Beth stood up. "I'll be okay."

"Promise me you'll tell Daddy."

Her sister nodded and opened the door. Cheryl's stomach told her Beth was more likely to buy a bus ticket to anywhere than to tell their dad.

Beth shut the door again. She asked, "Does your boyfriend know about you?"

Cheryl turned away. Without looking at Beth, she said, "Who told you?"

Silence, thick as a curtain, hung between them when Cheryl turned toward her sister.

Beth shrugged. Cheryl heard something that sounded like satisfaction when her sister spoke, "Mother said it was for my own good, so I wouldn't turn into a sinner like you."

Cheryl closed her eyes, took a deep breath. She'd wondered when it would happen. And now Beth probably thought she had a weapon. She was wrong. Cheryl didn't intend to be wounded ever again.

Beth renewed her crying; it came easily at her age, Cheryl knew. Beth said, between sniffles, "I didn't mean to upset you. I'm sorry."

"Wipe your face. We'll talk about all this some other time."

Her sister passed her shirtsleeve across her eyes. When Beth looked up, Cheryl wanted to laugh at the poor imitation of tragedy on her teenaged face.

Cheryl opened the door and stood back for her to pass.

In the kitchen, Aunt Jean corralled Beth in a big hug and put her to work washing the cookware. Cheryl left them talking about the high school volleyball team. She opened the back door and found her dad standing on the porch, looking toward the east, at the horse in the pen near the barn. He spoke softly, almost a whisper. "Ryder says she's a good mare, given her age. Gentle, not high strung. Did I ever tell you when was a kid I wanted to be a cowboy?"

She leaned against him, circled her left arm around his thin back. "Did Aunt Jean tell you about Beth calling?"

He nodded. She watched his profile, wishing she could erase the sadness that made his face sag. "I knew she was upset. Teenagers get that way a lot." He looked at Cheryl. She saw a trace of a smile. "I guess you remember."

Although she'd spent a lot of time trying to forget, she did recall all too clearly. "It's Mother she's worried about." She watched the mare amble around the corral. "Please talk to Beth. It's important." She waited, watching her dad watch the horse. "Especially at her age."

Her dad breathed out a sigh. "Sometimes I don't know what to do." He pointed out toward the barn where Uncle Skip stood with Ryder. "Maybe he'll teach you to ride. Seems like a nice young man. Not a boy."

"I should go help in the kitchen."

"Send Beth out here, would you?"

Ryder had watched Cheryl's sister, the teenager, moving from one person to another, skittish, not settling, staying just out of reach, since he'd seen her pull away from their father, out on the porch. This one felt threat, was sure something might down her at any minute. He wondered if Cheryl or her father knew she might break and run.

Her aunt pointed him to the chair next to Cheryl's when they sat for dinner. Reminded him of his mother. Her uncle, newly retired and planning to raise a few cattle, actually seemed interested in hearing his ideas about raising feeder calves versus starting a cow-calf operation. Good people. He could see why Cheryl liked living with them. Her dad and sisters seemed to get along fine with her. It must have been her mother that she'd had to get away from.

His deeper thoughts about Cheryl's family evaporated when she reached for his hand and held on while she made a wish over her birthday candles. The only thing he could focus on was that sensation that never failed to move through him when they touched—like a roar of applause that grew from his chest and swarmed to his head. He never trusted himself to speak when he felt it; he knew he would shout. Once in a while, she'd settle long enough for him to get used to the feeling; she might hold onto his hand, or lean on him. But more often she kept her distance—close enough to feel her breathing, not close enough to hold tight. Today she held on, stayed near. Almost like she needed him.

Cheryl ate slowly, watching Beth, thinking about how her mother had been right to warn her sister. When Aunt Jean lit the candles and told her to make a wish, Cheryl closed her eyes and wished to be thirteen again, and saw herself running.

She helped clear the table, even though Aunt Jean told her she should have the day off on her birthday. Beth and Lynette followed the three men out to the corral. Cheryl watched through the kitchen window. Aunt Jean asked, "Is she all right?"

"She's worried about Mother. I told Daddy." Cheryl rinsed the plates and placed them upright in the dishwasher.

"Anything else?"

"Mother told her about me, about why I left home."

Her aunt spoke from behind her, softly. "Beth should hear it from you, too."

Cheryl turned on the faucet, watched the water flow into

the sink, and the suds rise over the grimy skillet and saucepans. When foam covered them, she turned off the faucet. She faced her aunt. "She knows. Mother told her, warned her not to be a sinner like me. What else is there to tell?"

"Everybody's truth is different. Your mother sees one thing; you see another." Aunt Jean's hand on her back felt warm, a poultice.

Cheryl plunged both her hands into the dishwater, attacked the skillet with the Chore Girl. "She may be right."

"You both may be."

Laughter, from outside, bounced in the open window. Cheryl saw Lynette and Beth, each holding one of their dad's hands, pulling him toward the horse, urging him to get on. "She's still a little girl."

Aunt Jean said, "Promise me you'll talk to her."

Her dad and the girls began leaving for Iris—that's how it always seemed, like leaving anywhere took a lot of time and activity, and had to be done in steps—close to five o'clock. Cheryl followed the three of them from the porch to the car, carrying the baking dish. It now held half of the birthday cake and an envelope addressed to her mother. The note Cheryl wrote thanked her for the birthday gift—a Bible. It also said she wished her mother had been there with them for the cake. She'd signed it "with love."

Beth stood outside the car's rear door, after her dad and sister busied themselves buckling in. She whispered to Cheryl, "I'll do what you said, talk to Daddy. I love you, Cheryl."

Cheryl told her she loved her, too, reminded her not to do anything stupid, and said she'd call her.

Beth hung onto her hand. She said, "I'm sorry if I made you sad. Don't be upset with me."

Cheryl opened the Chevy's back door, kissed Beth on the

forehead, and nudged her into the seat. Then she stood and shut the door. "Buckle up."

Ryder watched from the front porch, with Cheryl's uncle, as her sisters and dad drove away. He could see, from her gait and the set of her shoulders, the day had worn her out. And it wasn't even dark. But by the time she got to the porch, her smile reappeared and the sparkle that came with it, that made him want to stand near, returned.

She said, "Hey, cowboy, let's go sightseeing."

He wished he'd brought her something better than a birthday card.

They spent an hour driving around Borger, with her telling stories she'd heard about the oil boom days and the rough place it used to be. Now it looked tame, changed by time and good intentions. A Sonic Drive-In provided all they wanted for supper—two Cokes and a shared order of french fries.

Now, as he followed her directions toward the river, north out of Borger, the stories stopped. Something about the silence and the distance that deepened her eyes, made him want to pull to the side of the road and stop the engine so he could hear what she was thinking, without her having to say it. He asked, "Did your birthday wear you out?"

"You can park over there." She pointed to a four-space parking area under a clump of cottonwood trees near the Canadian River. "I have something to tell you."

He parked facing west. Watching the sun set always calmed him down. Maybe it had that effect on everyone.

Now that they were stopped, the words Cheryl had been trying to assemble hung in her chest. When he heard them, he'd take her back to Aunt Jean's and she'd never see him again. Even now, every time he called, it still surprised her. These days, what guy his age dated and never went beyond kissing? He never asked why she held back, but surely he had to wonder.

She exhaled and then let the truth spill out—the drinking and general wildness, the pregnancy, the Gleason Home, her mother, leaving Iris—and once she began, she never slowed until she'd told it all. She finished with, "You deserve someone better, someone you can be proud of. It's time you knew so you can find her."

She had hoped he wouldn't say anything. And for a long time, he didn't. He reached for her hand and held it. She barely heard when he said, "What did you think I'd do or say when you told me all that?"

"What is there to say? It happened. It's who I am." She watched the last bit of day disappear over the horizon. "I should have told you sooner."

"Yes. No sense carrying all that around." He pointed to a dove settling into the nearest cottonwood. "It's the past. Doesn't matter to me."

She felt the fist that had lodged in her stomach unclench. He turned toward her and took off his hat. "I've done things I'm not proud of, too. I figure we get a chance to start fresh every day." He squeezed her hand and then pulled her toward him. "I'm sticking with you unless you run me off."

She wrapped both arms around him and kissed him, a deep, can't catch my breath, sort of kiss that for the first time she didn't try to control. When they parted for a second, he touched her face and smiled. He said, "No rush. We're going to be fine."

She kissed him again. He held her close, so near she felt his heartbeat, even though the console between the seats kept them apart.

Part III
2000-2006

CHAPTER 9

February 11-13, 2000—Ryder and Cheryl Sheldon
Caught in a Blizzard

Ryder watched the windshield wipers push fat flakes of snow to either side. The radio weather announcer's voice filled the pickup cab, making one more approaching winter storm sound like the blizzard of the century. "Bearing down from the west, moving rapidly from Arizona into northern New Mexico," the man said. "Stay tuned for regular updates."

So far, since Hereford, they'd only run into a few showers like this one, none of them lasting more than a couple of miles, and most of it melting when it hit the pavement. He shifted his eyes from the blades' slow, steady motion to get a look at Cheryl. From her profile, he guessed watching the snow hypnotized her a little, settled the jitters she'd said made her have trouble deciding what to pack.

He told himself he was calm, too. He'd driven this road, pulling a horse trailer, plenty of times—to Springer, Taos, other places north, rodeoing. But he'd never been headed to his own wedding before. They had taken four days off, including the weekend. Red River's ski area waited. They would race downhill on their first day as man and wife, tomorrow, Saturday to celebrate Valentine's Day a little early. Maybe he had been calmer when he was on his way to ride rough stock in some country rodeo. But the smile he couldn't get off his face reminded him of something he already knew—he could be excited and happy at the same time.

He touched her hand, and felt his own tingle. "You warm enough?"

She nodded and pointed ahead at the thickening snowfall. "This may turn into an adventure."

The way she said it, he wondered if the possibility of a blizzard was all she meant. "I expect it will. One way or another." Getting married definitely qualified. If the console hadn't been in the way, he'd have snugged her up under his right arm. As it was, he squeezed her hand, the left one, where he would soon put the ring.

Ten a.m. and they were close to Grady, New Mexico. If everything went their way, they'd be in Taos by two or three, Mountain Time, at the latest. They would stop at the Taos County Courthouse for a marriage license, and then be in Red River by five, at the condo they'd reserved. Tomorrow morning the Justice of the Peace would make it all official. They had planned it together, but getting them there was his job. He focused on the road, and flipped the wiper control up a notch.

An hour later, when they crossed under I 40 at San Jon, where a left turn would have taken them to Tucumcari, he wondered if his plan to take the scenic route, not the Interstate, might be a mistake. New Mexico didn't waste much money on clearing the state roads unless a real blizzard covered them completely. Interstates 40 and 25 got most of the attention. He sat up straighter and moved the heater control to defrost. They'd planned to stop in Logan for lunch. A trickle of melted snow cleared the edges of the windshield. He slowed from seventy to sixty. They could eat lunch and talk about whether they should change plans. Cheryl turned off the radio. He waited for her to say something. Most females would have started fussing about danger and sulking about delaying the wedding, back when it first started snowing. He wouldn't blame her if she did.

She said, "I love the way this feels—like we're in one of

those glass globes, in a whole different little world, insulated by snow and detached from everything except whatever giant hand shakes the globe."

He thought about pulling to the side of the road and kissing her.

Cheryl had never told Ryder, but she loved the smell of his pickup cab. Sweaty leather, old fashioned spicy aftershave like her dad used, hay, and the package of chewing tobacco lying open on the dash, all blended and smelled to her like security. She would ride anywhere with him just to inhale the air in there. During the past year and a half, she had made enough miles with him—to rodeos all over West Texas and New Mexico, to Central Texas to visit his mother, and up to her aunt and uncle's—to trust he would get them to any destination. Now, sealed in this comfortable space, lulled by the rhythm of wiper blades and swirling snow, she could easily have slept. If she closed her eyes, she would rerun the scene, for the hundredth time, of him saying last September, "Don't you think it's time we got married?"

She hadn't dreamed about some fancy proposal, but she'd nearly laughed when he said that, as if he were certain they would, and all that remained was to decide on a date. A look at his face told her he meant it. So she didn't laugh. Instead, she surprised herself by saying exactly what she felt, that before they decided on *when*, they had to talk about the *if* and *why* of it first. She had finished her degree in May and started work as a Registered Nurse in June. The girl she'd been at fifteen might have followed her first impulse and set a date that very month. She'd learned some caution since then.

So they talked. Because she'd often thought he hoarded words, unwilling to use them unless absolutely necessary, his carefully stated, often elaborate, answers and questions amazed her. She realized that one man watched from inside him while another, the cowboy of deeds more than words, ran the show most days. The other man, the one of complex thoughts and sentences, emerged only when needed. For several months, on no set schedule, they discussed everything from politics, to religion, to honor and fidelity, and a lot of other abstract notions. Neither of them mentioned having children. On many topics they agreed and on some they agreed to disagree. Nothing sounded like a deal-breaker, the cowboy told her. She agreed.

Then on January first, he pulled out a pencil and showed her the figures. According to his calculations, two could live cheaper than one, contrary to popular opinion. Instead of each one of them renting a house with two roommates as they had been, they would pay less living together. They would have money left over to save for a piece of land with a little house. One of the things they agreed about was eventually buying more land and him raising some rodeo stock; she would raise vegetables, like she'd always wanted. After staring at the numbers, she said, "The weekend before Valentine's Day." He grabbed her and waltzed her around the room, ending with a fancy twirl and a kiss.

She turned on the radio. The voice said, "Stay tuned for road closure information." The weather announcer sounded serious.

Ryder said, "We'll be in Logan in about five minutes. Going uphill to Mosquero from there may be tough, if it's coming from that direction. And I think it is. Might need to take a different route."

"You're the driver. I'm with you."

She patted her coat pocket, checking for the carved mesquite box holding the wedding band she would give him. She had made him promise he wouldn't buy her a diamond, and left the rest to him. Tiny surprises. The thought made her smile. Logan appeared ahead in the increasingly dense snow, which now clung to the roadside weeds and held onto last summer's bear grass. Maybe they should turn around.

Ryder made an effort to put a smile in place of the frown he'd felt growing as the snow thickened. He parked in front of a disreputable looking place with a sign above the door reading "Whiskey, Road to Ruin."

She said, "Sounds dangerous."

"Not in the daytime. Night's a different story. Especially if the place fills up with cowboys."

Ryder ordered burgers, fries, and Dr Peppers for them and talked to the woman tending to the bar and cooking. He went back to the table, shaking his head. "Guess I made a bad choice. The State Trooper stopped here about fifteen minutes ago and said they were closing I 40 west of Tucumcari and everything from Mosquero north and west."

Neither one of them spoke until the woman put their food in front of them and went back behind the bar. Cheryl said, "We can turn around. Get married some other time."

Ryder stared at his plate. He pushed his hat back from his forehead and looked at her, saw she looked serious and a little sad. He said, "I wanted this to be a holiday you wouldn't ever forget. Hadn't wanted anything as much in a long time."

"I won't forget that." She held up one of the french fries, but stopped before putting it in her mouth. "No one's to blame. You're not in charge of the weather."

"I intended to go back to work on Tuesday and surprise everyone I saw by telling them I had a great weekend—went skiing and got married."

"In that order?"

"First things first." He picked up one of the crisp potato strips. When he looked at her again, he winked.

She said, "Now I see where I fit in. Good thing we weren't headed to a rodeo."

They joked around like that a few more minutes, and he felt his shoulders relax a little. Then he stood and went back to the bar. After huddling with the bartender/cook, he returned to the table, smiling, carrying a to-go box. "Gather up what you want to take. We're going to Tucumcari to get married."

She thought about arguing, then thought again. Why not? Compared to saying "I do," riding to Tucumcari in a blizzard was no gamble at all.

As they stepped out the door, the north wind blasted snow against them and whipped up drifted piles, swirling it across the parking area in a dizzying pattern. He started the pickup and flipped on the wipers. "Ready?"

"Sure. I told you it would be an adventure."

Driving south the twenty-two miles to Tucumcari, Ryder explained that the county courthouse was where they would get the license and they could find one of the Magistrates there in the building to perform the ceremony. Probably be in and out in less than an hour. "Then we'll stay in town there or come back to Logan and wait until the storm passes and decide what to do. That motel next door with the horses' heads painted on the doors looked interesting."

Cheryl rolled her eyes for his benefit.

He said, "Maybe not the horses' head place. Okay."

It worked out altogether differently than he'd intended. By five o'clock they were Mr. and Mrs. Ryder Sheldon, one day earlier than planned. He found it hard to walk steady on the way from the courthouse to the pickup. He'd rather have skipped and jumped. Winning first place, a big jackpot, and a giant buckle in any rodeo he'd ever been in didn't come close to making him feel as tall and proud as he did right then. Later, when he told his mother and Albert, he'd have to try to explain that feeling. Or maybe they already knew how it was. So far, he and Cheryl had kept their plans a secret. She'd said eloping would be easier for everyone. He hadn't disagreed, partly because he suspected she didn't want to put her dad through having to tell her mother.

Back in the pickup, freshly married, he caught her wiggling her fingers, looking at her wedding ring. She'd told him to surprise her and he'd taken a long time finding one that seemed right—solid, not sparkly, beautiful in a way different from ordinary. The way her eyes widened and her smile shone, he knew she liked the broad silver band, inlaid with turquoise and lapis.

"I'm so happy," she said. Simple as that. It was the first time she'd ever told him she was happy that he hadn't wondered when she might say, "If only...." Today, no reservations tinged his wife's voice.

They sat in the pickup, the snow whispering against the windows, suggesting they stay put, holding hands. After a few minutes, he said, "I heard there's a wedding reception in Logan at the Road to Ruin. Want to go?"

"We shouldn't disappoint the crowd."

The feeling came as if the core of her, which for most of her life had spun like a top, whirled like a cyclone, and often threatened to explode in a molten mass, had stopped moving and taken on a steady warmth. A glow spread from it—happiness. Calm might never satisfy her again.

The heavy, wet snow fell intermittently in brief flurries by the time they parked at the bar. Ryder told her to stay put. She watched him situate his hat low over his eyes and stomp a path around the pickup and up the walk to the front entrance. Then he flattened snow back out to the pickup on her side and opened the door. He took off his hat and held it across his chest with his right hand, offering her his left—old fashioned and courtly. "Ma'am, there's a celebration starting in about two minutes. Do me the honor?"

Cheryl couldn't help laughing, when just inside the door, Ryder yelled to the woman behind the bar, "A drink for everybody, on me!" The only two other people in the place, sitting one each at two separate tables near the far wall, both saluted with their beer bottles.

The bartender said, "What's the occasion?"

While he and Cheryl stood wiping their feet on the mat, Ryder announced, "We just got married."

Cheryl said, her voice as strong and nearly as loud as his, "And it's for good!" Then she pulled Ryder to her and kissed him.

That long, breathless kiss lasted until the bartender yelled, "Are you two staying or should I get you a room next door?"

Cheryl said, "We're staying for the party. I'll have a Red Draw, doesn't matter what brand of beer. My *husband's* paying."

Ryder tossed a twenty on the bar. "Some jukebox change, please. There'll be dancing."

Ryder and the two men at the tables took turns dancing with Cheryl and the bartender, until a group of three men and three women opened the front door and stood in the entry, stomping snow off their boots. One of them yelled, "Storm's over.

Stars are out!"

The bartender raised the rag she used to wipe the bar and said, "You're just in time. We're celebrating. It's a wedding reception and dance!" She introduced the locals and Ryder and Cheryl, who each took a bow. After serving another round of beer, the bartender slid some more money in the jukebox.

One of the guys cornered Ryder, probably to pass along some wedding night advice, Cheryl figured. Happy to take a rest from dancing, she sat down in the only booth at the back of the room. Then Anne Murray's voice, singing "Can I Have This Dance?" filled the room and stopped all chatter. Ryder reached her before the second verse and swung her into a slow waltz step. The rest of the people in the bar, by now near twenty, stood back so she and Ryder were the only dancers. As they glided around the small, polished hardwood portion of the large barroom's floor, Ryder pulled her close and whispered, "For the rest of my life," echoing the song's lyric. Cheryl wanted to speak, but couldn't, for the tears. She clung closer and never missed a beat.

Everyone applauded them when the song finished.

The next morning, dawn light slid under the short curtains covering the window. They'd partied until the bar closed. He and Cheryl had walked next door to the motel and received the keys to the room with the leering palomino on the door.

Ryder rolled to his side, stood, and dressed without waking his bride. In a few minutes he came back with two cups of coffee from the motel office and a sweet roll in a cellophane wrapper. "His bride" —he liked the sound of that, he thought as he managed to open the door without spilling.

Cheryl covered her eyes with her right arm. "Bright out there this morning."

"I brought you some coffee. And here's a sweet roll, probably made in 1985. You ready to get up?"

"Sure." She slid up and leaned against the headboard. The sheet fell from her shoulders and dropped below her bare breasts. When she tugged at the cover, he caught her hand.

"No, don't. I want to look at my wife."

"You've seen her before."

"Not my wife. Not in the daylight."

She laughed and pulled the sheet to her chin. "Showtime starts at nine p.m., mister. Be there."

Luckily for them, the radio weather forecaster had been wrong. The road closures, more precautionary than necessary, were cancelled at eight a.m. They were on the road five minutes later. Instead of tackling the uphill drive to Mosquero, Ryder drove back to Tucumcari and on west. Then, as the day warmed and the roads heated, around ten o'clock, he turned north and aimed for I25 between Santa Fe and Las Vegas. If everything held together, they'd be in Red River by one and on the lift shortly after.

The hum of the heater created a comfortable background. He could drive along this way for hours, feeling like a glow surrounded them. He held up his left hand and said, "Did I mention how much I like this ring?"

"You did. I know you can't wear it to work or when you rope, but I wanted you to have it." She held her left hand next to his. "Mine is beautiful. Just what I would have chosen." He could feel her watching him. She said, "I love you. More than I can tell you."

They decided to wait until they got to Red River to eat. At one o'clock exactly, he parked in front of the condos. After unloading their three bags, he asked, "Lunch, Mrs. Sheldon?"

"Something quick. I'm ready to learn to ski." She had told him that the only time she'd ever skied was on the learner's slope at Ski Apache down south.

"I'll need a lesson, too. My only trip here was when I was a senior at WT. We spent more time at the Bull of the Woods than we did on the slopes."

Neither of them ventured beyond the easy runs, but skiing together, falling, and laughing made the afternoon speed by. At four p.m., they took the last chair lift to the top and skied a slow, lazy path down to the base.

In their room, he made a show of checking his watch. "I heard the show starts at nine here. What do you want to do till then?"

She threw a sock and both her gloves at him. "I'm taking a shower and scouting for food. I don't know about you."

Her cell phone made a strangled sound from somewhere under their toiletries on the bathroom counter. He handed it to her. Just after she answered, he watched her sink to the bed, listening. Her face tightened and she bit at her lower lip. He wanted to take the phone from her and throw it against the wall, to silence whatever had spoiled this perfect day. She said, "I can't get there before morning, Daddy. I'll be there as fast as I can. What room?"

She didn't say more. After she disconnected the call, she dropped the phone on the bed.

He sat beside her, put an arm around her. "What's wrong?"

"Mother's been in a car wreck. Critical condition in the hospital in Wichita Falls. Internal injuries, fractures, comatose."

He knew she needed to be there. It might be her last

chance. "When do you want to leave?"

"I'm sorry to spoil everything."

"Let's rest a few hours and then go. Weather's good. I know the road. We'll be there before noon." He wandered around the room, picking up jackets and gloves. He sat next to her again. "In a little bit, you call your dad and tell him not to worry, I'm driving you there."

She nodded, leaning against him, and started crying, sounding like a small child. He did the only thing he knew to do—stroked her hair and held her close until she settled.

The surgical intensive care unit at the Regional Hospital in Wichita Falls contained twelve rooms, each separate and equipped with a state-of-the-art Hill-Rom bed, monitors situated at eye level, a commode chair, sink, a shelf for preparing medication and supplies, a small closet, and a visitor chair. It was supposed to be efficiently organized. Mostly, it was small and cramped. As soon as she walked in and saw her mother, Cheryl felt a panicky need to gasp for breath. This place would smother her. A window covered the wall on the same side as the door and a desk hung outside from the wall below the window. A nurse sat on a stool watching; Cheryl couldn't tell whether it was her mother or the monitors that held her attention.

Her father had told her as soon as they arrived that the doctors said they just had to wait now to see how her mother was when she emerged from the coma. Cheryl didn't stop to ask that nurse anything about her mother's condition. She didn't want the burden of being expected to talk numbers and exchange code phrases the way nurses do. A family member has no expectations to live up to.

External fixators held her mother's right leg in place at the femur and tibia. Her right arm was casted from shoulder to wrist. Cheryl lifted the sheet and saw a wide bandage covering her abdomen. A chest tube snaked from between two lower ribs on the right and entered a Pleur-evac unit. On the left, a urinary catheter bag attached to the bed frame contained reddish brown urine and a few small blood clots. An IV with twin bags, one of which contained a dose of antibiotics, dripping slowly, hung above the bed near the monitor array at the head.

Cheryl initially avoided looking at her mother's face; when she did, she saw her face swollen and bruised and topped by a turban of bandages.

Apparently, she had no facial fractures, but there probably had been a skull fracture. Oxygen by nasal cannula told Cheryl she didn't require a ventilator.

She heard the cardiac rate monitor accelerate slightly. "Mother, can you hear me?" Cheryl held her left hand. Its dry corpse-cold feel shocked her. "It's Cheryl. Squeeze my hand if you hear me." She repeated it. Then, as if some long-delay switch had operated, she felt definite pressure against her fingers. "That's good. Can you speak?"

Her mother moved her head a fraction, but her eyes remained closed. Cheryl felt the air shift behind her. Someone had come through the door. A woman wearing a white coat and a name tag, "Dr. Anna Grayson, Intensivist," said in a soft voice. "Her daughter, the nurse?" Cheryl nodded. "Your father told me." The doctor beckoned her outside the door. "Your mother's neurological status is difficult to assess. According to the CT, there's a hairline fracture, but no intracranial hemorrhage, very little edema. All brainstem functions seem normal. She responds to painful stimuli, but not to verbal commands. Doesn't speak. She should be conscious. I'm most concerned about her liver and kidneys. She had three units of blood in surgery and the laceration of the liver was repaired the best the surgeon could, removed the crushed spleen. We may have to go back later to remove that left kidney. And if the other doesn't pick up the slack, dialysis. We just have to see."

"She squeezed my hand."

"When?"

"Just before you came."

"Well, that's good. We'll continue monitoring. Stay as long as you want."

Cheryl returned to the cell-like room and stood by the bed. "I think you can hear me. I have some news. I got married Friday. Daddy met him. You'd like him." She choked on the last words and couldn't speak for a long while. Then she found a breath and said, "Please, Momma, forgive me. I don't want to lose you."

She held the hand again, the one that had seemed for a moment to have had life in it. Nothing. She pulled the chair to the bedside and sat. "I'm going to stay here until you wake up. You have to wake up. Please try." The cardiac rate monitor accelerated again, briefly.

She held onto her mother's hand. In a while, when there still was no response, she put her head down on the bed beside their hands and closed her eyes. Fatigue seeped across her and she nearly drifted to sleep. A nurse entered the room, exchanged the larger IV bag for a new full one, and left. Cheryl roused herself and watched the nurse return to the desk outside the window. "Momma, you need to try to get well, for Daddy and the girls." Then, hating that her voice came out small and childlike, she said. "I need to know you forgive me." No response.

No use. Maybe Beth and Lynnette could get through to

her. Cheryl sat back in the chair. Then she heard, "Too much evil. I'm going now to be with Jesus." Her mother's voice sounded distant; her words came slowly, but distinctly. Cheryl stood, raised her hand to alert the nurse, then dropped it. Her mother said, "Only God forgives. Repent or be damned."

She walked to the door. If it had been three steps farther, she would have faltered. "Mrs. Magee spoke. Maybe you want to check her again."

When the nurse checked, she whispered to Cheryl that her mother's blood pressure had fallen. She pointed to the urine bag where several more clots showed, larger ones. When the nurse lifted the sheet, a swath of bloody drainage showed on the bandage. "I'm going to get Dr. Grayson."

Cheryl took her mother's hand again. "I'm sorry, Momma. I love you."

When she came out of the room, pale, head up, jaw tight, Ryder knew he'd gotten a glimpse of how she might look in twenty years, if he didn't make certain nothing ever hurt her again. The woman he saw was older, tough, so armored by determination that nothing and no one could touch her. "She's not going to make it, Daddy. She chooses to die."

Ryder heard her dad say, "The doctors…We can't know…" He took several breaths and turned away to stare out the waiting room window. Then he cleared his throat and focused on Cheryl. Like someone expected him to explain, her dad said, "There's a lot you'll never know about your mother. And a lot I guess I never understood." He shrugged and shook his head. "I'm going to get the girls, bring them here. They should get to say goodbye. Back in fifteen minutes."

He turned to Ryder. "Can you stay till then?" Ryder

waited for Cheryl to answer.

"We'll wait," she said. He hardly recognized her voice.

When her dad returned with the girls, both of them in tears, Ryder said, "We'll go now so Cheryl can get some rest. It was a long drive here. Call if you need us. Otherwise we'll be back in the morning." He wondered if Cheryl had the strength to walk to the pickup. That tough look had drained from her as they sat waiting. She hadn't spoken another word.

Two hours later, she was asleep and Ryder was watching television with the sound muted at the Motel 6, the only place nearby with a vacancy. Her phone rang. Ryder grabbed it before the second ring. Her dad said, his voice flat, weary, "She died. Y'all go on and get plenty of rest. I'll call you again around nine in the morning after we've all had some sleep. Tell Cheryl I love her."

Ryder turned off the TV and put out the lights. He'd tell her in the morning.

CHAPTER 10

February 15-16, 2002—Cheryl and Ryder Sheldon

Anniversary

Friday afternoon, four o'clock. Cheryl fussed with the new red and cobalt blue paisley cloth napkins until the fold creased perfectly. The indigo blue stoneware she bought last week would see its debut tonight. She set the plates on the table. Ruby red candles in star-shaped pottery holders stood in the center of the table, ready to light.

In less than two weeks, they would move to the country from this one-bedroom apartment in Hereford where they'd lived since they married. So tonight would be a triple celebration—their second wedding anniversary, Valentine's Day, and the upcoming move to the land they'd saved for every day the past two years.

Ryder had suggested they go out, because they hadn't made the time to in so long. But she told him she had a plan. Just the two of them, for one evening, neither of them working or too tired from work to move, a special dinner, and time to be alone together. She's splurged to buy a small tenderloin of beef, now seasoned and ready for the oven. The potatoes, scrubbed and wrapped, waited to be baked. Salad vegetables sliced, huddled under plastic wrap in the refrigerator. And for dessert, angel food cake with cherry sauce would top off their first fancy dinner in a long time. They both had tomorrow off and they could sleep late. Perfect. She straightened a napkin that didn't need it.

In the bedroom, she turned on a single bedside lamp, low, and lit a lemon-sage scented candle. New sheets, a light blue that matched the new quilt comforter and shams, covered the bed. She had hung the coordinating drapes at the new house already. Next week, each day after work, she would pack all that they had here to make ready for the move. She placed her royal blue satin gown against the pillow and smoothed a wrinkle from the comforter.

Now, she would bathe and then dress in her emerald wool slacks and silk shirt to greet the man she married just over two years ago. Some days it seemed like those years had passed in an instant; others seemed like two times ten hard years of work, with little immediate reward. Her steps slowed as she entered the bathroom, as if fatigue of those years had gathered on her shoulders and aged her legs.

A shower would cure that. She turned the water on and in seconds, her hair wet, her body soaped, she stood under warm spray. The relief that the first drops brought as they touched her skin disappeared. A rush of sadness ambushed her, coming from deep cover, looming until it darkened the space around her. Tears mingled with soapsuds and ran from her face onto her breasts. Catching her breath seemed impossible. It happened in seconds, she'd been snatched from happiness to a deep sorrow that clamped around her like something alive. She stood helpless against its force. Grief and despair mixed with the water and turned immediately to concrete. She fell against the shower wall, then slid as if pushed, to collapse near the drain, spray falling on her head.

Why today? She'd thought all this had passed, but here, today, a year since the last time, this emptiness brought her low again. Grieving takes a long time, the counselor she'd seen that once had said. And Mrs. Turner, the nurse from Gleason, had written her the same advice after her mother's death. Cheryl watched suds and her tears run into the drain until she imagined herself as a five year-old playing under a yard sprinkler, her mother laughing nearby. The she breathed evenly again. Standing, slowly, she shampooed her hair and rinsed all over. Toweling herself dry took a long time. She moved as if stunned, couldn't do otherwise. When she finished and stood straight, strength began to return to her arms and legs. The clock showed she'd been in the bathroom forty-five minutes. Last time it took her three days to feel normal.

Ryder walked in the front door of the apartment, set a paper bag on the end table near the couch, and took off his hat. He looked toward the kitchen, wondering if Cheryl had gone out and left the door unlocked. No sound greeted him, only the scent of her shampoo, which reminded him of a salad made of ripe fruit. He didn't raise his voice, but said, "Honey, you here?"

"In the bedroom. Be right there."

He was good at interpreting animal sounds, always had felt he understood them because of it. A colt tells its mother it's afraid with a whinny that's higher pitched than usual; calves bawl louder when they're upset, pitiful, close to a wail. Just now Cheryl's voice carried a brittle note, artificial, maybe to cover fear or something else. Ryder took three steps toward the bedroom and they met in the hallway. Without saying anything, he took her in his arms and held her tight for a minute before kissing her, first on the cheek and then on the mouth. She leaned into him.

He heard and felt her take a deep breath, and then let her go as soon as she pushed back and smiled up at him. He said, "My, you look pretty tonight, Mrs. Sheldon."

Now the smile reached her eyes. He felt the muscles across his back relax. His hand lay on her shoulder, loosely, as they walked into the living room. He pointed toward the candles on the dining table. "Someone's celebrating here."

"That's the plan."

He pulled her close for another kiss. Then he whispered, "Happy anniversary, Valentine's Day, new house, day off!" He felt her back stiffen.

Before he was ready to let her go, she moved away, toward the kitchen. She said, "I was just about to put the potatoes in the oven. The beef goes in in thirty minutes."

For some reason he couldn't name, he frowned as he tried to decide what to do next—clean up, sit down and take his boots off, or follow Cheryl around until she settled down and maybe told him what had her spooked.

He said, "No rush." He picked up the brown bag and lifted out a bottle of merlot. "I'll open this. We can relax a few minutes." He doubted he would. The same thing as last year, happening again, threatened to push him and his news, which he hadn't even mentioned yet, out of her mind.

The dark red wine waited in her glass. She hadn't tasted it as she busied herself tending to assembling salad and putting butter, sour cream, and horseradish on the table. Ryder had taken his glass and gone to clean up. Now she stared at the meat which she had rubbed with *herbes de provence*, as her cookbook recommended. He deserved a good meal and she should be cheerful and happy. She took a sip of the wine, and then another, and breathed in with the warm trickle as it passed down her throat and into her stomach. She finished the wine and considered pouring another glass.

In the bedroom, Ryder sat on the end of the bed, his left sock on and the right in his hand, thinking maybe he'd done something wrong, not encouraging Cheryl to talk more, to get the worst of it out of her system. After his dad died, for a least three years, Ryder woke from a dream, several nights around the date of the funeral, sweating, sometimes crying, his heart beating thunder against his ribs. The first time he jolted himself from sleep shouting to his mother to call the ambulance. The CPR he had been trying left him shaking. In another dream, a different year, he was sixteen again, arguing with his dad and knowing he'd never win. Even though it wasn't the same dream each time, it might has well have been, because he came out worthless or useless in all of them.

Showered and dressed in clean Wranglers and shirt, he walked sock-footed to the living room, to his recliner. He watched Cheryl sip her wine. She smiled at him over the rim of the glass. Dark circles under her eyes told him she'd been crying before he came home. He and she were different in a lot of ways, but he figured that they were alike about death—getting over it took time. He knew her strength more clearly the longer they were together, the effort she made to keep both their spirits up when they worked too hard. But the circumstances of her mother's death, and that God-awful funeral left some bad memories with him. No telling what kind of gouges it had made in her heart. The brief smile told him she would heal, but hadn't yet.

Hell of a thing to have to remember your mother dying after a car wreck coming home from a protest at a clinic her preacher said was an abortion mill. At the hospital in Wichita Falls, Cheryl's dad said he hadn't let her mother take their two other daughters along on the trip. But he couldn't keep her from going, short of locking her in the house.

Her mother had been riding in the front seat of her car, that wild-eyed, bible thumping excuse for a minister driving it. He got out of the smashed Lincoln without a scratch. The same fool, at the funeral, led his flock in a prayer for God to forgive her mother's lack of faith, saying in a loud voice that doubt was the only reason she could have been smitten. He'd used that word, smitten, like he was some sort of Jeremiah, sure that the woman had not been a true believer.

Cheryl's father had stood up in the middle of that prayer and walked out of the church, herding her two sisters along, tears running down their faces. Ryder sat perfectly still, waiting for Cheryl to move. She didn't, not until the members of the congregation, twenty-six in all—he'd counted as they marched by the open casket—left the two of them alone on the folding chairs in the makeshift sanctuary. He had walked behind her to that coffin, ready to lift her, carry her away, if she faltered. "I'm sorry," he heard her say to her mother.

He wanted to scream, "For what? I saw all the letters you wrote, watched you fall apart every time she refused to talk to you on the telephone. You tried as hard as you could." But he didn't say a word, just stood by hoping he wasn't failing her, waiting to catch her if she fell.

"I'm putting the meat in. It will be ready in twenty-five minutes." She lifted a relish dish from the countertop, so he could see it.

He walked the few steps to the kitchen and sidled up next to her, hung an arm loosely around her waist and hitched her close to his side. "You smell good." He pushed her hair aside and nuzzled below her right ear.

She hunched her right shoulder and shivered but didn't move away. "I know what you want."

"Tell me. I seldom know myself."

She pointed toward the dish of carrot sticks, olives, small green onions, and celery she'd assembled, colors alternating. "Grazing."

He popped two olives in his mouth. "What do you want?"

She backed away a couple of steps, shrugged. Then she inhaled deeply. When the breath escaped, no words came with it.

He pulled her to his chest and held her until he felt her muscles slacken. Right then he decided he'd wait to tell her his news.

The next morning, at the new house, Cheryl stood on a chair in the kitchen, putting up curtains. She'd already fit shelf liner into the cabinets and drawers, working at the chores for more than an hour. According to the deed, this house was thirty-six years old. Whoever owned it before had taken good care of it. The woodwork—cabinets, baseboards, and all—showed signs of frequent polishing. Sometime in those years they'd updated the bathroom and installed a dishwasher. All the ways she would make it homey had filled her thoughts the past two months since they had made the deal to buy it. A home of their own, together, one of the reasons people get married. Right this minute she had trouble feeling enthusiastic about the future. All that work together and they still might end up with a sad mess like her family.

She heard him call her name, from somewhere near the little barn. She hoped he wasn't still put out about last night. He hadn't said anything on the way out here. If he was upset, she couldn't really blame him. She'd fallen asleep soon after she cleared the table. This morning when she woke up with the dregs of wine coating her tongue, she expected him to let her know, in no uncertain terms, what he thought of her spoiling their celebration. But he didn't. He'd just looked at her like she might be a stranger who'd replaced his wife, and told her he hoped she could take time to come out here with him. He intended to get the horse's stall ready. She agreed; thought it was the least she could do, even though it meant the packing would have to wait. Apologizing would be right, too; try to make it up to him. But a headache and something she couldn't name kept her silent on the ride out.

"Cheryl." She heard him, but didn't respond.

Then she yelled, "In a minute." The headache's volume rose to a dull roar.

This was her first Saturday off in three weeks. Her schedule at County General in Hereford had her working ten hours shifts, eight days every two weeks. Because she wanted the weekend bonus pay, she agreed to be assigned one or more weekend night shifts every week. Immediately, she became her supervisor's favorite. It kept her from going with Ryder to most of the ropings and rodeos when he competed, but the result was the important thing. Her weekend pay added an extra thirty percent to every paycheck. Without that, unless Ryder had won the bronc riding *and* the roping in every rodeo he entered, which he hadn't, they would have had to wait six more months to get the house and the sixty acres it sat on.

He was dead set on paying at least half of the price up front, so the mortgage would be lower. And when he was determined about something, arguing did no good. Not that she didn't ever argue with him, and change his mind about a few things, but she'd learned he seldom gave in where money was concerned. He'd like it better if he could do it all alone, like men had to do when all of a woman's work was at home—cleaning and cooking and tending kids. As long as her paycheck was at least as much as his, it seemed only fair to her that they decide how to spend their money, together. Married people should agree on important decisions, together. When they found this house two months ago, they both agreed; it was the place for them to get their real start.

"Need some help here," he said, louder this time.

She slammed the scissors on the counter and walked fast from the back door toward the barn. When she got close, she yelled, "You in here?"

"Garage." She turned toward his voice and saw him standing near the top of a ladder leaning against the detached one-car garage, on the opposite side of the house. "Get me that hammer out of my tool box." He pointed toward the pickup that was parked near the barn, at least a hundred feet away. If he'd been a nurse, she'd have pointed out that for efficiency, if nothing else, before you start a procedure, you check to see you have all the necessary equipment.

"Anything else while I'm over here?" she yelled from the pickup.

He didn't answer. She turned the key, revved the engine, and drove the pickup over near to the garage.

He yelled, "I don't need the pickup, just the hammer."

She climbed two steps up the ladder and handed him the tool, then walked back toward the house. Without turning around, she said, "You might want something else when I'm not handy." She let the screen door slam when she went inside.

Three of the shelves still needed lining paper. She stood again on the only piece of furniture in the place, a kitchen chair, to reach the top shelf, holding a length of paper she'd cut. The screen slammed again.

"What's your hurry?" He said it before he got into the room.

"There's a lot do get done here. And I still have to pack at the apartment. I'm not off again until next Sunday." She continued fitting the paper on the shelf, didn't turn to look at him.

"I'm not doing enough?"

"I can't say. I don't have a clue what you're doing."

A long silence hung between them. "I feel sorry for you," he said. "Marrying a no-count who can't hire this moving done."

She turned and saw his face matched the words, grim. "Was I complaining?" She tried sounding reasonable, but wasn't sure she had it in her.

"Do you even remember last night?"

"What about it?" She felt her pulse accelerate. The chair wobbled as she stepped off it onto the floor. She caught hold of the countertop to steady herself. He didn't offer a hand; she could see both of them were clenched into fists.

"Tell me you don't remember saying to leave you alone, pushing me away, yelling at me."

"I don't." She didn't. She had to turn away, not look at his face where the hurt showed. She knew better than to have more than one glass of wine, but that hadn't stopped her. She remembered that much.

"Are you sorry you married me? Are you?"

"Sorry for you." There had been too many of these arguments in the last few months. Started over nothing, making no sense even before they stopped. She sat on the chair. He leaned against the cabinet near the sink, staring at the drain.

She watched him turn on the faucet, not speaking, heard the water rushing away.

He said, "If you want out, this is your chance, before you get in deeper."

Nausea that would have made sense first thing this morning swelled up. Swallowing kept her from vomiting. When she trusted herself to speak, she said, so quietly she could hardly hear herself. "I'd never leave. I love you."

He faced the sink, left her staring at his back, waiting. He turned off the faucet.

When he turned toward her again, he held out a hand. "Let's go to town and get a burger."

They ate at Bob's Diner, in a booth that contained the silence between them, electric with the energy of unspoken thoughts. Then they returned to the house and worked until near dark, around five o'clock. Ryder stayed outside; hammering sounds told her he wasn't far away. She finished the shelves, vacuumed both bedrooms, scrubbed the tub and the shower in the small bathroom, scoured the sinks, and cleaned the oven. Everything she could do was done. After stowing her cleaning supplies under the kitchen sink, she went out and sat on the front porch step.

Ryder came from the direction of the barn and sat beside her. He smelled of sweat and hay. He said, "You cold?"

She shook her head. He asked, "Are we gonna be okay?"

She nodded, stared at her shoes. "I hope so." She leaned against him, buried her head against his jacket. "I drank too much. I won't do it again."

"We'll celebrate next week when we move in here."

Looking toward, not really seeing, tumbleweeds caught in the front fence, she asked, "Did you mean what you said, about me leaving?"

"I'd have fought you on it if you said yes."

She held out her left hand. He took it in his right.

Dark came quickly in February. Ryder drove back to the apartment more slowly than usual, thinking about what his friend

James Royce had told him, making sure it was a good idea, the right time to tell her. "I have some good news."

"Good in general or good for us in particular?"

"Us, I think." He pointed at a coyote trotting across the road, and slowed for it to reach the opposite ditch. "Yeah, good for us." He nodded like he was certain. "The new prison out north of here, James Royce's wife's been working there in administration since it opened. Likes it real well. Pay's good and benefits are great." He paused, looked across at her profile. "Here's the part that's good. This week they posted an open position for an R.N., looking for someone with some experience. Plus, it's eight to five, Monday through Friday. Weekends off." He drove with both hands on the wheel, like he needed to concentrate. Looking directly ahead, he said, "Good for us."

Cheryl waited. If he talked more, she wouldn't have to. The heater fan hummed, the sound too low to be a real interruption. She knew it was her turn. He was waiting for her to say she'd do everything she could to get the job. But it might not be true. She wasn't sure she could spend the weekends watching him ride broncs and holding her breath the whole time for fear he'd be seriously injured. She took a breath and hated that it sounded like a sigh. "I'll call Monday to check on it. When I have some facts, we can talk about it more."

CHAPTER 11

September 16-17, 2005—Cheryl and Ryder Sheldon

Promise Me

A pril, Cole Cooper's wife, a perky blond who still wore big hair and favored tight knit shirts and Cruel Girl jeans with her boots, had talked more since they'd left Hereford than Cheryl had heard her say in the four years she'd known her. Riding in the pickup with her from Hereford toward El Paso, Cheryl had been subjected, thus far, to hearing April's hopes, wishes, fears, and resentments—and they weren't even in Roswell yet. Another three hours to El Paso.

Ryder and Cole had driven out together yesterday, pulling Cole's loaded two-horse trailer. She and April should get to El Paso before the rodeo dance wound down, before midnight for sure. If she ignored the sound from the driver's seat, Cheryl would enjoy the ride on this mostly vacant stretch of New Mexico highway from Kenna to Roswell, a road with few curves, no streetlights, and occasional coyotes and jackrabbits crossing.

"Every evening, it's the same story; he hangs up his hat, takes off his boots, and plops into his recliner. If I let him, he'd even eat in that chair," April said. She paused. When Cheryl didn't respond, April hummed a few bars of "Earl's Gotta Die."

Her chatter, weighted heavily on the side of irritations with her husband, would probably stop if Cheryl were to close her eyes and pretend to sleep. But April was younger and didn't work, even though they didn't have children, so she probably needed someone to listen. And besides, hearing another rodeo wife say the things she often thought satisfied Cheryl, in a way. It helped to know she wasn't the only one who felt like a minor prize on display, about as valuable as the drawer full of belt buckles Ryder had won—something he was proud to say he had, wouldn't want to lose, but didn't have much real use for.

Cheryl asked, "Do you want me to drive a while?"

"No, I like driving, doesn't matter where. Besides, you worked all day." April turned on the cab lights, steered with her left hand, and used her right to twist the rearview mirror to check her hair. She gave a nod to her reflection, then moved the mirror back into position, smoothly, like she had practiced. She said, "I just love your hair—so natural looking. I'm thinking about letting mine go back to its original color."

Cheryl closed her eyes. Her day at work paraded inside her eyelids. The same dull routine—passing out meds (lots of SSRIs and Xanax), bandaging minor wounds, checking sore throats and stomach complaints, avoiding personal questions, and ignoring suggestive comments. Men in prison stared at any female, even the nurses, like they were prey. She showered every evening when she got in, just to feel clean again. Ryder thought it was a good job, with its state benefits and all the guards watching over her.

She had to admit the weekends off were nice. Gave them time to be together when she went to his rodeos. But still, Emergency would have given her a chance to use her knowledge and would never be routine. Sounding way off in the distance, April said something Cheryl didn't quite follow about wishing she had a job and Cole's not wanting her to.

When Cheryl opened her eyes again, everything she saw beyond the road glowed white, lit by the full moon. She tried to speak and had to swallow so she could. "I've only seen pictures of this. White Sands. Never been over here before."

"We came when I was a kid. In the summertime, it looks like snow, but it's hot." April kept her eyes on the road ahead. "A deer jumped right in front of me back in the Hondo Valley. So fast I didn't even have time to put on the brakes. Lucky he made it across or I could have hit him."

"Let's get a Coke in Las Cruces. I'll drive if you want me to. Sorry I went to sleep."

"Probably the sound of my voice. Cole says I talk so much he can't hear me anymore." April was quiet for a couple of miles. Then she said, "I thought, when people were married, they didn't stop listening to each other until later, like maybe twenty years." Her voice lost its childlike lilt as she finished the sentence, came down flat.

Cheryl watched April's profile. From where she sat, seeing only the right side of the girl's face made her now somber expression even more pronounced, as if an older, disenchanted woman inhabited the unlined skin and held the firm jaw tilted upward.

As a nurse, Cheryl learned that silence is often the best response, maybe the only one that helps a patient find an answer. She knew, too, that keeping her mouth shut set her apart and was why she ended up with very few girlfriends. Not willing to share, people probably said.

April said, "Sorry, I didn't mean to be such a downer. I just wish I knew how to be, what to do. I want him to always be in love with me as much as I am with him."

"How long have you been married?"

"Since I was eighteen. Nearly six years." April slowed the pickup as a jackrabbit scurried from the ditch on their right to the other side of the road. "He's thirty now."

A cloud moved across the moon and the sand's color

changed to a luminous gray. Black fence posts exclaimed at the edges of the road, warning the sand about drifting from its assigned place. A green Border Patrol van, the driver the only occupant, met and passed them, the only vehicle Cheryl had seen for miles. This road seemed like it could be going nowhere, just straight and fast and empty, no end in sight.

April said, "I think we're not happy like we were when we first married. Sometimes I wonder if we're still in love." She paused.

Cheryl doubted it would do any good to tell her that happy isn't the opposite of unhappy and loving someone isn't the same as being in love. So she didn't say anything. Who can ever say that they and another person are happy and trust they are uttering truth? She knew there had been times, days, minutes when she was happy with Ryder but had he, at the same time, been happy with her? Did they share it or even mention it? Happiness may be like love in that way. But, like April, people speak of being *in love*, as if it's something one is a part of that wouldn't exist were the other person not present. Yet you never hear of being *in happiness*. Maybe it was too much to expect. Is being in happiness, or in love, so much like ether that it's inevitable that two people who start out with dreams that hold them on a path, moving forward together will, after a few years, begin to see possibilities in different, separate directions? Begin to drift. Her breath came out in a sigh as she closed her eyes.

Then, as if April had found the answer to a question, she said, "I think we should have a baby."

The wheels struck the road's corrugated edge, vibrating through Cheryl's feet. Her eyes wide open, she sat up straight. April said, "Sorry," as she corrected her steering.

Cheryl relaxed her hold on the armrest she'd clutched. She

pointed off to the right, at the outline of a hill, and beyond at higher peaks and a glow of lights. "Las Cruces. Soon as we get there, let's stop for the restroom. I'll drive on into El Paso."

They had found the rodeo grounds from the directions Ryder gave her and, even better, found a parking space near the arena. Here inside the barn that housed the rodeo dance, a live band sawed away at their version of "It's Getting Better All the Time." Cheryl watched April rise on tiptoe searching the dancers and the sideline watchers and drinkers.

"I don't see them," April said. "I hope they're okay, not hurt or something."

"They'll find us." Cheryl seldom had to look for Ryder. He always seemed to know where she was, and soon appear beside her.

Seconds later, Ryder turned up. He managed to ease in behind her, without her seeing, and made her jump by whispering, "Lady, you free for a dance?"

Without turning around, she said, "Not free, but worth the price."

Still behind her, he wrapped his arms around her waist. "I'll say." He squeezed her and she turned in his arms to kiss him.

Without stepping back, she asked, "You okay, no problems?"

"Not a one. Best time in this evening's roping and best ride in saddle broncs. My night!"

The band started another song, the singer belting out a pretty good version of "Tequila Makes Her Clothes Fall Off." Ryder said, "Want something to drink?"

She shook her head. He swung her out onto the dance floor. Dancing with him reminded her how much she loved being his wife. Over his shoulder, she saw April walking the edge of the dance floor, stopping every few steps to search the crowd.

The next night, after hearing the announcer stretched his name out to four very long syllables as final go round winner in two events, Ryder felt like partying till dawn, or at least for a couple of hours. Seeing Cheryl standing up, screaming his name when he jumped to the ground from his bronc ride, gave him a chest-bursting sensation. He would have run up in the bleachers and grabbed her right then if he hadn't promised to haze for one of the steer wrestlers.

The crowd at the dance threatened to make any movement hazardous. Packed shoulder to shoulder in lines at the four bars set up around the room, cowboys talked loud and jostled one another in the friendly, establishing my territory, way that young males do. Sweat and manure and sawdust created a familiar, encouraging smell. To Ryder it said he was part of something old-fashioned and wholesome and a little dangerous, and he'd made it through one more time and come out on top. It told him he belonged on horseback more than anywhere else.

He led Cheryl to a corner. The idea of being glad-handed all evening appealed to him less than drinking a cold beer, very slowly; admiring his wife, up close; dancing when the music struck him, and enjoying the feel of the wad of cash in his pocket. His payout had been bigger than he expected. Too bad he hadn't had anything to bet on himself on the side.

Pushing thoughts of money aside, he said, "Does me a world of good seeing you in the stands." He watched Cheryl's face as she watched the dancers. She turned toward him. It seemed like the moon had come up, just for him.

It was no surprise when the band switched from country

music to salsa. After all, they were in El Paso. If Ryder had ever danced to that music, he'd been drunk, for certain. Watching the people on the floor, he tried imagining how he'd do the steps without tripping. A cowboy all in black, too clean to have been in any event earlier in the evening, strolled into their corner and stopped at Cheryl's side. "*Quieres bailar, Senorita?*" His accent sounded genuine.

Cheryl glanced at Ryder. She said, "*Senora. Mi esposo,* Ryder." She offered a handshake and Ryder did the same.

The young man switched to unaccented English. "May I ask your wife to dance?"

Ryder didn't know how to refuse without being an ass. He nodded. "Her choice."

Cheryl gave a slight shrug and followed the man to the edge of the dance floor. Ryder watched as they began, the man holding her closer than any two-step, but not much different than anyone else on the floor. He drank his beer and watched the two of them, the rest of the dancers only a blurry backdrop, as far as he was concerned. By the time the man, who said his name was Alex, returned his wife, Ryder needed another beer.

He asked if she wanted one. She shook her head. He said, "Come with me. I don't want someone stealing you." His try for sounding light missed its mark, he could tell. She wrinkled her forehead and shrugged again, then followed him.

They stopped at the nearest of the bars spaced around the perimeter of the dance floor. Cheryl ordered a Diet Coke and Ryder got another beer, Corona this time. Cole and April met them as they headed toward the corner. Cole said, "Did I see the guy that hit on April dancing with you, Cheryl?"

"What are you talking about?"

"That bastard dressed like Johnny Cash. Speaking slick

Spanish. He's no more Mexican than I am. Probably an Aggie from up at Cruces, out hitting on women. He tries it again, he'll be sorry."

Ryder said, "Let's move over here out of the way." He steered Cole toward the corner, talking to him quietly, knowing drunks can't hear too well, keeping his attention that way. "No sense looking for trouble out of town. Just drink your beer and cool off."

Cole swigged his beer and turned back toward the dance floor. "No, I think I'll dance with my wife."

April's eyes skittered across the nearby dancers. "I'm about ready to get to the motel. We had a long day yesterday. I'll bet you guys are tired, too."

"Good idea, maybe something to eat first?" Ryder said.

Cole yelled, pointing into the crowd, "There he is." He turned back to Ryder. "Don't tell me he didn't piss you off, too. I'm going to explain to him how we do things in the Panhandle, keep our hands off other men's wives." Cole waded into the crowd, bumping dancers out of his way, plowing ahead.

Ryder watched from the corner, Cheryl on one side of him, April on the other. Cole was right; it had pissed him off. April leaned across in front of him and said to Cheryl, "All I did was smile at that guy. I swear. I wasn't flirting."

Cheryl nodded once. Ryder thought from the look on her face, maybe she'd smiled at that guy too. Or maybe something more while he was busy on that bucking horse. He saw where Cole stopped.

What the hell, he was through competing, just staying to watch the bull riding tomorrow. "Hold this," he said, handing his wife the half-empty Corona. "And stay put." He plowed into the crowd, toward where Cole now stood near the middle of the dance floor, toe to toe with the cowboy in black, surrounded by several other men dressed the same.

Cheryl said to April, "I'm leaving. You coming with me?"

April, looking near tears, said. "He'll be mad if I leave."

"He's already mad. They both are. No sense all of us getting arrested or worse."

April took a couple of steps beside her. Then she shook her head. In a little girl's voice she said, "I better stay."

Cheryl stalked toward the door. Two should-have-been-grown-by-now men, thirty-plus years old, showing less sense than a fourteen year-old high schooler on his first burst of testosterone, not smart enough to use words instead of fists. And about nothing—one dance, one smile. Let them find their own ride to the motel. She threw the Corona in a trash can on her way out.

She woke when she heard the door open, but didn't turn over or say a word. She saw the clock showing three-thirty. Ryder turned on the bathroom light. She pulled the sheet over her head, then added the pillow. The bed sagged when he sat on it. His boots hit the wall. She knew he'd thrown them. "Don't pretend you're asleep. From now on you can act like you're my wife or stay home." As far as she was concerned, he was talking to himself. He mumbled a few more things, none of them clear. Then she heard snoring.

The next morning, she got up around seven, showered, and left Ryder lying on his back, arms flung out, a large bruise on his left cheekbone. The coffee shop connected to the motel served a full breakfast. She ordered a big one—eggs, bacon, biscuits, and orange juice. She was halfway through, and reading the funnies, when Ryder sat at the table. He ordered coffee and picked up the sports page. From where she sat, he looked the worse for wear, but not seriously damaged. Neither of them spoke until the waitress returned and asked if he wanted breakfast. He didn't. Cheryl finished, paid for her meal, left him at the table, and went back to their room.

After packing her overnight case, she leaned against the headboard and flipped through the TV channels. She stopped on a Spanish language program, trying to follow the dialogue between the host and a woman he was interviewing when Ryder came in. He packed, still not saying anything to her. Then he took both of their bags out to the pickup. He came in again and stood at the end of the bed, in front of the television. "You coming with me or staying in El Paso?"

She rolled her eyes, making sure he saw her, and picked up her purse. He walked to the pickup and opened the passenger door for her. The plan had been to stay for the final events, the barrel racing and bull riding mainly, that would run this afternoon. Plus the all around cowboy winner would be announced. She knew, although Ryder hadn't mentioned it, that he stood a good chance of winning.

As they drove out of the motel parking lot, she saw Cole's pickup parked in front of a room a few doors from theirs. At least they got this far.

"It's two hours before the show starts. Want to go sightseeing?" he asked.

"Sure."

"You mad at me, still?"

"I never was. If you want to act adolescent, that's your business. I won't stay and watch is all."

"Jealousy got the best of me."

"I didn't do anything to cause it."

"Probably not."

"Definitely not." She wasn't going to take a speck of blame. She didn't deserve it. April may have; she didn't.

He pointed east. "We'll drive up toward the mountains." He drove without saying any more until they reached a small park, near a church. "It's hard for me to explain, getting jealous. I can't promise it won't happen again."

"Did I ask you to? Just don't try blaming me, imagining I'm flirting. Or cheating."

He nodded. They sat watching two small boys playing on a slide.

She asked, "Does your cheek hurt?"

"Just enough to remind me I ought to know better."

The barrel racing started at four and bull riding would follow at five. They ate supper at a Mexican restaurant, aiming to get to the arena in time for the bull riding. They both checked their phones and speculated about why they hadn't heard from April or Cole. She thought they might still be at the motel, making up. Ryder said he had a notion they had trouble that started way before last night.

When they got to their seats at the arena, Cole and April were waiting there, both smiling. If he'd have bet on it, Ryder would have lost. From the things he heard Cole shouting at her after the set to last night, apparently what usually followed included April running home to mother or him staying out for several nights, or both. To hear him tell it, she flirted with anyone who passed in range and was willing to follow up on it. Cole had told him some of the story before, and he heard them first hand trading insults about it all the way back to the motel last night. But here they were, smiling like a pair of chimps. He reminded himself people don't always mean everything they say.

The first bull out of the chute turned lazy after his second jump. The rider gave it his best but the bull didn't help. Eight seconds on a lazy bull meant a poor score. The next animal didn't show much better, but the cowboy lost his hold and the clowns had to cover to give him time to get out of the ring. The third bull out was a different story. He knew his business and intended to put that cowboy off his back and on the ground. The bull made a twirling turn, and the rider lost his grip and took to the air. As soon as he hit the ground, the bull hooked a horn into the cowboy's right side and flung him up and across the arena a good twenty feet. Looked like a rag doll thrown by an angry child. When he came down again, the sound could be heard across the entire arena. As soon as the awful crack echoed, a piercing wail escaped from Cheryl. She hunched down, her head in her lap. Her shoulders shook as she cried. Ryder pulled her to him and held tight.

The ambulance screamed into the ring just after the clowns ran the bull out the exit gate. When the EMTs picked him up, everyone could see the bone sticking out of the rider's thigh. He tried to wave, but fell back onto the stretcher. The announcer solemnly asked the crowd for a round of applause. "That's all this brave cowboy's getting paid tonight," he said.

Cheryl took some deep shaky breaths and sat up straight again. Her face had lost color and she held tight to his hand. She closed her eyes every time a bull sprang from the chute, until the last one had been ridden.

After the bull riding, the announcer called Ryder's name when the awards were handed out. "Best All Round Cowboy— Ryder Sheldon of Hereford, Texas" Cheryl let go of his hand, and he stepped across the bleacher seats and to get down to the arena floor. He took the check from the rodeo manager and waved at her. Her smile brightened her up and made him feel good, better even than the money, which he was proud to receive. That plus another belt buckle.

As they rode through the dark, taking Highway 54 across the Ft. Bliss Army reservation, instead of the longer way she and April had come, Cheryl thought how to say what she needed to. Trying to tell him what to do didn't seem right; she wouldn't like it if he did it to her. And she couldn't tolerate seeming afraid and pitiful. Finally, she blurted it out, uncomposed. "I need you to make me a promise."

"Anything, darlin', I'm the best all round. I can do anything you need."

"I'm serious."

He must have heard it in her voice. He said, "Tell me and if I can, I'll do it, whatever it is."

"Promise me you won't ride bulls ever again. That man could have died. He might still."

"Always that chance."

She knew riding bulls paid. But he didn't have to do it; he was doing fine, winning saddle broncs and roping. "I couldn't stand it if something bad happened to you." She hated the sound of her voice, weak. But she kept on, anyway. "I couldn't stand to lose you."

He reached for her hand. "Listen here, no way you're going to lose me. Trust me to always be careful. And I'm not going anywhere. Not without you."

She didn't say any more.

CHAPTER 12

June 20, 2006—Ryder Sheldon and Cheryl Sheldon

Signs of Neglect

Putting it off wasn't going to make it a bit easier. At first, Ryder thought he'd wait a few days to break the news to Cheryl about his new job. Regardless of when, she probably wouldn't take it well. This would be the third job he'd had since they married—not a problem if you improve your situation when you change. But quitting a job that mostly involved driving around the Panhandle, writing up orders for feed supplements and cattle medicine at dairies, and getting a regular paycheck wouldn't make sense to anyone but him. Except maybe Uncle Butch.

He pushed his hat back off his forehead, swiped at his face with his bandana. Six-thirty in the evening and still close to a hundred degrees. How Cheryl could run in this heat mystified him. She'd said on the first of June that she intended to run six days a week until she got back in shape. "Nothing wrong with the shape you're in, far as I can see," he'd told her. Meant as a compliment. She'd told him being in shape didn't have to do only with what other people can see. And then she trotted off down the county road and came back forty-five minutes later, red in the face and breathing hard.

This evening, she'd been gone since she set his supper plate down. Soon as he started eating, off she ran, more than an hour ago, headed south. She'd also stopped eating supper most nights. He squinted down the road. Then he paced back and forth across the porch.

He might have been able to tolerate that job, if he kept up rodeoing every weekend, but seeing all those dairy cattle penned up, standing in manure deeper than their hooves every day turned him against drinking milk for good. If he told the truth, he figured it wouldn't take long to start feeling the same way about feedlot beef. Plus, with all that needed to be done on this place, something had to give. He'd bought the adjoining half section in January. With the sixty they already owned, that made three hundred eighty acres. But payments had to be made, and before he could raise any roping calves or other rodeo stock, he had fences and pens to build, water lines to extend—enough to be a full time job itself. Hadn't even made a good start. Rodeoing had to go, at least for now.

But the thought of never having a chance or a reason to do anything resembling cowboying threatened to suffocate him, just like this damn dry heat. So he'd done it. Quit his job and signed on as a pen rider at a big feedlot. Starting two weeks from yesterday. At least he'd spend his time at work on horseback.

He opened the front door, then stopped and turned around to look down the road again. There she came, trotting, as if running slower for the last quarter mile would cool her down. He watched her smooth, striding gait. Her new routine meant she'd come in, clean up the kitchen, take a shower and be in bed before ten. Things had changed and he didn't know why. When he allowed himself to wonder, the only answers he came up with all pointed to the fact that the only way he'd know was to ask her. But the time just never seemed right.

When he let himself wonder about how far apart they'd gotten, he mostly thought about what he'd done or hadn't done, or he imagined her with some guy she met at work, or maybe in the grocery store. He didn't ever let himself go too far or he'd get jealous for no real reason; he shut it down and thought about land payments instead. At least money would solve that.

When she got within hearing distance, he said, "If you're going to go such a long way, you may need to have a dog with you, for safety."

She greeted him with a nod. "Dogs require more tending than I have time for. Eight miles today. I'll stick with that for a while." She walked quickly through the door he held open for her. As she passed, he inhaled the scent he thought of as hers alone. Even sweaty and dusty, she still smelled like exotic fruit—sweet and ripe.

Cheryl asked, "Are we going to see your uncle on Sunday?" She had to assume he was in his recliner. She couldn't see from where she was putting plates in the dishwasher.

"If that's okay with you."

A plate fell from her hand and landed on top of her running shoes. Still in one piece. Amazing. She had flinched when he answered from only a few feet away. Out of the recliner. She said, "Guess I'm still a little shaky after that run."

"Maybe it's too much, in the heat." He handed her the glass and the silverware he'd used at supper.

"Do you know if he likes apple pie? I could make one for him. And I thought I'd cook extra fried chicken so he'd have leftovers."

"Yeah, he'd like that a lot." He watched her profile as she turned toward the sink, started scouring a skillet that looked to him to be way beyond clean.

Ryder said, "I've wondered if he eats his own cooking or goes to Muleshoe. A man alone might not bother." After a silence, he said, "Yeah, he likes apple pie a lot."

She nodded, watching the suds disappear. As she wiped the sink dry, she heard his boots drop to the floor next to his recliner. She asked, "Need anything before the kitchen closes?" She intended it to sound like a joke. She leaned around the corner to see if he'd heard. Something on television had his attention. She said, "I'm going to shower."

Lying in bed, still awake, she heard the shower running and Ryder humming an off key version of "I'm an Old Cowhand." She moved close to the edge on the right side, her side, of the bed and closed her eyes. He didn't turn on any lights before he lifted the sheet and lay down. She was close to sleep when she felt his hand move near her hip, then slide away slowly, like stretching a tape to measure the distance between them.

Sunday morning, he still hadn't broken the news to her. If he didn't tell her soon, she'd hear it from April or that other friend of hers, Blaire. Around here, nothing's a secret for long. Their husbands, who would surely hear soon if they hadn't already, would pass it along.

He and Cheryl were both standing on the front porch, drinking the last of the morning coffee, before the day heated up. Looking off to the west, he said, "Doesn't look like it'll rain today. The grass could sure use it." He tried to remember what made him think he'd ever be able to raise calves on dry land, even if they did have a good well close to where he intended to build the pens. They'd need grass. Half the usual rainfall last year, and only three inches so far this year barely kept the buffalo grass and grama alive, much less put on growth enough for forage. Good thing he hadn't bought calves yet.

She asked, "What time should I be ready to go?"

"I told Uncle Butch we'd there in time for dinner. So we

better leave about ten-thirty."

By ten forty-five, in the pickup cab filled with the aroma of fried chicken and apple pie, he'd explained to Cheryl, the best he could. He'd told about how being a pen rider would make it tolerable to quit rodeoing, maybe not quit permanently, but for now. "I intended to talk to you about it before I signed on, but they called me Friday saying they needed a definite answer."

"So you've already signed on? Without even mentioning it?"

"I thought you'd be happy I'd stop rodeoing."

"You'll stop when you can't climb into your saddle." She flipped open a magazine she'd brought along, then flung it to the floorboard. "Kid yourself, but don't try to kid me."

He slowed for an intersection outside Friona. "See, that's why I didn't tell you."

"It's not about changing jobs. It's not discussing it with me, like I'm not important enough."

He pulled to the side of the road and hit the brakes, shoved the gearshift into park. "Aw, honey. Don't be mad. It's just till we can get the place in shape."

"We?"

"Yeah, we."

"Well, if there's still a *we*, then tell me more about the job, what it will do for *us*."

He leaned forward and put both hands on the steering wheel. He cut a quick glance at her and saw she didn't look as upset as she sounded. The pie's tart, cinnamony smell hovered, and made him wish they were already at Uncle Butch's having dessert.

"Well, I'll have to work some after weekends. He explained the schedule at the feedlot, working fifty to sixty hours a week. Then he said, "Now and then we might still be able to go to a roping if there's one close, but otherwise, when I'm not on the job, I can work on our place. Fences, water lines, all the things we talked about a while back."

She leaned down and picked up her magazine. "Makes sense."

"For *us*." He shifted into drive. "We okay?"

She nodded, but you had to have quick eyes to catch it. Then she flipped to the middle of the magazine.

After they passed through Muleshoe, south toward Butch's place, he said, because he didn't want her surprised by it later, "Money may be tight for a while. Mostly because of not having the rodeo winnings, but we'll save on gas and entry fees, so it should work out."

She was looking out her window. "I hope Uncle Butch has a microwave. These potatoes and gravy will need heating."

He'd driven one-handed for several miles, thinking about how hard being married was sometimes. Now he put both hands on the steering wheel as they passed through two gentle curves.

Cheryl had only been to Uncle Butch's place three times before. And the old man had visited them a couple of times. She'd always felt easy in his company. His stories about rodeoing and the people he "ran with," as he called it, were all told in a slow, good-humored way that made her wish she'd known him as a young man.

He was sitting on his porch in a metal rocker when they drove up. He rose slowly, using the chair's arms for a boost. Once he unfolded his skinny frame, he stood slightly taller than Ryder and several inches more than her five-seven. He opened the screen door for Ryder, who carried the cooler, and her with the pie. "Sure smells good," he said.

She said, "You two go back outside. I'll call you when I have this on the table." She heard Butch say, "If that's an apple pie, I'm going to recommend you do your best to keep that girl." Made her smile.

Once she figured it out, the system Butch used to organize his kitchen was clear. He kept one plate, fork, knife, glass, and a coffee cup in the dish drainer. Use, wash, reuse—simple. Everything else was put away, off the counters and out of sight.

Three other place settings and some serving bowls rested on a high shelf in the cabinet to the right of the sink. Dust had blown more than once since he put them away. She washed the extras and set the table. The microwave showed some use, wearing reddish-yellow grease spatters on its turntable.

Neatness, not cleanliness, seemed to be Butch's strong suit. But why should he bother? He lived by himself, had no one else to please, no one to explain to. Seemed like that would be an easy way to live, some of the time. Lots of days, more of them recently, she avoided discussing anything with Ryder. And she knew he did the same. This new job, for example. Two years ago, that would have upset her a lot more.

She shrugged. Then she placed the potato dish in the microwave. Fried chicken, slaw, and bread waited on the table. The turntable thumped softly with each rotation, just a little off kilter. Watching the potatoes spin slowly, heating, she felt a vague sadness lodge like a tiny ache under her breastbone. What little she'd seen of him, Butch seemed happy enough, but something made her want him not to be alone, even if it was easy.

She watched Uncle Butch take a bite of the thigh he'd chosen. He held it while he chewed, looking at it as if it held a secret. He winked at her like they were in on something together. "If I didn't know better, Ryder, I'd swear your momma cooked this. I see why you married this girl." After another few bites, plus several forks full of mashed potatoes and gravy, he leaned back in his chair. "I'm going to have to pace myself." Then he leaned forward and started in on the chicken again. "This is the best meal I've had in a long time. Sure am much obliged to you for cooking it. Bet your mama taught you."

"She did. "Cheryl ate slowly, thinking about her mother teaching her to have the fat hot before putting the chicken in, then turning the heat down to give it time to cook through.

It was a while before he said, "Only reason I'm stopping is to leave room for pie after while."

"I'll get this cleared. You two go on out on the porch." She made a pot of coffee and set out two additional cups. After washing the dishes, she wrapped some of the leftover chicken in foil, and put it in the empty freezer compartment. The rest, they'd have later, for supper. Someone needed to check on Butch more often. The cabinets held only coffee and cereal. The refrigerator contained milk, peanut butter, and canned biscuits.

"Would you like pie now?" she said through the screen. "I've made coffee."

They agreed they were ready. The three of them ate, sitting in the rusty metal porch chairs, without talking. The only sounds were forks against plates and an occasional "um" sound from Butch. When he finished, he sat back and took a deep breath. She patted his shoulder and said, "You may need a nap."

"I'm coasting."

Ryder was watching her. She could feel it without looking at him. "Me, too," she said. Closing her eyes, she let in the thought she'd been avoiding. How and when to tell him she was going to start working some weekends at Emergency in Amarillo. She hadn't actually signed on, had only sent her resume and interviewed by phone. But they had already offered her the job. All this time, she'd felt bad about not telling him she was considering it, not discussing all the reasons—interesting work, extra money, and if she told the whole truth, less time at home. Now, if she brought it up, it would seem like payback.

The afternoon heat and the chair's slight rocking movement encouraged her to relax. She woke, not realizing she'd drifted toward sleep, when her head dropped toward her chest. For a second, she felt completely lost and alone. She took a deep breath and stood.

She offered more coffee. Butch said, "I'll be awake until midnight as it is."

Ryder poked at him and said, "That first cup didn't keep you from nodding off just now."

"Hadn't had my exercise. Let's walk to the barn."

Ryder watched Butch haul himself out of the chair. He seemed to move slower than the last time he'd seen him. They walked side by side down the gravel road to the barn. His uncle produced a tin of Copenhagen from a hip pocket, offered him a pinch. Ryder shook his head. He asked, "You feeling okay?"

"Right now? I feel better than I have in a long time. Does me good to see you."

At the barn, Butch whistled, and one of his two horses walked toward the corral from the other side of the barn, taking his time. The horse sidled up to Butch, leaned his head against him, nuzzled at his shirt pocket. "He's a beggar." Butch produced a sugar cube from that pocket. "Maybe a little spoiled," he said. He pointed toward the other one, trotting back and forth out of reach. "That one's going to the auction. Too much vinegar in him."

Ryder told him about the new job, his reasons for taking it. Butch didn't ask any questions, but he did raise an eyebrow at the mention of his leaving off rodeoing. "What are you thinking?" Ryder asked.

"I'm thinking it's hard letting go when you're doing pretty well. Your wife have anything to do with you quitting?"

Ryder laughed. "Nope. She didn't know until today. Probably should have talked about it with her before I took it." He thought about what he'd just said. Then he added, "She never asked me to quit. I decided."

Butch said, "I bought a horse once, a quarter horse a guy intended to race, but decided to sell. Real fast horse, but like racehorses are, high strung, skittish. I bought her thinking she'd grow out of it, once she got used to me. At first I could see she wanted to belong to me, like when I tended to her. But I got too busy with my ropin' horse, not paying her enough attention. Ruined her. She broke out of the corral, tried to go wild—must have had mustang blood. Had to hunt all over for her."

Ryder knew his uncle had a point, so he asked, "Did you ever find her?"

Butch nodded. "I did, but she wouldn't load in the trailer. I finally realized she'd hurt herself before she'd do it. Had to sell her. Needed more attention than I could give her."

Ryder felt his heart speed, a quick run of too many beats too fast, like he felt coming out of the chute on a bronc. "That's too bad. She'd have probably been good stock. Some good colts."

"That's what I'd hoped." His roping horse came up and nudged at his pocket again, wanting more sugar. They stood, leaning against the corral, watching the horse. Neither one of them said anything for a while. Then they talked a little about the weather and how Bailey County seemed to be in greater favor than

Deaf Smith, far as rain was concerned. "A man could do worse than to have this place," Butch said.

While the men were at the barn, Cheryl took the opportunity to look in the bathroom medicine cabinet. A nurse checking an elderly person's circumstances wouldn't be snooping. She found the usual things—mercurochrome, which no one sold any more; Campho-Phenique, the label soaked in oil that made her nose burn; Band-Aids; Sloan's Liniment; toothpaste; Johnson's baby powder; Gold Bond powder, guaranteed to stop foot itch; and a bottle of Old Spice Aftershave—vied for space. But no pain medicine or anything else gave a clue of serious ailments. A side drawer contained saw palmetto capsules and an electric razor. The commode surprised her by showing evidence of recent scouring. Maybe the main thing he needed was a good multivitamin. Or a companion to share meals with.

The one bedroom, bed neatly made, and the second, smaller room he used as an office, could use dusting, as could the blinds. His closet made her smile. Like a lot of cowboys, he took his Wranglers and shirts to the laundry. Seven pairs of starched jeans and ten shirts hung in a neat row above a pair of work-worn brown cowhide boots and a barely-used pair of black belly-ostrich ones. Belts and award buckles lined a shelf. If she were a public health nurse, she wouldn't have found anything here suggesting neglect. Still, the feeling that something was off- kilter lingered.

She stepped outside and watched the two men walking slowly up the drive. Butch definitely favored his left hip and leaned forward like a man heading into a strong wind.

Ryder went inside as soon as they got to the house. He said, "Everything okay here?" Said it mostly to find out where Cheryl was and what she was doing.

She came from the bedroom, wiping her hands on her jeans. He pointed to the porch and opened the door, held it for her.

Uncle Butch had settled in one of the porch chairs. "Let's sit out here and visit some more. That walk did the trick. No nap needed," Butch said. He patted the seat of the chair nearest him. "This one's for the cook." Ryder followed her, sat in the chair on her other side.

She said, "The pie's in the freezer, and some chicken, too."

Ryder figured she was thinking about Butch eating, worrying it wasn't enough. He asked, "Uncle Butch, how often you eating these days?"

Butch said, "I ever tell you about that old boy I used to know down at Rotan?" He waited until Ryder shook his head.

"See, he got to where he couldn't stand his own cooking, so he went to town looking for some woman to do it for him. Trouble was, he wasn't much on bathing, so most of the women turned their noses up at him." He waited for a second, didn't move on with the tale until Ryder nodded.

"Then he heard about that dried food the army uses now instead of C Rations. Just add hot water. So he went to the Army-Navy store in Abilene and bought up three cases of them things— enough for six weeks or longer if he stretched it." He paused. Ryder thought he practiced his timing. Never moved along until he had a clue his audience was with him.

Ryder asked, "So how did it work out for him?"

"Musta been all right. Folks said last time they saw him, he weighed twenty pounds more and had taken to saluting anything that moved."

Cheryl rolled her eyes and shook her head. Ryder laughed. He could tell Cheryl wasn't going to let it go. She asked, "So, where's your stash of those dried meals?"

"Haven't bought it yet. But I'm getting pretty close. My cooking appeals to me so little that some days I just eat peanut butter." Ryder noticed his uncle said that with a straight face.

They stayed until six o'clock. She made sure they all three snacked on the extra chicken and gravy before they put the cooler in the pickup. She also managed to extract a promise from Butch to buy a bottle of One A Day vitamins and some frozen dinners. He said, "Okay, I will. If you're as good a nurse as you are a cook, you probably know what you're doing."

On the way back toward Muleshoe, Ryder said, "Thanks for working on him about eating. He probably took it better from you than he would from me."

"We need to come see him more often. A person his age shouldn't be alone." Then she said, sounded like it was as much to herself as to him, "No, alone isn't the word. Everyone probably needs some time to themselves, that's alone. *Lonely* is what I mean. Having no one near to care about or to let him know he's loved. That's lonely."

He drove slower than the limit heading home, the sun sinking on their left, twilight creeping up on the other side. Neither of them said any more all the way to their house, and not much when they got there.

Part IV
2008

CHAPTER 13

July 26 and 27, 2008—Ryder Sheldon

Rough Stock

Two Tylenol and four Modelos (he wouldn't have spent that much on beer, but she'd said it was her treat) had finally got Ryder where he could sleep. Now this. A woman yelling, "Oh, Jesus!" Sounded frantic, a woman in trouble. A pain shot through his left side, all the way down to his hip when he tried to move. He rolled to his left side and regretted it immediately. That damn bull probably broke a rib. Maybe he'd dreamed the cry for help; maybe he'd yelled it himself. If she needed saving, surely someone closer would call the police.

Earlier that night, just outside the rodeo arena a campfire had lit the edge of the dusty road like a small beacon as he drove slowly away from another disappointment. Piñon smoke hung in a cloud that looked like a fist over a small ring of rocks. Flames the stones encircled looked weary, tired of flickering, just barely producing a fading blue and orange glimmer. As he passed, a wisp of smoke rode a sudden breeze into the pickup cab. It cleared as quickly as it entered, in the time it took him to blink. And when he opened his eyes wide, he saw her—on his right, standing on the edge of the road, a backpack leaning against her left leg, her right hand waving slowly, as if she knew him, expected him. He rolled to a stop about ten yards past.

Picking up women at rodeos wasn't something he made a habit of, but he'd done it a few times in the last couple of years, to have someone to dance with a little, to celebrate after a win, before he headed back home. Picking up hitchhikers was even less typical of him; he might not be lucky, but he tended to be fairly cautious. Something about that wave made him stop. That and the fact that he could barely steer and had no idea where he intended to go.

His wife never knew about the other ones, and he didn't even recall their faces. Although that one who was so quick to show off her purple underwear turned up in a dream once in a while. He'd never done much to feel guilty about, far as he could remember. But he sure never mentioned other women to Cheryl. Some things a wife didn't need to hear about. If he didn't go back, she'd never know about this one. Wouldn't matter then anyway.

Staying upright in the seat took most of the energy he could muster. So when the hitchhiker leaned in the passenger side window and said, "Need a driver?" all he could do was nod. She took her time getting to the driver's side door, walking the way everyone does wearing above the ankle hiking boots and carrying a backpack slung over one shoulder, a sort of rolling trudge, as if she might have been keeping to the beat of a slow march. After she adjusted the seat and the rearview mirror, she asked, "Bad bull, huh? Where to?"

With some considerable difficulty, he'd moved over to the passenger seat. He told her he didn't care where she took him, as long as he never saw another bull. "I'm getting way too old for this shit," he said. Then he pulled his hat brim down near his nose and tried to imagine not hurting and not being broker than when he left Texas.

Those were the last words they said for about fifty miles, long miles for him because every bump or turn shot a new pain through his body or his head, or both.

A woman who can drive a pickup and knows when not to

talk owns two major assets. Not the most valuable ones, land or
cattle, but an understanding of men and good sense. He realized
he'd been close to asleep when she said, "Santa Fe okay with you?
I know a good place to stay."

Her voice didn't match her face, what he could tell of it in
the dash lights. She looked to be about seven or eight years older
than him, forty or so. But her voice sort of tinkled, like a young
girl's, full of music. He dredged up the strength to say, "Have to
be free or else sleep in the truck. I'm broke."

"I'll pay."

He nodded once and slumped back down in the seat, his
hat over his eyes, pain he'd gotten familiar with pulsing in his left
side. He tried for a deep breath and all he got was a short whiff of
manure; probably stepped in it getting out of that last bull's way.

Light poked a finger under his hat brim. Even in pain, a person
can lose consciousness and think it's sleep. He came to and his
eyes focused when he rose up and looked through the windshield.
La Quinta Motel.

She pointed to a six-pack in the floorboard and then shook
two pills from a bottle that said "acetaminophen 500 mg." in big
letters on the side. She said, "I stopped in Espanola. You slept
through it. Take these. I'll be right back. You got a name?"

"Ryder."

"Amy."

About then he'd have believed her if she'd said she was a
saint and her name was Mary.

She repeated his name and laughed. "Your momma had a
sense of humor."

He wasn't up to laughing, just made a little sound in
his throat.

As soon as they got into the room, he sat on the bed and next thing he knew, he'd fallen over on his right side, ending up in a sort of wad in the middle of the bed. He rolled back to a sitting position and leaned forward, elbows on his knees, head in his hands. Damn, everything he had hurt.

She handed him a new beer to replace the one he'd finished in four long gulps when she disappeared into the hotel lobby. He turned just as far as his misery allowed and saw her fiddling with her backpack, then heard some zippers opening and closing behind him before he heard the bathroom door close.

He had time to put away that beer and one more, hoping they would take him away from the gouging and grinding that seemed to have taken over his body. At least his head had quit hurting. A start. He'd just opened another Modelo when she said, "You need help getting out of your boots?"

"Guess it's that or sleep in them."

Besides a girl's voice and a nice laugh, she possessed a gentle touch. Maybe she worked with horses. He managed to sit upright and then to stand and lean on her shoulder while she got him out of his boots and Wranglers and down to his undershirt and shorts. "You sure your name ain't Mary?"

"That your wife's name?"

He'd have answered, but didn't have the gumption. The clock notified him it was twelve forty-three. He lay flat on his back and she pulled the sheet and bedspread up, all the way over his face. Not many women know the value of cover.

The clock on the bedside table showed two a.m. Dark outside. It took a minute, but the hum of the in-room refrigerator reminded him of where he was, La Quinta Inn, Room 112. Santa Fe. Hoping he'd go back to sleep, he remembered she'd gotten handicapped access, ground floor. Technically, he didn't qualify, but the stiff-kneed limp on his left leg and the bruise on his right cheek probably would have convinced the clerk. And since she offered to pay, and the pickup would be right outside the door, and that meant he didn't have to worry about some thief getting in the saddlebox that hadn't locked since he'd pried it open the last time he lost his key, he agreed when she mentioned getting a room intended for the lame. Maybe if he groaned real loud, that would shut down all those useless thoughts. But that would be inconsiderate. He closed his eyes, found a position that didn't make him want to scream.

"Oh, Jesus!" His eyes sprang open again even though he wanted nothing more than to sleep.

He looked to his right. There she was, exactly where she placed herself not long after they finished off the six-pack. Didn't look like she'd moved at all. Way to the far side of the king-sized bed. Breathing slowly, regularly. Definitely not the one who called for Jesus. That came from above.

He told himself he didn't have to worry about the unnecessary saddle out in that unlocked box. Just get some sleep. The woman shifted, just slightly, and made a sound like the start of a laugh, "Ha." Then after a deep breath that ended in a sigh, she lay still.

Bull riders don't need a saddle. But he'd loaded his bronc-riding rig in the saddlebox when he left, mainly to avoid having to answer questions. His wife would have had a shit hemorrhage if he'd told her what he intended to do. Riding broncs was one thing; bulls were a different matter entirely. No saddle required, only lots of guts and plenty of luck. Sometimes, especially if the clowns weren't fast enough, some speed getting up off the dirt and onto the fence helped, too. He'd been about a half-step off tonight. If it hadn't been for the clowns, he'd have more than a rib busted.

The only way he was going to make any money was riding bulls, finishing eight seconds on every one he drew, making it to the final go round and coming out in the top three. All that plus some heavy side bets and he just might make it away with enough to buy a new horse. Otherwise, he'd lose his job. No feedlot kept a pen rider who didn't have his own horse.

Maybe he could get to sleep if he tried that deep breathing his wife was always practicing. Said it helped her relax and relieved stress. The first deep breath he tried got as far has the middle of his chest before it felt like a knife under his heart. Not relaxing, by a long shot.

The explanations he had manufactured never did satisfy her, but it kept her from asking him anything else. He'd sort of bow up like he might be getting upset when she tried being reasonable, telling him she would work extra shifts at the hospital, enough to replace the horse he'd had to put down. It didn't hurt to let her think that grief had him all sensitive. Goddamn, he already depended on her for the house payment. What kind of a man let his wife buy him a horse?

No more sounds from above. He lay perfectly still on his back, breathing carefully, hoping for sleep, or if not that, maybe an answer. So far the only one that made any sense involved heading west instead of going back to Texas.

His wife would do better without him. Ever since they'd been married, eight years now, he'd poured money down one rat hole after another—first dragging Clint in that beat up old horse trailer to ropings all over the Panhandle every weekend, sleeping in the pickup, just to get enough money together to chase that first dream, the half section of land where he imagined raising cutting horses and some roping calves.

Well, he got the land and the note that went with it. He

added saddle bronc riding, which he'd been good at before he turned twenty-five, so he could get on the big money circuit, planning to pay off the note fast, and start building corrals. Five years had passed and he'd never even dug a posthole. The money he saved for fencing went to replace the pickup that gave out. He'd had to buy another used one instead of the Dodge three-quarter ton flatbed he'd need for the ranch—he'd taken to thinking of their 380 dry acres as a ranch. But he never quite won enough riding broncs to ever get ahead. So a couple of years ago, he took the job pen riding, making a steady wage, able to keep up with the note.

Then last week his only horse had to be put down. He'd told Cheryl he would just do this one rodeo in Taos and he'd bring back enough to get another horse. Then they'd get everything back on track.

She never said so, but he could tell she'd about had a sack full. Some men just weren't cut out to be married, couldn't manage to take care of anyone but themselves. Besides, even if she didn't actually complain, he could see it on her face. The smile she used to never be without had changed to a sort of faintly-dismayed-but-never-actually-grim sort of expression. A lot like the martyrs on holy cards.

He meant it when he said, just before he pulled out of the driveway, "Just this one more and then I'll quit, I promise you."

She'd said, "Don't make promises you can't keep."

He didn't have an answer for that. He had pulled his hat down, straightening it low over his eyes like he always did for luck, and driven slowly west toward the county road. Funny how he could feel miserable around her even when she didn't seem to expect anything from him.

Three-thirty, according to the clock. Up above, thumping

sounds—like someone running on small bare feet. Then, sounds he recognized for certain. Rhythmic, pulsing toward a crescendo, the bed hitting against the wall, again. And that woman's voice, again, "Uh, uh, uuuhhh." On and on. Maybe there were more than two people up there.

Gangbangers? Probably not. She hadn't screamed, not really.

The rhythmic thumping continued, the beat of drums in some ancient ceremony. The pitch of the woman's voice rose; "Uh, uh, uuh, uuhhh, uuuhhh," up the scale, steadily, toward high C. He twisted his neck toward the clock see how long she held the note. Then, "Oh, Jesus!" Followed by a long, loud sigh. Silence, briefly, and then afterward, more thumping, quieter at first, but steady. Wore him out, just thinking about it.

Turning to his left side again reminded him why he shouldn't, even if that was the only way he could ever sleep. Tonight he'd have to forget it. Just stay awake and wonder who those people upstairs were. And wonder where they got all the energy. Probably weren't married.

He looked to his right. The hitchhiker hadn't moved and her breathing remained steady and slow. Some people can sleep through anything. His mother would have said she must have a clear conscience.

He pulled a pillow, carefully and slowly, from under the arm of the woman who'd paid for the room. That maneuver, which he managed with his right arm, announced another bruise or sprain or something, this one at the right shoulder joint. At least the new pain took his mind off the rib on the left side that he knew now, for sure, must be broken.

On the pillow, the woman's scents, piñon and lemon, competed, reminding him of the high desert. Instead of covering his head with the pillow as he'd intended, he clutched it to his chest and relaxed against it. For a brief second, his left side forgot to hurt.

Sleep must have finally overtaken him, or he fell unconscious; one or the other, because light now shone around the edge of the drape and the clock told him six a.m. had arrived. He hadn't heard anything more from the room above. As soon as he roused and realized and then tried to forget who and where he was, his body took over reminding him; he was a guy who hit the dirt after two seconds on the biggest bull in the pen, in the third and final go round; the cowboy who didn't have a horse and by Tuesday wouldn't have a job either. The pain had gathered in one spot this morning, his left side toward his backbone. Otherwise, soreness, but not actual pain, blanketed his entire body. He'd probably live.

His hitchhiker lay in the same position as he'd last seen her. She stirred only briefly when he sat up and felt around for his clothes. His Wranglers slid on without causing him to scream and he managed to angle his right arm into the sleeve of his shirt without too much strain; the left one presented a challenge so he let it dangle and stepped as lightly as he could to the bathroom. He didn't turn on the light, mainly because he didn't want to see himself in the mirror. But there also was no need to wake Amy or whatever her name was. After he peed and saw it contained no blood, he took a deep breath and wasn't struck dead by the effort. He'd definitely make it, although what *it* was, he didn't know.

The door to their room opened without any creaking and he slid out slick as a burglar. No word sounded from the woman he'd shared the big bed with.

About six-thirty, he heard someone whistle, a piercing single note. He turned, slowly, hoping not to start his body sending a new round of signals his bull riding days were over. From where he sat on the tailgate, he saw the hitchhiker, her head anyway, peeking from the door to the room she'd paid for.

He could barely hear her when she said, "I made some coffee. It's not great, but it'll do for a starter. Want some?"

He nodded and she stepped out, carrying two paper cups. She handed him one and said, "Can you make it over there?" She pointed to a pair of large landscaping rocks on the other side of the parking lot.

"Getting my boots on convinced me I can do anything." He eased off the tailgate and followed her to the rocks. Eased himself down again. A groan that embarrassed him escaped before he could stifle it. He lit a cigarette, raised the pack in her direction. She shook her head.

They sat side by side, apart. He smoked and stared back toward the door to room 112, disability access.

After about half a cup of coffee, she said, "Any bets on what went on upstairs last night?"

"You heard?"

"Seemed like all night." She drank some more coffee.

"Honeymoon."

"Five dollars?"

He stubbed out the cigarette, lit another one. "If I had five, yeah."

She pointed to the rooms on the second story. The door to room 212 opened slowly. A plump, long-haired young woman, with no visible injuries, wearing a flowered sundress, looked both ways, then walked to her left across the balcony. She didn't seem to notice them as she came down the stairs and went directly to a crew cab pickup parked in front of 108. Seconds later, she slammed the pickup door and climbed the stairs again, now carrying a tote bag over her left shoulder. She stopped at the door to 208, knocked, and disappeared inside, then reappeared quickly and returned to 212.

He said, "The best man and maid of honor in there." Although to him it had sounded like the best man was in 212.

"We'll see. Want any breakfast? It's free."

He shook his head; curiosity kept him in place. The door to 212 opened again, and the same young woman stepped out, followed by a slim man, about the same age, wearing a dark suit and a blue shirt, who followed her to 208.

Ryder lit another cigarette. He and the woman he'd found beside the road —or did she find him?—both stared at the upstairs doors and sipped their now lukewarm coffee.

The door to 208 opened. The young man exited and turned right. The female emerged pushing a toddler in a stroller. An older woman and man followed, carrying luggage. Ryder looked at Amy and raised an eyebrow. She leaned forward and frowned, studying the scene as closely as possible without leaving the rock.

The older woman and man stopped long enough to add the stroller and child to their burdens and struggled down the stairs. The young woman who had called for Jesus returned to 212, but only briefly. She reappeared in the doorway with an infant in her arms. She stopped, shifted the infant to her right arm and managed to pull her dress strap and top down to bare her left breast, all in one smooth motion. The baby latched on to the food supply and quickly disappeared under a small blanket the woman produced, apparently by magic. She proceeded toward the stairway, followed by the suit-clad young man. He carried nothing other than a wide smile.

Ryder tried looking certain. He said, "See there. Honeymoon."

Amy cut her eyes at him the way people do when you raise a bet and then call for five new cards. "Wrong, cowboy." She turned again toward the group now piling into the crew cab pickup. "They were renewing their vows."

He heard her laugh her young girl's tinkling laugh as she walked away toward the motel's dining room.

She brought him back orange juice and a sweet roll from the free breakfast buffet. He felt like he should do more than thank her, but didn't know what to say or exactly why. She stowed all she had in the backpack. He watched, ate, and wondered how long before checkout time.

"Well," she said, "thanks for the ride."

"Hell, thank you for driving and for the bed. You probably saved what's left of my life."

She shrugged like it was nothing. "Got to go. I promised to meet some people here."

She waved as she closed the door.

He stood under the hot water in the shower a long time, thinking about how tough it would be to take a shower in a wheelchair, using the low mounted spray nozzle in the odd-looking stall. Trying not to think about what to do next.

At Clines Corners, he stopped for gas, intending to use his only credit card, which he hoped hadn't reached its limit. A voice on a speaker at the pump told him he'd have to come inside and pay before he could get fuel. Souvenirs, scratch-off lottery tickets, Slim Jims, and tiny cellophane packets of Quick Energy and Hangover Remedy pills surrounded him as he signed the card receipt. This truck stop attracted people from everywhere, travelers of all sorts, not only truckers. He noticed a lot of them could easily pass for fugitives—wearing unmatched clothes, walking like their shoes didn't fit, shifting their eyes away if you caught them watching.

Tank filled, he stared down at I 40 where it passed going east and west. He could join that steady stream headed to his right and he'd end up in Albuquerque and then could go south until he found a ranch needing a hand. Or he could skip the big highway and the fast trucks that always followed him too close and go back north fifty miles and then over east a little ways to the cattle land near Las Vegas. He could look for work around there. Hell, possibilities waited everywhere. Or he could go left on I 40 and end up back in Texas before dark. He drove north.

In Las Vegas, he had to break his next to last five-dollar bill to buy a Coke. His Tylenol had worn off and every step he took convinced him he had more than one cracked rib. He took two more of his drug of choice and wished for some more Modelo. He closed his eyes for a minute, heard the hitchhiker's laugh in his mind. That was one smart woman, a woman who knew how to treat a man. Just let him be. Help out when he needed it, but nothing more. No expectations.

Not a single head of beef grazed anywhere near the road at the first ranch he came to outside Las Vegas. Dry everywhere this year. He prowled around for over an hour before he drove on.

The soreness that had been a hint before was now a fact that assaulted his entire body. His own bed might be a place he could heal up. No doubt there'd be no one up above calling for Jesus. He laughed, a quiet, "Ha." About a mile later, he said under his breath, "Renewing their vows. Hmmph."

He turned east and drove slower than the speed limit. Seven o'clock became eight when he crossed the New Mexico line into Texas and the Central Time Zone. He thought the pressure in his chest increased about the same time. Forty-five minutes later he parked at a strange angle behind his wife's Toyota, because what strength he had just seemed to evaporate when he saw their house. Steering past the gate and across the cattle guard had taken his last speck of concentration. He couldn't help limping as he crossed the yard.

She came out on the porch. "You're hurt. Here, lean on my shoulder."

He did.

"How many bulls did you ride before the one you didn't?"

"Two. Number three had different ideas."

She told him to sit on one of the straight-backed kitchen chairs. He pushed back his hat and let her look him over; emergency nurses know about cracked ribs.

After she had thumped and pulled around on him and put her ear to his chest and had him breathe as deep as he could, she stood back. "You should see a doctor."

"No, I don't need one." He tossed his hat on the kitchen table, took a few more slow, deep breaths on his own. Taking his time, looking at her and at the clean, neat little kitchen, thinking about how good their bed would feel. "What I need is a horse. A man's gonna work as pen rider, he's got to have one he can always rely on."

CHAPTER 14

July 27, 2008—Cheryl Sheldon

A Simple Test

A hospital bathroom should be clean. This one, off the waiting room for the Emergency Department, smelled like dirty diapers and vomit. The stall she'd just closed herself into, smaller by half than the one in the nurses' lounge, lacked both paper seat covers and toilet tissue. But it did contain a message, Cheryl noticed.

There on the floor, inscribed in the grime missed by housekeeping's occasional mopping—FUCK YOU—all capital letters. What tool had the writer of that message used? A finger? How long had it gone unseen, unread? Any other day she would have laughed; irony, usually at least, made her smile.

She replaced the box in the deep pocket of her scrub top and left the stall, left the bathroom, stopped at the information desk nearby, and called the housekeeping department. A visitors' area bathroom should be especially clean.

When she returned to the ED, two other nurses and the unit clerk occupied the chairs at the nurses' station. Only three patients so far and before she left the unit she transferred the last one, a pregnant woman, twenty-six weeks, who presented with contractions and spotty vaginal bleeding, to the OB floor for observation. Sunday mornings often started slowly. But even on slow days, Emergency never bored her like her regular job at the prison infirmary. Locked in from the time she signed in until she left. Might as well have committed a crime.

The unit clerk looked at her and raised an eyebrow. "You feel okay?"

"Sure, why?"

"You're pale."

"Something I ate's not agreeing. I'm fine."

She would be as soon as she could get to a clean bathroom, open the box, and pee on that little stick. All she needed to know was that she wasn't pregnant, and her color would return to normal, along with her heart rate. And the headache at the base of her skull would disappear. She recognized anxiety when she felt it.

The ambulance radio emitted a shrill beep, and rapid chatter notified them six patients were inbound from an MVA on I 40—chest wounds on two, possible fractured femur, and a long list of other injuries caused by a cattle truck veering into a slow moving Sunday School bus.

The Unit Clerk placed the first of several calls to alert surgeons, anesthetists, and the on-call surgery supervisor. Then she knocked on the door of the Doctors' Lounge to wake the ER doc who always stayed out of sight until a real patient arrived. Cheryl and the other two nurses raced to check supplies in the Major Trauma rooms.

Three o'clock arrived just as the last patient was dispatched to surgery. Cheryl finally looked up from the computer screen when Marsha Carson said, "You angling for overtime?"

Cheryl laughed. "I didn't even hear you come in. I'll give you report in just a minute. One more entry on that last patient and I'm done." She quickly typed a description of the pre-transport condition of the six-year-old with the fractured femur, pressed ENTER, and exited the record. "Calf rope!" She flung both hands up high the way they did in the rodeo, to show a clean finish. "That's it. No report to give. We shipped them all out.

You'll get fresh ones."

Was it too much to ask, just ten minutes alone in the restroom? She had barely slid the lock on the stall door when she heard, "Cheryl?" The voice belonged to Danette.

"What? Did I forget something out there?"

"No, I just wanted to say hi. You working next weekend?" The door to the stall on Cheryl's right banged closed. "I thought maybe we could go out dancing again after shift, if you are. That guy you danced with last month was there again last night."

Cheryl took a deep breath and let it out slowly, as quietly as she could. She stuck the still unopened box back in her pocket and flushed the commode. "I probably won't be here. I need to rest a weekend or two." She stood at the sink, watching the water swirl down the drain, listening to Danette pass gas, daintily, the way pretty girls like her always seem to do everything.

Cheryl said, "I'm out of here. Have a good evening."

Ordinarily the shifts she worked in Emergency at Med Center Hospital in Amarillo lasted either ten or twelve hours. A few of those each month, at between $300 and $400 per shift, put quite a bit in the account at the credit union and still left her a few weekend days at home. Today she drove the forty-three mile trip home, which she usually made in thirty-eight minutes flat, as if snow and ice covered the road, very slowly and cautiously. Ryder wouldn't be in before eight. Three hours at least. All she needed was ten minutes alone.

She reached, with her right hand, into her purse and found the envelope from the credit union. Twenty-five stiff, new one hundred dollar bills. Right where she'd put them Friday. Numbers had haunted her every day and night for the past two weeks. Twenty-eight days; four weeks, an uncounted number of tequila shots and margaritas; two weeks late, as of today; thirty minutes at the rundown Knight's Rest Motel on the Amarillo Highway; one smooth-dancing, slick talking guy with dimples, who probably hadn't believed her when she said her name was Lucy.

After she turned south from I 40, she set the cruise control on fifty-five. Still hot from the afternoon sun, the pavement danced with mirages of wavy water. A dust devil whirled across the brown pasture to her left, growing larger with each rotation, advancing directly toward her. She tapped the brake and slowed; a dervish vortex that size could shove a vehicle off the road. Before she'd gone a half mile, the devil veered away and dissipated, the dust and plastic sacks it carried all dropping to the ground like beings deprived of spirit. Maybe she'd imagined it.

She resumed speed and punched the radio on. Spanish, spoken too rapidly for her to understand, intruded into the Toyota. The usual sound of accordions and bass, the staples of conjunto music, quickly gave way to conga and bongo drums, piano, and trumpets playing salsa. She abandoned the AM band and switched to NPR. *Prairie Home Companion's* segment "Lives of the Cowboys" stopped with Lefty in mid-sentence when she turned off the radio. Wondering how to explain to Ryder taking a weekday off if she had to spend the crisp new money at the only abortion clinic within two hundred miles took those bumbling cowboys' place.

Until that Friday last month, she'd always told Danette, the ringleader, she had a long drive and had to get home. She suspected they all wanted to get her talking about herself. That wasn't going to happen; she never talked about her personal life, never wore her wedding ring at work. Danette and one of the other nurses from Emergency had asked her to go out after their shift several times, said they knew a great place to dance salsa. That afternoon she agreed.

It would be her secret. Ryder had some of his own. She knew darn well he didn't dance alone at the rodeo dances she knew he stayed for when he had a win to celebrate. And she never asked about the purple bra she found under his pickup seat last July— all of hers were black or white. Sure, she thought about it, tried to pinpoint a cause. Eventually, she decided that what kept people tied started to unravel after eight years married. Fighting about underwear and deciding whether to believe whatever story he'd come up with didn't seem worth the trouble. But since then, they spent more and more time being polite to each other, like strangers seated next to one another on a plane, staying as far apart as possible in cramped quarters.

He had told her when he left that weekend for another rodeo, somewhere down near Vernon, that if he didn't finish in the money this time, he'd quit and just stick with his day job. And she couldn't even recall the last time he'd taken her dancing. Besides, she loved salsa and he preferred waltzes and the cowboy two-step.

She said, "I'll bring a change of clothes."

Danette said, "I'm not on tomorrow, so I'll meet you here when you get off at seven."

That Saturday night, when Cheryl walked out of the nurses' lounge wearing high heels and a shiny, red, off-the-shoulder dress with a flounce around the bottom of its tight skirt, Danette said, "Wow!"

Even the E D doc, who seldom looked up from the computer, if he ventured out of his room at all, whistled and said, "I'll second that."

Her cheeks heated. She knew her best features and how to emphasize them. Even though her face was nothing remarkable, racehorse ankles and a firm butt, when displayed properly, usually fetched some second glances. That, plus wearing eye makeup, bright red lipstick, and gold hoop earrings, and sporting a short, slinky dress, made her pretty certain she wouldn't miss too many dances.

Danette offered her a high five and said, "I hardly recognized you! We won't sit out many tonight."

"Who's going with us?"

"Just us."

"I'll follow you in my car. So I can leave for home from there."

They were hardly in the door (no cover charge for unescorted ladies) before a short, swarthy man wearing a bright yellow shirt stepped out of the crowd near the bar, walked directly to Danette, and led her to the dance floor.

Carrying Danette's purse and her own, Cheryl took her time finding an unoccupied table. As she made her way from near the door to the farthest corner of the room, she smiled her nurse-smile, the one that said, "You interest me. You can trust me." Nothing sexy, nothing seductive, just a smile she knew made people feel good and want to talk to her. Or in this case, maybe ask her to dance. That's what she came here for.

After that first dance, Danette turned up alone at the table. She fanned herself with both hands. "Whew! Hot in here. Makes me glow," Danette said. She dabbed her neck, all the way down to her cleavage, with a paper napkin. "I love salsa. Even women who aren't look beautiful when they dance salsa. Like tropical birds, preening, doing mating dances." She reached down and loosened the ankle strap on one of her emerald green, high-heeled sandals.

A husky, red-haired man stopped at their table just after Danette's margarita and Cheryl's Diet Coke arrived. He introduced himself as Frank. Danette raised an eyebrow and cocked her head like she misheard when Cheryl answered, "Lucy Harmon. Not from around here. Just in town for the weekend." She extended her right hand to the man and watched his smile reveal a deep dimple on his right cheek.

They danced their first dance when the next song began, "Valio La Pena." He'd obviously done this before. Most anglo guys danced like they'd prefer pushing a partner counter-clockwise around the floor in a two-step. Too self-conscious. Not this one. He partnered like he was born making a woman look good. Never too close, leading with just a touch at the small of her back or on her hip. Besides that he smelled like some expensive cologne Cheryl didn't recognize, pleasantly masculine, definitely musky.

After two more dances, Frank, or whatever his name was, said, "I don't want you to get away from me, but I need to sit one out. Will you have a drink? Margarita?"

"Yes, thanks," Cheryl said. Why not? Just one wouldn't cause a problem.

The temperature in the room climbed as people arrived and the dance floor filled with smiling couples, the women swirling their skirts high, flirting with their partners, moving as if their feet and bodies had told their brains to take the night off. Drink orders changed from margaritas to tequila shots; drums sounded a beat that lodged in Cheryl's chest and made her eager to dance every dance.

Danette beckoned her to go with her to the restroom. Cheryl watched as Danette blotted her damp face and neck, then reapplied lipstick. Danette said, "I'm going to leave pretty soon. It's nearly eleven and I have to work tomorrow."

Cheryl knew a lie when she heard one. Danette and that

yellow-shirted guy would leave together. She said, "Careful on the way home. One or two more dances and I'll be ready, too."

Back at the table, before she could sit down, Frank handed her another shot and pulled her toward the dance floor. She downed the shot; she'd lost count a while back.

She twirled near him, then away. He said something she couldn't hear. She moved near again, keeping the beat with her hips and staying in place. "What?"

He asked if she would leave with him. She danced away, feeling her hips exaggerate the rhythm and wondering why they weren't connected to the rest of her. She twirled back and said, "I'll meet you."

He told her where and said he'd be in room 146. She hoped she'd remember the number.

When he left, she danced one more dance, choosing a partner from the three men sitting together at the next table. She waved to Danette as she and the yellow-shirted man walked out the door. After telling her final partner she would soon turn into a pumpkin, Cheryl surprised herself by walking like a sober woman to make a final visit to the restroom. The condom machine offered her a choice of colors.

The Knight's Rest occupied a large lot only seven blocks away. She knew it was seven because she counted them as she drove slowly and very cautiously toward the large sign he'd described, never exceeding thirty miles per hour. As he'd promised, he waited in room 146. Music with the same beat they had danced to minutes earlier poured from the bedside radio. They danced again, more sedately than before.

She handed him the condom. "My bad luck I can't take birth control pills. They make me sick. It's this or not at all." She heard herself being bold. Reckless but not completely stupid.

He nodded. "Not a problem." Then he helped her gently from her dress, and she twirled around once on her high heels while he stripped off his shirt. They danced again, she in her panties and bra (she wished for a second she'd bought purple) and he without a shirt. She felt sweat pooling between her breasts. With her eyes closed, for just a moment, she danced on a bridge in Iris, Texas, with a boy whose name she'd put out of her mind long ago.

The beat from the next song accelerated. They stopped dancing. She let him lead her to the bed. He used the same subtle touch he used on the dance floor.

With the beat in the background, they moved together as if choreographed. Neither of them held back, and to her surprise, they came at the same time.

She laughed quietly when she heard him snoring seconds later.

Midnight was still fifteen minutes away. He didn't move when she opened the door to leave.

Driving in the dark, west on I 40, she wondered why she couldn't stop smiling. Tequila. It had gotten her in trouble before.

By the time she turned off I 40 south toward home, her face felt stiff and her stomach reminded her she hadn't eaten since lunch. Jackrabbits flitted across the highway, one seeming to move in a syncopated rhythm, dancing up from the ditch on the left toward the center stripe. A faint, dull thump told her he hadn't moved fast enough.

She slowed at the intersection of two county roads five miles from their house, rolling through at a crawl. When she parked near her front gate and opened the car door, she vomited onto the ground, tasting lime and tequila and bile as her stomach tried to empty its memory of the hours before. That wouldn't be the last of it. She wobbled on those stupid high heels and stepped in the puddle before she managed to stand up straight. The sidewalk felt like it angled up an incline. Slamming the door, she yelled into the dark house, "Damn you and damn that purple bra!"

The next morning, working against a headache that made her squint, she had pulled the red dress out from where she'd shoved it behind her pile of dirty scrubs in the closet floor. She'd bought it at a cheap store in the mall knowing it would never stand much use. Minutes later, smoke swirled upward, smelling of the diesel she lit in the incinerator to be sure the evidence turned to ash. Ryder liked her better in blue than in red, or used to when he paid attention.

When Cheryl called the next day, the Emergency Department supervisor accepted her excuse of stomach flu, but only after she promised she would work the entire first weekend of next month, one twelve-hour shift and an eight. Irrational as Cheryl knew it was, she convinced herself that if she stayed out of the ED for a few weekends, Frank would have left town and she wouldn't run the risk of his being rolled in on a gurney and recognizing her. Although she knew she probably wouldn't recognize him, every bit of the rest of that night had stayed with her in detail.

Ryder had made a rodeo each of the following weekends, winning a little, roping at the first one and finishing out of the money, riding saddle broncs the other three. In between he worked from daylight until late in the afternoon riding pens at the feedlot close to Hereford.

There wasn't much occasion for talk during the weekdays. By the time he ate supper and fell asleep in his recliner, she was in bed. She had to be locked in at the prison Monday through Friday at seven a.m. and that meant she had to be up early. Except for one evening, over the chicken fried steak she'd made because it was his favorite, he said out of nowhere, "Things will get better soon. We'll have enough saved to get this place in shape. You won't ever have to work extra anymore. Maybe not work at all. Maybe start a family."

"We're fine. The only thing I worry about is you getting hurt riding rough stock."

"Nah, not gonna happen. I'll be okay." He took his plate to the sink. On the way to his recliner in front of the television, he kissed her on the cheek, briefly, like a short stopover on a long trip.

Fine was nowhere close to how she actually felt. By then her usually predictable period was six days late.

At the county road intersection, she stopped abruptly to avoid being T-boned by a manure truck whose driver apparently thought his cargo deserved the right of way. The truck rattled past and left a feedlot odor in its wake. Cheryl inhaled and reminded herself she'd done what she did—the past was history. Getting herself killed by a manure truck might be ironic, but all she could do now was go forward. She drove straight ahead toward home.

In the methodical way she had learned to perform nursing procedures, she reviewed the steps she would take. First, confirm her suspicion. A simple test. Second, if the strip showed +, she would call tomorrow for an appointment for the abortion to be done this week, next week at the latest. Termination of a pregnancy before fetal viability was no crime and not a sin, as far as she was concerned. Seeing the many abused and neglected, unwanted children who turned up as patients in Emergency convinced her of that a long time ago.

She reached into her purse again, reassured herself the

envelope hadn't disappeared. Ryder never asked how much she made working extra and never knew how much of it went into her savings at the credit union. Maybe he didn't ask for the same reason he insisted he should be the one to pay for what he called "all the essentials." That meant he should pay for land and taxes and whatever else he needed to, to feel like a man, she supposed. Trying to discuss money with Ryder tended to always leave them both upset. So she quit trying. Just as well, he'd never know about this money or where she spent it.

They had talked about having kids, about three years ago, before it quit raining. Since the dry spell turned into a drought, neither one of them had brought it up. In the way that married people do, neither of them changed the routine—condom plus foam, just to be safe, because birth control pills put her in bed with blinding migraines and non-stop vomiting. Even that double protection could have failed. It hadn't in eight years. And the fact was, with going their separate ways so much of the time—her work, his work or rodeoing—sex had become infrequent. Something else they didn't talk about. If she did turn up pregnant, and he got to thinking about it, he might have doubts. She didn't have a doubt that she didn't want to be pregnant, at least not now, not with the way things were with them.

A wave of nausea, something she hadn't felt since that night after the tequila, reminded her, if she had ever had a doubt, that a dimple-cheeked, red-haired baby would be impossible to explain. There had never been a reason for her and Ryder to discuss their views on abortion. But he'd been raised Catholic. Besides, it was her body, her decision.

She pulled into their drive and parked in front of the sidewalk. Straggly clumps of native grass and little bits of Bermuda dotted the space she intended to make into a yard. One day, eventually, it would rain and she'd plant some shrubs, too.

Trudging toward the front door, a third step occurred to her—never repeat the mistake that got her in this mess. She promised herself, no matter what the result of the test was, she would never, under any circumstance, drink tequila again.

Still moving slowly, Cheryl locked the front door, took the test kit box into the bathroom, locked that door, and removed her scrub suit top and then the matching blue pants. Her bra fell next on top of the small pile. Pressing her breasts methodically, like a clinical exam, she noted that they weren't tender, not the least bit.

The packaging on the test stick resisted, as if it were protecting a secret. She jerked open the top drawer below the sink, felt around for her extra bandage scissors. She handled them expertly to slice the cardboard box and the plastic wrapper.

A person who said prayers would have begun to utter one about then, but her doing it would be hypocritical, she knew. She jerked the elastic of her panties, moving them down her thighs as she stood above the commode, positioning the test stick as instructed. She felt warm, wet liquid oozing on her inner thigh. Berating herself because she failed at such a simple procedure, unable even to control her own urine, she sat, actually sort of collapsed, onto the commode seat, crying.

She blew her nose so hard her left ear stopped up. Intent, she jerked her underwear off her right ankle, then the left. The panties landed on top of the other dirty laundry, showing her a strip of dark red blood, menstrual blood. She stared at it, shook her head, and reached for a washcloth, then for a tampon. It was several minutes before she managed to find something clean to wear and leave the bathroom

Sitting at the dining room table, she opened her purse and took out the envelope. Ryder would be back soon, if he made it back. Riding bulls—that's what he'd gone to Taos to do, even though he acted like it wasn't—would be the fastest way to make enough money to buy a new horse. He'd looked lower than she'd ever seen him when he had to put his down. Said he'd lose his job without a horse. And just when they were close to getting even again.

She stared briefly at the envelope, then wrote on the front and put it on the table where he'd see it. If she had written a check, he wouldn't have cashed it. Being stubborn seemed to be what held him together a lot of the time. But actual cash would be harder to turn down.

He parked at an angle, like he didn't have the strength to turn the wheels straight. His stiff-kneed limp told her he needed help; she hurried off the porch toward him. After she got him on the straight-backed kitchen chair and examined him and told him he probably had a cracked rib, he didn't move.

Going to the doctor didn't appeal to him, never did. That didn't surprise her. He'd probably been told all his life that the thing to do when you got hurt was to "cowboy up." Said he needed a horse, not a doctor.

She set out a plate of leftover chuck roast and vegetables, put it next to the envelope. She'd written *New Horse* across the front. Most of the roast and all of the potatoes disappeared quickly. The smile he showed her across the table looked kind of weak and didn't last long. "That was just what I needed. Thanks."

He hadn't touched the envelope, just stared at it. He said, "I hate for you to do this. We were saving up for later."

"That's extra. I put it away from the shifts at the ED. A stash for emergencies. My secret."

His eyes focused on hers for a long time and she didn't look away. He said, "Well, I guess I qualify. A pen rider without a horse is an emergency. I'm much obliged."

Getting him to bed involved helping him from the table to the bedroom, pulling off his boots and jeans, positioning him for comfort, and propping him in place with pillows. Just as she reached to pull up the sheet and bedspread, he caught her hand, pulled her close. He said, "I know I'm a lucky man. Thank you."

She kissed him on the lips. Then she pulled the cover all the way up over his head.

CHAPTER 15

July 28, 2008—Ryder Sheldon

A Good Horse

Cussing wouldn't do a bit of good. And neither would crying. But when he woke up in his bed at home and saw the time, five a.m., Ryder gave a second's thought to doing one or the other or both. When, after lying still listening to his heartbeat, feeling pain with every breath, dying didn't seem imminent, he rolled carefully to a sitting position and waited for things, like his lungs and ribs and whatever else that bastard bull had displaced, to settle. Then he stood and faced Monday morning.

Cheryl twitched and the quilt covering her shoulders moved. He waited until she settled before he took careful steps to the bathroom. He avoided the one floorboard near the door that always squeaked. No sense waking her before five forty-five. She didn't have to report to work until six-fifty for lock in at seven. She never harped on it, but he knew she hated that part of her job. What she did like were the pay and benefits and evenings and weekends off, she said. But she could be lying. Just to make him feel good.

He stood in front of the commode for what seemed like a long time before a stream of urine finally started; only it looked suspiciously like blood. No surprise; it had happened before when he rode bucking horses or bulls. It would clear up on its own if he drank enough water. If he mentioned it, she'd get lathered up and insist on that doctor visit. Flushing seemed like the only logical move. He had to find a horse. Today.

"You okay?" He heard her talking to him from the bed. She always woke up slow, didn't usually say much.

"Sore." He rinsed his hands. "I'll live."

"You getting up?"

"If I'm going to buy a horse, I've got to get started." He watched his reflection in the mirror as he talked, worked on not frowning. She'd be on him like a buzzard if she got a clue how much he hurt. He worked up a smile and opened the bathroom door.

There she stood, blocking his way, not two feet in front of him. She had that look on her face, the one he'd seen her use when someone complained about some ache or pain, like she could see through you without the aid of x-ray. Made her a good nurse. And hard to lie to.

She rubbed her face and stepped aside.

He managed to get to where his clothes made a pile on the floor on his side of the bed without limping much. "I think I'll be fine when I walk off the soreness," he said, even though she hadn't asked him a question. He was glad she didn't, but couldn't figure why she wasn't mad. Seemed like the nurse in her had replaced the wife these days.

"With any luck at all, I'll be able to find a horse today and be at work tomorrow like I'm supposed to."

She didn't say anything. He could feel her eyes on his back. He kept talking. "It's my turn to work Tuesday through Saturday this week, so…"

He trailed off while he pulled on his Wranglers and shirt, and struggled with his left boot, holding his breath so he wouldn't groan.

From the bathroom, over the sound of water running, she

said, "You'd be better off not smoking until those ribs are healed."

How did she know every breath made him grit his teeth? He tucked in his shirt, felt in his pants for the envelope she'd given him, and touched a bottle cap in the right pocket, stuck down in the bottom. Modelo might not taste as good this morning as it had Saturday night.

She came out of the bathroom holding an old sheet and some safety pins. "If you wait a minute or two, I'll bandage you so it won't hurt so much." She produced bandage scissors from under the folded sheet and cut the fabric into several wide strips. "You'll have to take your shirt off and hold your arms straight out."

Five minutes later she had swathed three of the homemade bandages around his chest and secured them with the oversized pins, restricting him from armpit to belly button. "See if you can breathe. It might be a little too tight."

He drew in a hesitant little gasp. "Nope, that helps." He tried again, deeper. "Yeah, a lot. Thanks."

She nodded, went to the kitchen. He followed, trying hard not to limp. Working fast, she turned on the coffee maker and set out two cereal bowls. She asked, "Will you be here when I get in?"

"Depends on whether I run onto a herd of wild horses looking for a home." He buckled his belt. She poured a bowl of Grape-Nuts and pointed to the other bowl and asked a question by raising her right eyebrow.

"I'll get something later. Coffee's what I need now."

"And a Tylenol?"

She handed him both before he could answer.

Neither of them said another word. She took her coffee into the bedroom. He knew her routine—shower first, then eat, then dress. Then she'd be ready to talk. With any luck he'd be down the road before then. He finished his coffee and poured a second cup, this one into an insulated mug.

The horse trailer didn't cooperate on his first try at getting it hooked to the pickup hitch. A two-pound sledge hammer usually remedied the stubborn latch and got it seated on the ball. Finally, after squatting down, a move that shot a pain through his left knee, and whacking the connection a good one with the hammer, muttering, "You no-hooking son of a bitch," he got it done. Then he managed to stand up straight.

Carrying his coffee mug, and dressed in her uniform, Cheryl came out on the porch and down the walk to the horse trailer. The fine wisps of dark hair that always slid out of the clip at the nape of her neck caught the early morning light. She stood between him and the sun, surrounded by a golden aura like the church window saints that always glared at him when he ducked out of catechism classes. "Am I right? It was a bull?"

"Yeah. Could have won big. Two high point rides, made it to the last go-round. Then barely out of the chute on the last one." He stuck his hands in his back pockets, stared toward her and beyond.

"If you'll take these every four hours, that pain will be manageable." She handed him three more Tylenol in a sandwich bag.

"You think I'll hurt that bad?"

"Just a guess." She glanced in the direction he'd been looking. "Maybe you were yelling, 'Oh, Jesus,' in the night for some other reason." She didn't smile the way she used to when she joked. "Might have had something else on your mind."

He took the coffee mug, raised the bag as a toast, and showed her the best he grin he could muster. "Thanks. See you this evening."

He pulled out of the yard, checked the side mirror to be sure the trailer was pulling straight, looking normal, as he went through the gate.

He pulled the empty horse trailer north nearly to Channing, with no luck, then headed south and took 214 down to Friona. By the time he pulled in for a burger at the Tasty Cream, the only place he'd seen that had enough space for a horse trailer in the parking lot, he'd stopped and talked to seven people. They all had extra horses, and none of them wanted to sell for what he wanted to pay. He'd be damned if he'd spend every bit of that money if he didn't have to.

The cowboy who belonged to the other horse trailer in the lot nodded when Ryder walked toward him with a cheeseburger on a little red plastic tray. So Ryder sat down across from him at the table in the back of the small joint. The table wobbled when he leaned forward on his elbows to talk about horses for sale. The cowboy told him that with the price of feed, everyone willing to sell thought they were going to make back some of the money their horses had eaten in the past six or eight months. "I'd sell you mine, but it's the only one I've got," he said.

"Doesn't make sense," Ryder said. "If they're costing them so much to feed, why not sell them cheap?"

"You never know what some people are thinking," the cowboy said. "Me, I make what living I can by tending other people's cattle. So between that horse and my pickup and trailer, it's what I have to have to run my business. My overhead, you might say." He stared at Ryder's uneaten french fries. "You gonna eat those?"

Ryder pushed the paper dish toward the cowboy. "Help yourself."

He remembered to take another pill, followed with a big drink of iced tea. The cowboy snorted a little laugh. He pointed with a limber french fry at something behind Ryder. "That a by-God fact. My wife's a teacher. Good wage, great benefits."

Ryder twisted in his chair to look where the fried potato was aimed. A sign above one of the tables next to the wall read, "Behind every cowboy, there's a wife in town with a good job."

He said, "Yep. Mine's a nurse."

The cowboy gathered all the evidence of their meals onto his tray. He said, "Better get back on the road. I spend more time driving my truck than I do on horseback these days." He stood looking at Ryder, like he might have something else to say. Then he touched the brim of his hat and said, "Good luck." He dropped the trash in the bin by the door on his way out.

Ryder eased out of the booth. He didn't bother hiding his limp as he crossed the lot, knowing he looked like an old man one way or the other. By the time he checked his taillight connection and watched several cattle trucks pass on Highway 60, he'd come up with an idea. Uncle Butch might know someone who had a horse. Ryder was pretty sure that even as old as he was, his uncle still went to the café in Muleshoe every morning, just to hear the latest. He'd be home by now.

Or maybe he had a horse. Uncle Butch was always going to country auctions and buying or trading for a calf or a horse, sometimes even a pig, just to have something to talk about. Usually sold 'em the next week. And if you could believe what he said, he usually made a little something in the bargain.

It was forty-two miles out to his uncle's place from Friona. Ryder could have called, but the old guy usually didn't bother to answer. He'd told Ryder more than once, "Anybody wants to talk to me, they can come and visit."

Ryder found the old man who'd bought him his first pair of real cowboy boots standing out by the gate when he drove up. "Headed somewhere?" Ryder asked.

"Nope, just takin' a little walk. Need the exercise."

"If you've had enough, I'll give you a ride to the house."

Ryder got out and limped around to close the gate, then got back in the pickup at about the same speed—slow. Uncle Butch took a while getting in, pulling at his pants to get his right leg situated after he sat. "Looks like we're a pair," he said.

"You lame too?" Ryder asked.

His uncle pointed to a mesquite tree with a bunch of little ones coming up around it. "That damn thing needs killing. Going to take over."

They passed several more clumps of mesquite as Ryder drove the road the half mile to where the little house sat. He parked in front of Uncle Butch's pickup. The stock trailer he always hauled to auctions was still connected. Ryder asked, "What did you buy this week?"

"Couple of little feeder calves. Might raise one of them for meat for winter." His uncle got the door open and turned sideways in the seat. "Come on up on the porch. Visit a while."

They headed for the two metal rockers on the front porch. Ryder watched while his uncle took longer than usual to get into the chair. He looked like he'd lost weight since the last time he'd seen him. "You getting enough to eat, Uncle Butch?"

"All I want. Been a little off my feed the last few weeks. I think it's the heat."

Uncle Butch always said his bunkhouse style place was exactly what he needed. It sat on a concrete slab and sported a metal roof. Low maintenance. Two big rooms and a smaller one plus a garage with a washer and dryer and an old upright freezer.

A four-strand barbed wire fence marked off a small yard. He sometimes grazed a few mother cows and calves in years when the pasture grass grew. That explained the fence. "Keeping them off the front porch," is what he'd said.

From where they sat, the two of them could see the low hills on the south half of Butch's 640 acres. Butch pointed in that direction. "Sometime when we're both in a little better shape, I'll take you down there. There's things you need to see."

Ryder nodded and kept his mouth shut after that. He knew it wouldn't get him anywhere to come right out and ask if Uncle Butch knew anyone with a horse for sale. He might as well relax. He was going to hear all his uncle had on his mind, whether he wanted to or not. It had been at least three months since he'd been out here, maybe more. He leaned back and rocked a little. The chair squeaked, sounding the way he felt. He rocked again and it quieted down. A breeze kicked up the smell of manure from the pen down near the barn.

Instead of starting in on a story about the latest funeral he'd attended or last week's auction, Uncle Butch leaned back in his chair and rocked a couple of times, not taking his eyes off his nephew. "Riding bucking horses again?"

"Bulls, this time. Except the last one. He pretty much rode me."

"Where?"

"Taos."

"Anything broke?"

"Maybe a rib."

His uncle nodded. Then, as if he'd been waiting for just the right cue, he told a story about a cowboy he knew who lost an eye up near Gallup when he'd been stomped by a bull. "They get some mean animals over at those New Mexico rodeos." He pointed down toward the barn at a chaparral bird strutting up the road. "That's Gus. Stops by every day about this time and again in the evening."

"Where's your dog?" Ryder asked.

"Had to put her down." He shook his head. "Hated to but she was old, sick." He hauled a can of Copenhagen from his shirt pocket and inserted a hefty pinch behind his bottom lip. "Sure hated to. Missy was a good dog." He spit and resituated the dip. He pointed at Ryder's empty horse trailer. "You lose your horse?"

"Had to put him down. Just the other day."

"You still pen riding? Or did you get your fill of bein' fenced in?"

"Yeah. Still at it." Ryder found a toothpick in his shirt pocket, stuck it in his mouth instead of the cigarette he wanted. "You know anyone who has a horse for sale?"

"Let me think about that a little bit." He spit again. It landed on a grasshopper near the edge of the porch. The old man smiled. "Beat him to the draw."

Ryder rocked again and closed his eyes. Uncle Butch had also given him his first cigarette and taught him how to rope. He'd asked Ryder, when he was about ten, if he intended to be a farmer like his dad. He remembered telling Butch something like, "Not if I can help it."

After that, it seemed his father's older brother took every opportunity to teach him all he could about cattle and horses. By then, Butch had stopped rodeoing when he was in his fifties, but was still team roping with his friend Clay most weekends. Ryder went with them every time his dad let him. Although it had seemed to him that he managed to save up an awful lot of plowing for Ryder to do every Saturday.

Uncle Butch rocked, little short movements that could put a person to sleep. He stopped. "You still married to that nurse?"

Butch was giggin' him, he could tell. He said, "So far," and shifted in the rocker to stretch out his stiff knee. "Did you ever think about marrying, Uncle Butch?" He'd asked him that before and always enjoyed whatever bullshit answer his uncle came up with. Usually a different one every time.

For a while, when he was younger, Ryder had wondered if his uncle didn't like women. But later on, when he listened to Butch and Clay reminisce about their rodeo days, he heard plenty of stories about girls they'd gone out with, whorehouses they'd visited in Wyoming, and a couple of near misses with the threat of shotgun weddings to convince him that Butch liked women just fine. He just didn't want to marry one.

His uncle's shoulders twitched to match a silent laugh. "Yeah, I thought about it a lot of times. Even got close once." He leaned back and stretched both arms above his head, then relaxed them and shrugged both shoulders—apparently the rest of his exercise routine. He resumed rocking. "I decided I'd rather want what I didn't have than have what I didn't want."

Ryder smiled. The bandage made it easier. "I think I understand. Some days more than others."

Butch stopped rocking. "I know a fella who's got a horse."

"Think he'll part with it for a decent price? Seems like everyone I talk to thinks theirs is premium stock."

"You can get it for nothing."

Ryder frowned. "I need a horse good enough for work. I'll lose my job if I don't turn up with this trailer full of horse tomorrow morning."

"You can have mine."

"Not George Perry. He's your favorite horse."

"My only horse. I've just been keeping him so nobody can mistreat him."

Ryder knew George Perry was good for roping, well trained and still in good shape. Was the last time he saw him. "What would you ride if he's your only one?"

"Back in April, on my birthday, was the last time I rode him. Eighty-two that day. Took him out and prowled around the whole place. I decided that day a man who has to hang on to the corral to mount his horse has no business riding." Ryder could see he was serious. Some people could never be certain with Butch as he usually wore a half-smile no matter what. They'd spent enough time together that Ryder never had a doubt.

Butch rocked forward and used the momentum to help him out of the chair. He stood, leaning against one of the cedar porch posts. He pointed down toward the barn. "I've been exercising him on a lead rope since then. You go bring him up to the corral and you'll both have a job come tomorrow morning."

"Uncle Butch, that's not why I came out here."

"I know you didn't. But I want you to take him. And you have to promise me when it's time to put him down, you'll bring him back here."

Ryder nodded. "Sure, Uncle Butch."

"There's a place I've picked out on the west edge where I'll bury him. He won't go to the rendering plant."

"Yessir. I'll tend to it." Ryder couldn't seem to raise his head.

He had trouble seeing right then. Tears clouded his eyes

all the time he was loading George Perry in the trailer. Uncle Butch was right. He was still a good horse.

Ryder had the urge to hug his uncle, but like always, just shook his hand when he left him sitting on the porch. As he pulled away from the house, he looked in his side mirror and saw Butch wave. Ryder stopped and leaned out the window. He wanted to say something, but just waved and headed toward home.

CHAPTER 16

July 28, 2008—Cheryl Sheldon

It'll Heal

Men putting on an act, pretending they weren't hurt when they were, made Cheryl want to yell, "Who do you think you're kidding?"

But she never did. Her football-playing guy friends in high school had made a good show of toughness—lying, denying double vision and headache, repeating the coaches' mantra, "Play through the pain," and she'd cheered at them to get back in the game. Now she tended to prisoners' wounds every day and showed a concerned, but never skeptical, face as each one boasted and complained that treatment was unnecessary.

She bit the inside of her lower lip as she wound the first of three strips of bed sheet around Ryder's chest. She stood back from him at the same cautious distance she learned at the prison, the arm's length that argued with her instinct to touch, to comfort anyone in pain. She met his eyes with a bland expression in which he'd never be able to see pity or blame.

"You'd do yourself a favor not to smoke until your ribs heal." She gave the advice she'd give a stranger, resisting an urge to slap some sense into him. Then she tightened the final two bandage strips in place.

He couldn't wait to leave. She knew because he had rushed out to get the horse trailer ready, off to look for a new horse. She sped through her routine too, stopping only briefly when she heard him cussing the obstinate, inanimate metal hitch. Without looking she imagined him crossing himself as he slammed the pickup door. Probably invoking one of the saints he hauled out when he thought she wasn't watching, in some ancient ritual imprinted in his childhood.

The first time she'd seen him cross himself before a bronc ride, she'd puzzled about it, given that they both avoided churches. "Just for luck. A habit." That's how he described it, when she asked.

She catalogued it then as one of the few signals of stress he ever showed. She'd come to think of it as his only visible evidence of any emotion these days, aside from the smile he wore most of the time. Most people read his open, faintly amused expression as pleasure. On the contrary, she knew by now the smile was not voluntary; it only registered neutral, a condition from which he seldom allowed himself to vary much.

Why this controlled predictability irritated her, she wasn't certain. Lots of women would trade places. A husband who didn't raise his voice and could not be provoked to argue? The man of their dreams. Maybe so, but Cheryl hadn't heard him laugh out loud in so long she wondered if he'd forgotten how.

And that fact, if she let herself think about it, seemed like a splinter—maybe insignificant, but uncomfortable, even painful, that would heal faster if you did something about it—dig it out, clean it up—but also might remedy itself it were left alone. Or it could fester, a source of systemic infection.

As Ryder crossed the cattle guard, drove on out the gate, she walked slowly into the house. Might as well get on the road, too.

Cheryl opened the refrigerator to retrieve one of the diet meal drinks she substituted for lunch. Her purse and a paperback mystery completed her necessities for the day. The aroma she thought of as rich brown velvet reminded her to turn off the coffee pot. She filled a thermal cup, stirred in a spoonful of sugar.

Looking out the small window over the sink, toward the barbed wire fence that marked the western boundary of the yard, she imagined Ryder dragging his empty horse trailer from one ranch to another, looking for a horse to buy, and hating the fact she'd handed him the envelope that would solve the problem. She'd bet every dollar in that envelope that he'd spend most of the day avoiding asking his Uncle Butch to sell him a horse, or give him one.

She imagined Ryder telling himself it wouldn't be right, that at his age he should be able to rely on himself, and maybe his wife if he had to. Couldn't go through life expecting people to take care of him. Or maybe he wouldn't even be aware he was thinking about any of that; maybe the Uncle Butch idea would sneak up on him, out of the blue. Regardless, she knew he'd spend the day proving he tried everything.

She slammed the car door and told herself to quit thinking about her stiff-necked husband. He wasn't about to change. The fishtail her car did when she accelerated surprised her. She watched in the rearview mirror as the house disappeared in the cloud of dust she raised.

Radio stations seldom played old rock at six-fifteen a.m. She twisted the tuning dial, hoping to find ZZ Top or something else loud. Just as she glanced up from the radio at the always empty road ahead, a movement on the side of the ditch ahead and on her right took her mind off of searching for distraction. She squinted against the early sun's glare, scanning as she slowed from seventy to near forty. The animal raised its head, struggling get out of the ditch. Just as she passed, the dog, yes, it was definitely a dog, fell to one side and slid back down. It could have as easily been a child.

Her brakes squealed. She halted the car, shifted into reverse, and backed up, slowly.

A curly-coated brown and white dog howled as she stopped just in front of where it lay with its head on a clump of bindweed. In seconds, Cheryl knelt in front of the animal, speaking softly, her mind running through a mental comparison between canine and human injuries—breathing: appears to be okay—bleeding: no external hemorrhage—spinal cord injury: purposeful movement of all extremities apparent—fractures: no way to tell—internal hemorrhage: ditto. Her assessment interrupted by a pitiful howl, Cheryl obeyed her impulse. She stood, hurried to release the trunk lock, and pulled out a blanket she kept there for emergencies.

Howling gave way to moaning. When she returned and spoke again to the dog, its eyes followed her movements, but the animal didn't resist as Cheryl pushed the edge of the blanket under its left side. As she moved into the ditch to get to its right side, she slid, covering her scrub pants with dirt. It wasn't a large dog, maybe thirty pounds, and looked young. If she could get the blanket all the way underneath it, she should be able to pick it up and put it in the back seat.

Ordinarily she hated the manure trucks that sped the roads, odor and fertilizer dust in their wakes, but today she would have welcomed one, would have stood in the road and waved it to a stop. She wouldn't mind having some help right now.

No sense waiting. Never a manure truck around when you need one. She laughed grimly at her own little joke. The dog stopped moaning and licked at her hand when she petted its head. Cheryl took a deep breath. Now that she had the blanket under the dog, which she saw was a male with no collar or tags, she returned to the car and opened the passenger side back door.

A combination of strength, awkwardness, and determination on her part and some passive cooperation by the dog, that she now called Buddy, got him deposited on the back seat. It took about five minutes, and she felt certain she'd not worsened his injuries, whatever they were.

"Whew!" Now she had to make some decisions.

Her cell phone showed two bars and not much battery. Not a surprise since she hardly ever used it or bothered to check. Since she seldom missed work, an absence shouldn't be a problem. After a long wait between the prison switchboard's answer and her supervisor's voice, she quickly explained that she had responded to a roadside emergency and was going to accompany the patient home. Never once did she lie, at least not directly, and the supervisor didn't press for details. Ever since the woman had announced her upcoming retirement, she didn't seem too concerned about anything. "I'll be in tomorrow and will make up the day later if you need me to," Cheryl promised.

The dog's panting accelerated, eyes closed. He surely must be in pain. She spoke some nonsense to him, in her best reassuring-nurse voice, and turned the car toward Hereford. Any vet would do, at this point.

Thirty miles and twenty minutes from that ditch, she turned left across 25 Mile Avenue and stopped at a hardware store on the north edge of Hereford. The dog's breaths came slowly and irregularly, with an occasional low moan escaping when he exhaled. Cheryl refused to think about internal bleeding, but if he had been human and she was his nurse, and if this car were a cubicle in Emergency, he'd have a liter of D5 NS running wide open right now.

If she hadn't stopped, she would be safely locked in by now. Routine would have taken hold again.

She left her door open when she ran into the store. "I need to know where the nearest vet's office is, now."

The woman behind the counter stopped chewing her doughnut long enough to direct Cheryl to a clinic three blocks south. Cheryl mumbled her thanks and sprinted to the car.

Before she buckled herself in, Cheryl saw the dog's front paws twitch, as if he were running. But the dog didn't raise his head or make a sound. Cheryl said, "It's going to be okay. We're nearly there."

The sign stenciled on the door told her she and Buddy had arrived too early for help. **Veterinary Clinic hours—8 a.m.—6 p.m. M-F.** She banged a fist against the door. Thirty minutes until this place opened; Buddy might not last that long without help. She had to pray someone was already in the back. This time she banged on the door with an open palm, four times. No one responded. She shaded her eyes with a hand on either side of her face, leaned close to the barred window beside the door trying to see in. Dark.

Cheryl walked to the car and sat in the back seat, next to Buddy and patted his head, rubbed his short ears, gently. She'd done all she could do and didn't understand why she'd done any of it. And crying about a dog she found in a ditch close to dying made even less sense, but that's what she was doing. Cheryl pulled more of the blanket over him, hoping it made him feel safe.

She talked to the dog, said she was sorry someone hurt him and left him alone. His heartbeat, when she put her hand on his chest, felt rapid and birdlike, a flutter, his breathing shallow and rapid. The calm she often felt when there was nothing left to do took over.

It seemed like a long time, but according to her watch, it had only been ten minutes when a man parked a pickup next to her car. Gravel crunched under his boots as he hurried to her open door. "Emergency?"

She told him what she knew about the dog's situation, which was nothing much. He scooped up the limp animal with the blanket and walked toward the building.

"I think he's in shock," she said, then wished she hadn't uttered it. It seemed like inviting the worst, like he might hear and give up. Humans did that; maybe dogs did too. She trailed behind the vet to the clinic door.

"You'll have to get my keys—in the pickup," he said. She ran for the keys and rushed back to unlock the front door. The vet held the dog close to his chest. "You can come with me."

Buddy lay like a bundle of dirty rags in the center of the exam table, not moving as the vet listened to his heart and lungs. The dog whimpered when the vet moved his back right leg. The man had large hands, but his touch looked tender. "I'll need to x-ray, but first I'm going to start some fluid. That leg's fractured, for sure, and some of his ribs. You're right about shock." All the time he was talking, he gathered equipment. Without looking up at her, talking quietly to the dog, he started an I.V. and hung the bag on a hook above the side of the table.

"My assistant's going to be late this morning. I hate to ask you, but can you help me get the x-rays? All you'll need to do is hold him still while I set up." Cheryl nodded. He pointed to a long lead apron hanging on a peg on the wall. "Put that on and then hold him while I get the machine."

Buddy didn't offer to move. She watched as his respirations deepened and slowed a bit. She told him to hold on, everything would be better soon. Maybe the fluid was helping. The vet rolled the portable x-ray machine in and positioned it. "I don't think he'll move now. You just step back and be ready to catch him in case he changes his mind." He turned some dials and rechecked the position of the x-ray plates. "You're a nurse?"

She nodded. It took no time at all. He said, "I'll check these and be back in a few minutes. Can you stay with him?"

"I named him Buddy."

The vet looked toward her with a sad smile. He repeated, "Buddy."

He came back and said, speaking toward the dog, not looking at Cheryl, "There's free air in the abdomen. The intestine's perforated somewhere. The leg is fractured, but might heal. And I think his liver is probably lacerated." He shook his head. "If he survives the shock, I would be surprised if he survived the internal damage. I mean without surgery."

"What would you do?"

"I could do an exploratory lap, but to tell you the truth, I doubt he'll survive it. No telling how long since the injury and his abdomen's already getting rigid—peritonitis." He stopped talking and looked at his hands as if they held some answer.

She waited for what she knew he would say. The silence hung over the limp dog.

"I'd recommend putting him to sleep. He'll be in severe pain soon. If I do it now, he'll go peacefully. Or I can watch him to see how he does for a few hours on fluids."

Cheryl didn't know what to do about the tears that kept her from seeing the man clearly. Buddy wasn't even her dog. She wiped at her eyes and said, "Sorry. It makes me so mad. Hitting him and leaving him there. Could have been a child."

The vet nodded. Cheryl said, "That's the humane thing, I guess. But I could wait here in town a while and come back."

The vet didn't answer. She continued patting the dog's head until the doctor came to her side of the table. "I'll take that apron off you now. It's heavy."

Cheryl wandered the aisles at Walmart. She couldn't think of anything she needed, they needed. Due to the drought, and not wanting to tax the house well, she hadn't even made an effort to start a garden. And she hadn't baked in several months because neither of them had an appetite for sweets. Like everything else, their meals had taken on a bland sameness—roommates eating in a dormitory cafeteria.

The receptionist asked Cheryl's name and address, for the bill, she said. Then she took her to a room where Buddy lay on a large cushion in a crate on top of a large table. Cheryl could see he'd stopped breathing, even though the IV line still tethered him to the vet's attempt to save him. She touched his curly head.

The vet said from the doorway behind her, "I'm sorry. He couldn't hold on. Too far gone."

Heaviness against her chest made it difficult, but she managed to stand up straight. Somehow it made her feel better that the vet looked stricken, his shoulders slumped.

He asked, "You want me to dispose of the body?"

"Buddy," she said. She took a deep breath. "No, I'll take him out to the ranch and bury him."

He wrapped the dog in the blanket. "I'll take him to the car for you."

Driving the vacant miles back to the ranch, Cheryl wondered what Ryder would say if she told him what she'd done, wondered if the expression on his face would even change, wondered why they'd never had a dog. It seemed like something married people without kids would do, but they never had.

The garden plot offered the only place where the dirt was

soft enough to dig in, dry as it was. She tied the bundle—Buddy and the blanket—into a black plastic trash bag and squatted to place it on the ground next to where she'd dig the hole.

The barn smelled of mouse turds and horse feed. She pushed the door open wide for light. Ryder usually hung the tools on the walls, but she couldn't see a shovel anywhere. She walked farther into the barn, trying not to inhale, thinking of hanta virus, and pushed aside a pile of feed sacks where she saw a glint of metal. Somewhere they had a new shovel, but this old one would do.

Digging the hole in the midday heat, she stopped several times to rest. A dog's grave didn't have to be six feet deep, but after she got past the few inches sandy topsoil, the thought of coyotes unearthing the body kept her digging.

Something clanked against the shovel tip and jarred the handle as she pushed on the blade with her foot. Stinging shot through her right palm. "Dammit!" She cussed herself, not the fist-sized rock the shovel had hit. If she had any sense at all, she'd have worn gloves.

She raised her hand close to her face, searching for the source of the pain. Nothing showed except for a tiny puncture below her third finger. She picked up the rock and flung it as far as she could. Telling herself to slow down, Cheryl rested with her foot against the shovel blade. A few more shovels full and the hole became a rectangle long and wide enough to hold Buddy. But the depth didn't satisfy her. Next, she dragged the garden hose from the back porch, connected it to the all-weather faucet, and pulled the end to the shallow hole. She imagined a slurping sound as the dry ground soaked up the water.

After two more rounds of wetting and digging, sweat ran down her forehead and into her eyes. She nodded as if answering. That should do. She cradled Buddy in his plastic shroud in both her arms. She nodded again after she placed him in the hole, satisfied it was at least two feet deep. Covered and smoothed flat, the burial site blended into the drought-brown landscape. Another layer of the dry dirt that would have been the garden made it finally seem a proper resting place.

She'd told herself the heat and sadness accounted for the wave of weariness she'd surrendered to after that. No sense lying to herself, though. The dog was only part of it. After she buried Buddy and cried some more, sitting in the heat next to the grave she'd dug, thoughts about that night in Amarillo clutched at her. What if Ryder knew?

Getting cleaned up would settle her and a nap would revive her. She rolled up the hose, put away the shovel, closed the barn door, shook the dirt and ditch grass out of the car's back floor mat, and went in the house. At the kitchen sink, scrubbing with liquid detergent and a brush meant for vegetables, she moved from left hand to right, then up her forearms, punishing every inch of skin until it reddened. After rinsing, she inspected the puncture on her right hand. The puncture site had swollen and reddened slightly. No amount of pinching and pressing brought the sliver to the surface.

Running the water as hot as she could tolerate, she stood staring out the window above the sink, seeing only the horizon and nothing of the detail nearby. Her focus turned inward to the question that had been in her mind since that night in Amarillo— would she confess to Ryder? No, and she would have to tolerate the guilt. Yes, and she would have to suffer whatever the result would be. She'd deserve it. He could leave her; he would hate her.

The water stopped, although she didn't remember turning it off. She wouldn't tell Ryder. Wounding him by telling would be worse that what she'd already done. The only thing left to do now was take the nap she'd prescribed.

Not long after she woke, Cheryl heard Ryder's pickup and trailer cross the cattle guard. After he stopped, she watched him limp to the trailer, open it, and lead out a tall brown horse with a white blaze on his forehead. He was talking to the horse as he led him to the corral.

And when he came in the house, he kept on talking, lots more than usual, mostly about all the people he'd seen on his journey around the Panhandle since sunup that morning. She didn't interrupt; registered maybe every third word. He pulled off his boots as he delivered the punch line of his long story about searching all day for a horse. "Uncle Butch. I can always count on him."

Enchiladas she'd made and frozen saved her from cooking from scratch. Spanish rice and Ranch Style beans turned it into a meal. Halfway through his second helping of everything, Ryder said, "This hits the spot." A full-fledged grin lit his face and he told one more story, something about a cowboy whose horse went with him to the Tasty Cream. Talking the way he used to a long time ago, like a person who knows how to be happy.

She smiled toward him and carried some of the remains of the meal to the kitchen. He picked up his empty plate and the bowl of beans and followed. He said, "Nobody makes enchiladas like you do."

Loading the dishwasher occupied her for a few minutes. He stood staring out the back window, a toothpick in his hand. Then as if he'd come to some decision, he said, "Yep. Nobody like you." He reached into his hip pocket and pulled out the envelope she'd given him. "You'll be able to put this away for later. For us."

Cheryl took the envelope and put it on the kitchen counter. "Think you're in shape to work?"

"Oh yeah, I'm fine, just sore. I'll heal in no time."

He might be fine, but on his way to the living room he limped with every step.

He sat crooked in his recliner, favoring his cracked ribs, turning the pages of *The Livestock Weekly*. She could tell it wouldn't be long before he'd be in bed. If she didn't say something now, he'd be asleep in a few minutes.

She went into the bathroom and returned carrying a bottle of alcohol, a large-eyed sewing needle, and a cotton ball. Holding her right hand toward him, palm facing up, she said, "I think there's a splinter in there. Can't get it out by myself. Will you help me?"

Part V
2008-2009

CHAPTER 17

December 1-10, 2008—Cheryl and Ryder Sheldon

Heartbeats

Monday morning, Cheryl finished handing out the last of the meds to the herd of inmates rounded up by the first-shift Correctional Officers for their scheduled doses. Most were drugs that treated anxiety or depression. Others stamped out infection or kept assorted pains to a tolerable minimum. As the final officer and his charge left, she locked the medication room door. The infirmary echoed the squeaks of her rubber soles on the finished-concrete floor.

Next on her list of routine duties was ordering medications from supply. She sat in front of the computer terminal, opened the program, and logged in with her password. The program welcomed her, "Hello Nurse Sheldon," from a message in the upper right corner of the screen which she knew meant, "You are being watched, no Internet surfing allowed." That blinking cursor set out immediately to annoy her as it urged her to fill in the blanks on the supply form, another of the thousand tedious necessary tasks she thought a monkey could do.

Today, she couldn't clear her mind of the weekend; one more alone while Ryder worked. Since his ribs healed, and he promised, back in July after the Taos rodeo, not to ride bulls again, he'd worked as if doing penance. If he wasn't at the feedlot, he picked up day work tending cattle on places that raised stocker calves. Any time left over, it seemed he filled with cussing the drought and worrying. That left her too much time, even if she did work some weekend E D shifts. Too much, because hours alone invited sadness. It threatened to ambush her.

She left the cursor blinking and rummaged in the desk drawer for the Amarillo telephone book. The list of counselors in the Yellow Pages ran three columns, including some display ads. The hallway door opened and a guard stuck his head into the room. "I'll be back in ten minutes with the inmate."

Cheryl stuck the phone book back in the drawer. "I'll be waiting here." She'd forgotten about the nine-thirty "teledoc" neuro consult. At least it was not routine. She'd get back to the form later. And the counselor, maybe never. Everyone feels sad sometime. It would pass.

Her job in the "teledoc" room where she'd take the inmate for his neurological consult was to follow directions from the doctor at the other end of a video hook-up in Lubbock. She was the robot that made it possible for him to perform a neuro exam by remote control. He would tell her which reflexes to try to elicit, where to move the camera, and anything else he would do, himself, to examine the patient, if he weren't safely 110 miles away.

She'd done it many times. The correctional officer brought the inmate to her in the large infirmary room. She explained the procedures, asked if the patient had questions—they seldom did—and he shuffled down the hall in his orange jumpsuit and flip-flops, guard at his side. She always followed a few feet behind. Today her steps seemed as shambling as the prisoner's, one foot slogging behind the other, mostly going nowhere, particularly since she'd quit running a while back.

This morning, when their little three-person parade got to the video-equipped exam room, she had the patient sit on the exam table, facing the monitor. The procedure required that the inmate would have to be uncuffed for some parts of the exam, so the guard unlocked him and stood nearby, a hand on his Taser. Cheryl switched on the system. A nurse, all smiles, in Lubbock, appeared on the screen. She explained the doctor was running a bit late and they would be back on camera when he arrived.

At the moment inmate 43560 grabbed her from behind, Cheryl's thoughts fled in several directions. She smelled his sweat and felt an overdeveloped bicep grip her neck and a steely hand twist her right arm behind her back. He whispered in her left ear, "Bitch, you don't do everything I say, I swear you're dead."

In her six years at the prison, Cheryl had learned to ignore suggestive remarks and to limit her natural compassion to a cautious sort of bland kindness. She never liked that about the job—having to be a sort of robot, not a real nurse, one who cares. At that minute, having the machine's lack of emotion would have been her choice, rather than the chest-thudding sense that her heart might stop before her breathing steadied. She said, "I will."

He hadn't asked her to do anything. She did her best to relax so his choke hold wouldn't crush her larynx. She didn't resist when he pushed her forward, out of range of the video camera.

Then it all started. The inmate, 43560, put the guard down with one blow of his right fist. The sound of the officer's head hitting the tile-over concrete floor, the sensation she might choke or vomit or scream, and immediately after, calm flooded over her and muffled everything.

"Turn that thing off." He pointed toward the monitor. She tried, but couldn't reach the switch pad without his grip closing her airway.

She said, "I'll choke. Take me closer." His hold on her neck released slightly and he leaned forward a few inches. A groan rose from the crumpled guard.

The inmate reacted by shoving Cheryl's right arm upward. A sharp pain in that shoulder made her gasp. Then he pulled her toward the floor, near the guard. "Take that walkie-talkie off his shoulder, rip the mic off." She did. "Don't move." She didn't.

He released his grip on her neck and continued holding her right arm with his left hand. He aimed his right fist like a piston, and with a short stroke, punched the guard just over the ear. The officer went limp, looked deflated. Cheryl hoped he would continue breathing. She watched. He did, slowly.

Her head jerked upward when the nurse in Lubbock spoke. "Hello—I have a picture here of an empty room. Are you there?"

He whispered, barely audible, "Don't move. Answer her. Don't let her see you."

Cheryl raised her left hand in a what-do-I-do gesture. He mouthed, "Say something. Now." Another push against her right arm made his the last word into an exclamation.

She said in a voice that seemed to belong to a fearless woman, a voice that sounded nothing like her own. "A problem with our video. I'll turn it off and then back on. See if that helps."

He stood and pulled her to the side of the monitor, farther out of camera range. With his eyes and a nod, he gestured toward the switches. She covered most of the switch pad with her palm as she turned off the video and muted the incoming speaker. If the nurse in Lubbock stayed in the room, she'd hear what was happening.

He shoved against her, moving her away from the guard and toward the door.

Cheryl said, "What is it you want me to do? How do you think you're going to get out?"

"Don't want out."

That didn't make sense. His name, what was it? Charles Turner. He wasn't on psych meds. "Charles, I don't understand. Why all this?"

"Shut up. I need to think." He clamped his arm around her throat again.

Cheryl felt herself sag. She struggled against him, useless effort. Again, he twisted her arm. A muffled squeal escaped from her throat. "Do that again, I'll break it." His hold on her neck loosened briefly and she breathed a full, deep breath. Then a blow from his fist exploded against the side of her head. Pain pierced her ear, sped across her skull, and gripped her entire head. She didn't immediately lose consciousness, and didn't understand why. Then the world went silent; her legs failed.

"Cheryl. Cheryl, can you hear me? If you hear me open your eyes." The voice sounded familiar, female.

She opened her eyes and followed the commands—move your arms, now your legs. And then she answered the questions that showed she was oriented times three. Fully conscious. She rolled to her left side and raised herself to a leaning position. "Where is he? The inmate. Charles?"

"Solitary. Soon as he opened the door, they cuffed him. He didn't really resist." The nurse put a hand on Cheryl's back. "Lubbock heard. They called."

She sat up. Her head hurt and she touched a painful lump on the left side behind her ear. A brief dizziness nauseated her, then subsided. She pulled against the nurse's arms to stand; her right shoulder protested. She stopped still until the pain ebbed.

"Think you can walk?"

Cheryl nodded. Her brain seemed to rattle in her skull. Holding her head very still, with both hands, made it stop.

"Lean against that table. I have a wheelchair outside the door."

The nurse pushed the chair, Cheryl riding with her head in both hands, down the hall to the nurses' station of the infirmary. After she locked the chair's wheels in place, the nurse said, "They'll want to examine and debrief you. Then you can call someone to take you home. You ready?"

"In a few minutes."

The nurse brought a paper cup of water, but Cheryl's hands shook so she couldn't hold it. She slumped back against the wheelchair. The nurse pulled up a chair, and stayed there sitting next to her with a hand on her shoulder.

Ryder had left his cell phone in the pickup. He could barely hear on it in the wind and he'd surely not be able to hear today with the wind from the north at about thirty miles per hour. Damp, but no moisture falling, not yet, at least. He'd been on horseback since six a.m. loading cattle. They had finally finished. He opened the break room door and before he could close it against the wind, the manager said, "I just got a call for you. The prison. Something about your wife. Call back right away." He handed Ryder the receiver of the office landline and turned the phone around. "You know the number?"

Ryder nodded. She never called him from work. He told himself it was the cold that made his hands shake. As soon as he said his name, the prison operator put him through to the warden's office. He listened as the man tried to explain and to assure him his wife was in no danger. As soon as the warden stopped talking for a second, Ryder said, "I'll be there in thirty minutes." He got to the door, had his hand on the knob, before he thought to tell the manager why he had to leave.

His first thought was that if anything happened to her, he'd die. The next one was that he'd kill anyone who'd hurt her. After that, he wouldn't listen to any of the others that crowded for his attention. He focused on the road, pushing the speed limit all the way to the prison.

After the P.A. conducted a complete exam and pronounced her fit to go home under family observation for signs of concussion, Warden Johnson came and talked to Cheryl. He spoke slowly and very distinctly, like she might not understand. He explained, the way he had it figured, Charles Turner feared he was marked for death by one of the prison gangs. He faked a sudden severe headache and tremor to get to the infirmary and continued it to get someone alone as a hostage. It had turned out to be Cheryl. Turner's goal was to get put in solitary, where he thought he'd be safe. He'd told the warden he didn't intend to hurt her, didn't even have a weapon. He would be charged with assault and a raft of other things including attempted escape. For a second, Cheryl felt sorry for the prisoner. But mostly she just wanted Ryder to come take her home, and then she didn't want to come back here ever again.

The other nurse insisted on pushing Cheryl in the wheelchair out to the pickup. Ryder might have been embarrassed if he'd thought about it, because as soon as Cheryl stood and he opened the pickup door for her, he started crying. Embarrassed or not, there was no stopping the tears. And right there in the prison parking lot, before he knew it, they were standing out in that cold wind, holding onto each other crying like they were lost and telling each other that nothing and no one else mattered as much. The nurse said nothing, just hustled the chair back toward the administrative building.

It took a few minutes for Ryder to satisfy himself that the

knot on her head and the red mark on her neck didn't need further medical attention. It would take her a while to get over it. He could tell by the way that she held onto him. It had been a long time, if ever, since she seemed to need him as much as she did then.

They'd just pulled outside the second of the double layer of gates at the prison. He turned right onto the Farm-to-Market Road that would be the quickest way home. Cheryl grabbed his right arm. She said, "Stop, I'm going to faint or vomit." He braked and stopped at the edge of the ditch, turned off the ignition. He could see she was breathing too fast. He unbuckled her seatbelt.

"Hold your breath, now. Hold it till I say let it out." He watched as she did what he said while he counted silently to eight. "Now let it out slowly. Hold my hands." She followed his instructions and the next thing he knew, she'd started crying again. He said, "I'm coming over to your side."

He opened the passenger door. "Scoot over a little. Now, baby, you sit here on my lap." She slid into his lap, still shaking with sobs. He rubbed her back in circles. It seemed like a long time, but finally the crying settled into sniffling and ragged shudders.

She said something, but he couldn't understand the words muffled against his chest. Then he did hear her speak, torn fragments of thoughts separated by tiny silences. "Hate this place.—All my fault. I'm so sorry. Everything. Secrets…too many."

The tears on his face now were his. He said, "Won't let it happen again. All wrong. You deserve better than me." Sounding like kids who hadn't learned to make sentences, both of them. He didn't know if she heard. It didn't matter; he'd said what needed saying.

She shook her head, heaved another breath. He still couldn't see her face. He heard, "Wasn't paying attention.—Locked in all day.—Feeling…sorry for myself."

He rocked her gently. The sniffling stopped and a bit later, she sat up straighter and leaned her head on his shoulder. Then he said the thing that had been on his mind for a long time. Just above a whisper, "How did we get this way—apart?" She didn't move or make a sound. "Don't try to answer. Neither one of us can."

She put both her arms around him. She said, "Let's go home…start over."

When they got to the house, she wandered around, not seeming to be certain of what to do. He settled one of the questions that might have had her roaming by telling her they both could use a little bit to eat and then a nap. "I'll heat up some soup. You get out of that uniform and into something you can sleep in."

Without a word, she went toward the bedroom. When she came back she wore a one of his sweat suits, long and oversized on her, and a pair of blue and white striped socks. He said, "Let's eat. When we're through, I'll make an ice bag for your head."

The tomato soup and crackers warmed him and made the story about nap the truth. After she finished what she would of her meal, he took her hand and led her to the bed, then placed the makeshift ice bag, wrapped in a towel, gently on her head. He shut the blinds and shucked off his clothes down to his underwear. "Let me get in here beside you."

She said in a voice with not much force behind it, "Hold me close so I can sleep." So he did.

Wednesday afternoon, after taking another long nap, Cheryl stood in the kitchen with her cell phone in her hand. She had unlimited minutes she never used, so why not? Digging around in the junk drawer, she found a pencil and a small spiral notebook, the size that fit a man's shirt pocket. She flipped through to see if Ryder had written something in it he might want to save. It was empty. After staring at the blank page for a long time, she pressed 1411 for directory information. She told the operator, "Luling, Texas. Karla Rene Holder." She doubted there would be a listing. After fourteen years, Karla probably had a new name and lived in Houston or someplace far from her hometown.

The operator said, "I have a K.R. Holder in Luling. Hold for the number." Cheryl wrote the ten digits and listened dumbly as the voice offered to dial for her, for fifty cents. She pressed the button to hang up. She laid the phone on the counter and looked in the cabinet for something sweet, then gave up and peeled the pink-cheeked apple waiting in the fruit bowl next to the phone.

Two bites later, still standing at the counter, she pressed the numbers and listened to the distant ringing sound. On the ninth ring, a voice she recognized answered. Cheryl said, "Karla, it's…"

"Cheryl! I'd never forget your voice. Where have you been? I've looked for you so many times." Karla still rushed her words together and every sentence had the air of an exclamation.

"I didn't ever call because I thought you wanted to start fresh."

"Not without you. What made you call today?'

"You always understood me; back then I could tell you anything."

"You still can."

Cheryl didn't speak for a few seconds; they both had so

much to tell—fourteen years' worth—there was no right place to begin. "You first. What have you been doing, how's your life? Everything. I'll give you five minutes."

Karla laughed. Cheryl sat in a kitchen chair. She said, "I'm waiting."

It took about ten minutes, but in short order, Karla sketched the outlines of those years as she had lived them. Went to college at Incarnate Word in San Antonio, worked as a high school counselor, a job she loved, lived six blocks from her parents, and so far had never married. But that was likely to change before long. "I've been dating the best man I've ever known, for the past two years. He's a veterinarian, has a small ranch, and…"

"And what?"

"He understands me and he makes me laugh. He's asked me to marry him every six months since we started seeing each other. He doesn't know it, but if he asks again next month, I may say yes."

"Being married's not always easy," Cheryl said. Karla didn't say anything. She was waiting. Something a good counselor would do, or a good friend. So Cheryl ran through the list of facts—college, job, location, husband.

"Is it worth the trouble?"

"Being married? It's complicated. But yes, it's worth it, with the right person." After a pause, she said, "I wondered…oh, never mind."

"What?" Karla asked. "What did you start to say?"

"To ask something." How could she, out of the blue after fourteen years, ask Karla if she still thought about those months at Anson Gleason? "But I'll wait until I see you. I will see you won't I?"

Cheryl felt herself relax when Karla said, "What about this

weekend? Can we meet somewhere? Ft. Worth?"

"Have you been back there?"

Karla's voice fell near a whisper. "No, but I think it's time."

Cheryl told herself, if she could survive being choked and held hostage, she could do anything. "Yes. We could check for flights to put us at DFW on Saturday sometime. Are you sure?"

"I'm sure I want to see you, talk with you."

They exchanged e-mail addresses and promised to make definite plans no later than Friday morning. Karla said, "There's one thing I want to tell you now, wanted to a long time ago. It may not mean anything to you, but it was important for me to hear it." Her voice had gotten soft again.

"Okay, tell me." Cheryl closed her eyes and recalled how it felt to have Karla and her baby sleeping behind her when she had felt so lost. Remembered the comfort of their friendship.

"For at least three years after I came home, I spent a lot of time making myself and my parents miserable. I won't go into it now, but I screwed up a lot." She hurried through an explanation of how she eventually met a counselor when she was in college. "What I wanted to tell you was the most important thing that counselor told me. He said, 'All these bad choices you make are ways of punishing yourself for a mistake you made when you were fifteen. Asking others, or God, to forgive you for that mistake, for being human, is your choice. But you will only be whole when you forgive yourself.' It was as if he'd handed me a key that let me back into a world where I could see colors and where I could stop defeating and punishing myself." She paused before she continued. "I wanted you to have that key, too."

Cheryl needed to hang up or she would spoil their visit by breaking down again. "Thank you. That means so much to me."

Before Cheryl could try to speak more, Karla said, "Count on me for email tomorrow morning."

Cheryl said, "I'm so glad I found you. I'll see you this weekend."

Ryder said he understood why she needed to go, and he drove her to the airport in Amarillo on Saturday morning. When he picked her up on Sunday night, he hugged her like she'd been gone a month. She saw him searching her face for a clue, making certain she was as okay as she'd told him she was before she left. He didn't ask, but she told him. "Seeing her, going back there, it's hard to explain, but I feel stronger, better now. I want you to meet her. You'll like her."

Ryder drove without talking. The silence on the trip home seemed right. It gave her time to think. Later, as they neared home, she said, "She wants me to be in her wedding, matron of honor."

"When's the wedding?"

Cheryl laughed. "She's waiting for him to ask her one more time before she says yes. It'll be the fifth time he's proposed, unless he's given up." After a few miles, she said, "She asked if I had any advice about being married."

"What did you tell her?" He reached for her left hand, gave it a squeeze.

"Said I wanted to think about it. Maybe you have some advice to give her, too."

The following Sunday, after spending the days cooking, cleaning, running, and letting Ryder hover over her, she felt like herself again. Or the other, stronger self she preferred. She told him she would go back to work the next morning.

During that time away from work, and after seeing Karla,

she had thought about a lot of things—how being in danger puts every small thing far into the background like in a snapshot of a pair of travelers, the figures out front in sharp focus and all the mountains or the amusement parks or crowds only a backdrop, how it makes you focus on what's really important to you. An answer came to her question of why until now she hadn't believed that Ryder was ever in love with her. She hadn't believed she was worth it, thought he didn't know who she really was.

There had been lots of thoughts about the future, how it didn't matter as much as the present. She intended to make every day the future of the day before and never let herself be anything other than grateful to be alive. She thought about saying those things out loud, to Ryder, but decided he would know without her telling him, because he would see and feel it all.

They sat down to supper. She'd cooked chicken fried steak and mashed potatoes and green beans and made a salad. And there was gravy, even though neither one of them needed it. Her Aunt Jean's recipe for devil's food cake furnished dessert.

Before they began eating, Ryder's cell phone rang. He frowned and muttered, "Don't they know it's suppertime?" His frown deepened after he answered and a few seconds later, said, "Yes, I'm his nephew." He listened a while longer, then said, "Tell him we're on our way. It'll take an hour and a half."

He told her Uncle Butch was in the hospital in Lubbock. Had been taken by ambulance from Muleshoe. "Must be serious or he wouldn't have let 'em take him."

She hoped he was wrong, but dreaded he might be correct. The last time they'd visited, when they took Thanksgiving dinner to him, she'd told Ryder she didn't like the way the old cowboy looked. "I'm sure he's losing weight and he seems weaker," she'd said. "He needs to see a doctor."

Neither of them speculated aloud as they drove toward the hospital in Lubbock. Somewhere close to Littlefield, Ryder said, "I sure hope it's not his time."

She said, "Maybe it's something simple. Maybe he took a fall and just needs to eat more. They'll check him out before they let him leave, regardless. Especially if you encourage him, tell him you want him to do what they say. What you think matters to him." A few miles later, she said, "He's a cowboy. One of the old kind. He's tough."

The people in Lubbock had put him in a bed on a step-down unit, monitoring his heart. Wearing oxygen cannulas in his nose, and lying against the white pillow and sheets, Uncle Butch looked pale and old. After Ryder and Cheryl let him know they were there, she stayed in the room, sitting by his bed, and Ryder went out to find out what he could from someone medical.

He got a little information from the nurse at the desk, surrounded by monitors, and some more from the doctor who turned up just as he'd about decided they'd have to wait until morning to get the full story. When the doctor explained the situation, Ryder felt himself sort of fold forward, like a kid does when he gets the air knocked out of him. He knew he'd breathe again, but wasn't sure how, or if it would be soon enough. He sat down and the doctor did too. She was a gray-haired woman with a kind face. Just seeing the concern in her eyes made him feel a little better. But the thought of leaving Uncle Butch seventy miles away from his own place and ninety from theirs worried him, even if she was a nice woman. He hadn't had much experience with hospitals, but even to him, young and in good health, it seemed like a dangerous place. Uncle Butch was old and sick. Ryder wanted someone there to watch out for his uncle every minute, until they could take him back home.

Maybe Cheryl could convince him he was worrying needlessly. He called her to come out of the room. Butch didn't need to hear all of this, sick as he looked. "That doctor," he pointed toward her sitting at a computer at the nurses' station, "is the one in charge of his case. She says he fell and was semi-conscious and nearly hypothermic when a friend found him. She thinks he probably needs a pacemaker and to be checked out for anemia." He shook his head, not to disagree, just to try to think clearly.

Cheryl said, "I'm going to stay here with him. Anyone in the hospital, especially an older person, needs someone watching. An advocate. That way you can get some rest and go on to work tomorrow." She nodded her head like it might convince him. No need. The knot that had balled up in his stomach released as soon as she finished talking.

"I know you'll do a better job at it than I would, but I feel responsible. He's my uncle."

She said, "*We're* responsible. Let me do this part. There'll be other things that only you can do."

Before he left, Ryder said, "I'll call you first thing in the morning. And I'll arrange to get off early so I can come back. What about your job?"

"I hadn't told them when I'd be back. I'll just leave things as they are; go back when this settles down."

He hugged her close and whispered he loved her. She told him she knew it, and she loved him, too. Driving back, alone, with the radio turned off, he had a feeling things would work out, just the way they were supposed to, but he wasn't sure how that might be.

Close to four a.m., Butch said, "Someone over there?"

Cheryl moved to his bedside from the recliner where she'd

been dozing. "Me, Cheryl. Been here all night. How you feeling?"

He lifted the cannulas from his nose and studied the plastic harness. "Oxygen?"

"Yes, they thought it would help. Anything hurt?"

"Sore all over. That's not unusual." He raised both hands and touched his head. "Think there's a knot somewhere up here."

"They said nothing was broken, nothing new. You had a lot of rodeo fractures, apparently."

"Yeah, I had some of those." He closed his eyes. She thought he might have drifted back to sleep. Without opening them, he said, "If it wasn't for that pup, I'd probably be dead right now."

"What pup?" There hadn't been any dog on the place when they visited at Thanksgiving. A stroke doesn't usually cause hallucinations. "Do you see the pup here in this room?"

He opened his eyes, then winked at her. "No dogs allowed in the hospital." He patted the hand she'd placed on his. "He's out at my place. A little heeler somebody dumped out, I reckon. Is this Monday?"

Cheryl relaxed a little. He was more aware than she'd thought. "It is. They brought you here to Lubbock yesterday." She watched him nod slightly.

"I fed the pup yesterday morning. He'll need to be seen about."

"I'll let Ryder know. He'll take care of it." She waited, watched him close his eyes again, holding onto her hand. "You might want to sleep some more before the doctors come. I'll be right here."

Uncle Butch's doctor, trailed by a kid she introduced as a medical student and a girl she said was a resident, appeared in the room at seven a.m. on the dot. The doctor said, "Good news, Mr.

Sheldon. We looked at the pictures of your skull and brain we took when you got here. That's all fine. No stroke, nothing fractured. But we do need to give your heart some help. A pacemaker, so it will beat often enough to get plenty of blood to your brain. We get that working, you'll feel lots better."

"Think I'll be good for a few more miles?"

She said, "I do. Are you up to hearing about how we put in a pacemaker?"

The doctor explained about the procedure and the hardware. Cheryl thought she breezed through it a little too fast for Butch to fully understand. Then the resident examined him and said aloud what she would record, so the student could hear. She turned to the doctor, as if the exam were over. Cheryl walked to the bed and pulled the sheet up from the bottom so her patient's feet were visible. "You'll probably want to document the extent of pedal edema, too."

The resident glanced at the doctor, then pushed her index finger against the top of each of Butch's swollen feet. She said to the student, "That's one plus pitting edema." To Cheryl she said, "Thank you. I should have included that." Sounded as if she meant it.

The doctor beckoned to Cheryl from near the door. "You work in health care?"

"I'm a nurse. His niece by marriage."

"I'm glad you're here. The pacemaker's going to be essential. I'll come back at noon to get a permit signed, if he agrees. Do you have questions?"

Cheryl shook her head. "I'll go over it again with him. If he has concerns, I'll let you know."

She straightened the sheets on Butch's bed and helped him find a comfortable position. When she asked, he agreed he could use something for the soreness. "All over my body," he said. She managed to get a nurse to bring acetaminophen and encouraged him to drink some water. When his breakfast tray came, he ate a little of everything on the plate, and drank the coffee. He said, "I've had worse coffee. But I don't recall when."

Not long after he ate, he closed his eyes. In seconds, soft snoring told Cheryl he'd drifted to sleep. She walked into the hall and called Ryder. She explained about the pacemaker and Butch's concern about a pup that needed feeding. She told him tending to the dog would be as important to Butch as getting the pacemaker. Ryder said he'd take care of everything and promised he'd be at the hospital by one.

She heard voices from Butch's room. He'd found the switch and turned on the television. Staring up at the wall-mounted set, he said, "You reckon they have the Rodeo Channel here?"

After switching through several stations, he turned the set off. "What do you think I ought to do?" he asked.

"Lots of people have pacemakers and they help them feel better and live longer."

"I'd hate to be a burden, to not be able to do for myself after that."

"You'd be less likely to need taking care of if you have the pacemaker than if you don't. Everything—brain, muscles, digestion—works better when your heart pumps correctly."

"Looks to me like it quit beating. Doesn't that mean it's time for me to give up the ghost?"

She told him his heart didn't quit, just got erratic and slow, even though his question made perfect sense to her—what message do we get that tells us it's time to die?

He said, "Maybe that's why that dog came up. If he hadn't been there, licking on my face, yipping in my ear, I'd probably have just let go, gone on. It got damn cold laying out there."

She didn't say any more. He closed his eyes again.

When Ryder got there, Butch's first question was about the dog. Ryder assured him he'd been fed and was outside in the pickup. "Looks like a good little dog. Real young."

Butch perked up. He said, "I hear I'm going to get a new battery. What do you think about that?"

"I think it's a good idea," Ryder said.

Four days later, with a heartbeat the doctor pronounced normal, Butch was ready to leave the hospital. In the hall, Cheryl, who hadn't left the entire time, and Ryder, had come up with a plan. Uncle Butch and Speck, the name he'd given to the spotted heeler pup, would come to their house and stay. After that, they'd all three decide on a more permanent arrangement. Ryder said, "Think he'll go for it?"

"He likes my cooking. Maybe that will be enough to convince him."

"He won't want to be any trouble. He's been on his own a lot of years." Ryder thought if anyone could talk him into it, she'd be the one to do it. But it wouldn't be because of the food.

Last night, he'd seen his uncle hanging on to her hand when she sat in the chair by his bed, and watched him relax when she rubbed his back and talked to him about how she liked the way puppies' breath smelled and about enjoying going to ropings, and telling him her plan to grow a garden someday. She said she'd plant tomatoes and peppers and squash. With marigolds and hollyhocks around the edge.

"My mother used to grow hollyhocks," Butch had said. Then he'd gone to sleep again.

CHAPTER 18

January 25, 2009—The Sheldons

New Year

Cheryl stood looking at the three large cardboard boxes of Christmas decorations. She parked them in the utility room when she took the tree down January sixth. She remembered the date because in the middle of packing them, thinking about the start of another year, she made a big decision. The odd thing was that she hadn't even been conscious of thinking seriously on the subject. As if some unseen force sent her a message to which she must respond immediately, she had walked to the telephone, a string of tinsel garland draped around her neck, and called her supervisor in Emergency at the hospital in Amarillo. "I won't be able to come back to work on the weekends. My family situation has changed. I'm needed here."

The woman had tried to convince Cheryl to wait a while, just be left off the schedule until she could come back. That would have made changing her mind easy. She said, "I'm sorry. I have to do this now." Then she asked whom to address her resignation letter to and where to send it. When she lifted the tinsel garland from her neck, a weight went with it.

After they brought Uncle Butch and Speck to the house, everything changed. Each afternoon, the pup greeted her before she stepped on the porch. No matter what the weather, he and Butch waited for her there. The aroma of fresh coffee, boiled the cowboy way, encouraged her to visit and rest a bit before thinking about cooking supper. And when Ryder returned in the evenings, the pup celebrated by racing around his boots, jumping on his pants leg. No matter how tired Ryder was, he pretended to race Speck to the porch while she and Butch cheered them on.

Even though she still flinched each morning when she heard the locks close behind her at the prison, coming in from work to a no-longer-vacant house, seeing Butch gain weight, and watching his energy return, rewarded her. It seemed like a family lived there. Like most homes, it wasn't perfect by a long sight—Ryder still worried about money and lack of moisture—she sometimes woke in the night, startled by an arm gripped around her neck, by a phantom whiff of tequila, her mother calling her name—the pup gnawed a fretwork pattern around the edge of a leg on the dining room table one afternoon as Butch napped—but she knew that what she felt there now was happiness.

Until this year, they hadn't decorated at the holidays, never even a Christmas tree. Putting things up just to take them down a few days later seemed sort of pointless—Ryder said that the first December they were married. She hadn't argued; he'd said aloud what she'd thought. Besides, they had always traveled to see family if the December weather allowed. This year, the first week Butch was with them, while Ryder was on the phone giving his mother an update on their patient, Cheryl whispered to him, "Ask them to come here for Christmas dinner. We'll invite everyone." He stopped talking, raised and eyebrow and cocked his head, then shrugged and passed the message to his mother.

Two days later, they had yeses for seven guests. She, Ryder, and Butch spent two evenings putting up and decorating a tree. Planning the menu made her feel like a hostess. By ten on Christmas morning, her dad, both her sisters, Aunt Jean and Uncle Skip, and Ryder's mother and her husband arrived. Their three additional vehicles crowded the drive. Several wrapped packages they brought plus those from Cheryl's shopping trip filled the space under the tree. Her sisters, both now out of their teens and in college, helped her finish cooking the meal she'd begun the night before. Aromas of roasting turkey and dressing, sweet potatoes, and pecan pie lured everyone to the table.

Her sisters volunteered to help with clean up. When it was just the three of them in the kitchen, Lynette told her their dad had a girlfriend. Cheryl looked up from scrubbing the roasting pan. "What do you think about that?"

Lynette shrugged. "She's a nice woman, a widow. You should see them together. Cute."

Beth focused her attention on drying the sweet potato casserole dish.

Cheryl said, "He hasn't mentioned it to me at all." She talked to him at least once a month. "Think it's serious?"

Beth found a spot on a high shelf for the casserole dish. She closed the cabinet door. "I hope so."

Cheryl scrubbed the final speck from the roaster and placed it in the dish drainer. "That takes care of everything."

After the others left that evening, Butch told her and Ryder he couldn't remember when he'd had a nicer time at Christmas. When he said that, Cheryl decided to leave the tree up for a few days. If Speck hadn't tried to eat the garland and knock off the colored balls, it might still be standing. That night, in bed, Ryder said, "You worked hard making it a good day for all of us." She moved closer to put her head on his chest. He said, "In case I haven't mentioned it lately, I'm glad you're my wife." No dreams woke her that night.

Coming in the back door, Cheryl heard Butch speaking to her from the living room, starting up as if they were in the same room, in the middle of a conversation. He said, "I've been thinking. It's about time for me to get back to my place. Don't want to wear out my welcome."

She stopped in the kitchen and said, loudly, so he'd hear, "Just a minute. I'm going to wash my hands." She'd come in from taking the Christmas decorations out to the garage, a place she never attempted to clean. Fitting the boxes on a shelf there left her grimy. She went to the living room, wiping her hands on a kitchen towel. "Now what's this about wearing out your welcome?"

His place needed seeing after, someone to be there, he told her—check the house, be sure the heater kept running so the pipes wouldn't freeze, things like that.

"Who'll make me cowboy coffee in the evening?" She made a big frown in his direction, made sure he saw it, and tried to think how she might convince him to stay.

"That could be a problem. Mine's probably is the best you'll ever get." He leaned back against the couch cushions, put his feet on the ottoman she'd bought for him. "I'm pretty sure you and Ryder don't need me supervising you."

"And you know you don't need any more looking after, right?" Now that he felt better, getting him to stay was going to require some fast talking. "I'm just beginning to get some meat back on you. Regular meals. I'd consider a favor to me if you'd stay a while longer."

He shrugged. "This dog's gettin' in the way, too. Needs to learn to sleep outside." Speck raised his head and wagged his tail when Butch pointed toward him.

"He's just a puppy. It's cold." She would miss the dog nearly as much as she would Butch.

She sat in the chair across from him, leaned forward. "Seriously, I want you to be as well as you can be before you leave here. Your hemoglobin is coming back up, but the doctor said you're still anemic." She patted his knee. "Would you think about staying a while longer, not decide until tomorrow, anyway?"

He nodded. "It'd be an imposition. Me staying much longer."

"Is it me? Do I make too much noise?"

Butch laughed, a single, "Ha." Then he said, "Hardly. Near deaf as I am, I couldn't hear it thunder. Not that it ever does."

"I'll be back in a minute. You want the remote?"

He took the control she offered and concentrated on changing channels. Since he'd been at their house, he'd figured out how to find the bull riding from McKinney, Texas, shown at several times each day.

Ryder stood inside the barn with his back to the door, grooming his horse to the sound of country classics coming from an old transistor radio. He dropped his currycomb, startled by a touch on his shoulder. Before he could turn around, Cheryl kissed him on the back of his neck, and finished by running her tongue from there to his right ear. Goose bumps paraded down his right arm. He reached to grab her. "Hey, my wife won't like it if she finds out some woman's kissing my neck in the barn."

"Then we won't tell her." She backed away, just beyond his hand, laughing.

"What's up?" He resumed brushing the horse.

Cheryl watched a muscle ripple the length of the animal's back as Ryder stroked his spine. "Butch is talking about going back to his place."

"You think it's too soon?"

She nodded, stared at the floor.

"For him or for you?"

"Both." She shook her head. "Me, mostly."

The tiny wrinkle between her eyes told him the subject pained her. He said, "Tell you what—soon as I finish here, I'll come in and see if he wants take a ride over there this afternoon. All of us."

"What do you think?"

"I don't think he needs to be living by himself. Not anymore. But I also don't think that's entirely up to us."

He let the horse into his stall. "This is a good horse." He turned to Cheryl. "That place of his is real important to him. He may not be ready to admit it's time to leave there." They walked toward the house, side by side. "I don't think we ought to try to make him do what he doesn't want to."

"I just want to be sure he knows he's not any trouble here with us. And that we mean it when we say we want him to stay."

Ryder watched his wife move efficiently around the kitchen putting together a meal they could have as supper before they returned. As soon as Butch agreed to the trip, she'd started making sandwiches. Now the cooler held all they'd need, including half of an apple pie.

"I'm sure glad that swelling in my feet went down. Thought I'd have to give up on these boots." His uncle pulled on the left one. "What about the dog?"

"Far as I'm concerned, he can come along." Ryder figured that would suit both Butch and the dog just fine. He saw, from her profile, Cheryl smiling at that exchange. It seemed to him she truly meant it when she said she'd be happy if Butch lived with them. But then she seldom said things she didn't mean.

None of them talked much on the way to Muleshoe. Speck rode calmly in Butch's lap in the back seat. As they headed south out of town, Butch said, "Cheryl, you never have seen the whole place. Want to take a look when we get there?"

"I'd like that." Men and the land they got tied to made her wish she really understood how it felt—to want to take care of a place and watch it flourish, to turn it into something better. Her dad didn't own the land he farmed and never took on a lot of acres. For him, farming was a way to work outside and add a little to the income he made as a mechanic; she'd heard him say he pitied the guys with land payments, but loved to have an excuse to work in the sunshine.

As they neared the road to turn west toward his place, Butch said, "Notice how the land looks different here, more little hills. Well, the soil's different too. Better for raising grass instead of crops. One of the reasons I bought the first half section back in the fifties. Never was too interested in driving a tractor."

She turned in the seat and watched Butch as he looked intently at the land on either side of the road. "Water's pretty good out here. I put in new pumps on my house well and the stock wells a few years back." He sounded like a real estate salesman. Pointing out the best features. Coming out here was good for him. Maybe he'd be willing to stay put with them for a while after he'd seen everything.

As soon as Ryder stopped the pickup and opened the doors, Speck hit the ground running, stopping to mark every pole and bush in the vicinity of the house. Then he collapsed, panting, on the porch. They took the food inside and when they got in, Butch walked slowly through each room, opened and closed the refrigerator and its freezer. "Looks like everything's working okay." He turned on the faucets and let them run and she heard him flush the commode. He came into the kitchen where she was putting the food in the refrigerator. He asked, "Need to rest or are you ready to see the place?"

He had a purpose, but she hadn't yet figured out what it was. "I'm ready."

As they rode the mile-long east perimeter of Butch's property, he told about buying the front 320 the first year he won Best All Around Cowboy, 1950. "Twenty-four years old and I was riding high, had visions of staying on top for about five years and then setting myself up in a big ranching operation." He leaned forward from the back seat and said to Cheryl, "I learned pretty fast that there's lots of others dreaming the same dreams and staying on top is harder than getting there." Ryder had heard that same story when he was a kid. Now he understood what it meant a lot better than he had then.

Butch pointed out that the fences were all in good repair. "I done a lot of that work myself. Fixing fence isn't cowboying, but it's damn sure part of ranching." They passed a long stretch, maybe a quarter mile, of mesquite. Butch shook his head and didn't say anything.

Ryder said, "You taught me when I was about twelve how to mend fence right down there." He pointed to the four strands of barbed wire stretched between weathered cedar posts to their left. Set me out with a box of staples and a fence tool and took my horse with you. Only way to get it back was to finish the job." Butch looked toward the fence and smiled as if he saw the whole scene replaying.

Ryder drove on. Butch said, "You always did a good job. Whatever I tried to teach you."

When they reached the south fence line, Ryder turned right and drove slowly as the road crawled up a slight hill. Butch said, "Keep your eyes open for a surprise." Ryder crept along for a half mile. The road leveled briefly, then dipped slightly. Off to his right, he saw an earthen dam across the little creek that had sometimes run through the draw. He stopped the pickup. "Well now. That's something you don't see too much around here. Catch any water?"

"You two take a look and tell me. I'll sit here."

Cheryl asked, "You feeling okay?"

"Sure am. Go on down there with him. We don't want him to get lost."

The stock tank had been built in exactly the right spot. Hard to tell how deep it was, but water stood within two feet of the top of the dam and extended for about twenty by fifty feet in a long thin strip of water. Trouble was, this tank had been in place long enough for some mesquite to start growing into the bank. It would need work. Ryder said to Cheryl, "This is worth a lot, if a person was raising livestock."

When they got back to the pickup, he asked Butch when he'd had the dirt work done. He could tell his uncle was proud of the tank.

Butch said, "Government program a few years back. Cost share saved me a lot of money. It'd come in handy if I ever had any calves grazing out here."

Cheryl felt a warmth in her chest as she listened to them talk and saw Ryder's glances toward Butch—intent, not about to miss a bit of wisdom from a respected teacher.

A fence running north to south stopped their progress. She offered to open the gate. Ryder said, "Go ahead and close it when we get past." The gate had been made of fence wire, four barbed strands, with a fixed post on one end, a support post in the middle and a final post that fit into two wire hoop latches attached to the end of the other fence. Getting it closed took a hefty pull. She looked up and saw Ryder watching her in the side mirror as she wrapped her left arm around the top of the post and used her body weight as leverage to hitch it close enough to fit under the latch.

Back in the pickup, Butch pointed a thumb at her and said, "She'd make some rancher a good hand. Knows how to close a gate." They continued slowly driving west. Brown clumps covered the ground without any interference from mesquite or other trees. Those clumps, thick with thatch from last summer's growth, showed the native grass remained healthy. Butch waved a hand toward the park-like expanse. "Any rain or snow at all and this will green up nice come summer." She watched Ryder's face and wondered what he was thinking.

"From that gate back yonder, down to the next fence, this is the second half-section I bought. Got it in fifty-five. Mainly wanted this big pasture and I like that the boundary is straight as a string. Not a foot of this ground's ever been broke out. That's why the grass is so good." Butch paused as a jackrabbit zigzagged away from them. "All these fences are in good shape." He pointed at the jackrabbit as its path straightened. "He's headed to New Mexico. It's just fifteen miles that direction." Ryder wished now he'd taken his time more when he came out here with Butch the past few years. He had reason to be proud of his place, and nobody to show it to.

When they reached the western boundary, Ryder turned north and drove on slowly, close to the fence. The pale winter sun glinted off the blades of a large windmill as they turned lazily in the intermittent breeze. Ryder said, "You must have put that tank and windmill up after I left for college." Butch nodded and told him it was in 1995. A half-mile later, Ryder stopped below the windmill, near the stock tank it fed. He got out of the pickup, walked slowly around the tank, wondering what else he'd missed.

At the north fence, after Ryder turned right again, to make the last leg of a full circuit around the rectangular property, Cheryl turned so Butch could hear her. She said, "I can see why you like to keep an eye on this place. It's beautiful." His smile told her she'd said the right thing.

Speck roused from his nap in Butch's lap, shaking his head like he'd been in deep sleep. He stepped across Butch's legs to stand with his nose to the back window. Butch patted his head and told him he'd be able to get out soon.

Nearer the house, he said, "You might like this story, Cheryl. Fact is, I don't know if you know this either, Ryder. How I got that second piece of land. It was the second, also the last, year I was Best All Around. I came home with money burning a hole in my pocket. And wouldn't you know, there were people waiting, ready to relieve me of it. First there was a neighbor thinking to sell out." He pointed west. "But I wasn't too sure about that, thought he was asking too much an acre.

"Then there were a couple of widows, grass widows, if I recall, interested in finding a husband." He paused and smiled like he might be recalling the divorcees. "And then a wildcatter came to town, saying he was going to deep drill some of those old shallow wells around Sundown. It had been a big boomtown back in the late twenties. My, he was convincing—promising a sure pay off, willing to sell big royalty percentages for small investment, and carrying a briefcase full of seismograph logs. Laid out those logs on a table at the café, pointed to a lot of lines that told him there was still lots of oil down below.

"Give me a couple of weeks to consider it, I told him." He paused again, then said to Cheryl, as if the conversation was between them alone, "Give you three guesses what I did."

"Bought the land, but only after negotiating the price down?"

"Nope, I gambled. Threw in with the wildcatter, almost everything I had." He sat back like he'd finished the tale. Cheryl watched Ryder's face. She knew he wouldn't be happy until he heard the rest, but wouldn't get it out of Butch unless he asked. Storytellers like Butch never gave away their ending too soon.

Back at the house, liberated from the pickup, Speck made another circuit of everything that was standing still, raising a leg to pee so often he started wobbling when he did. Cheryl followed Butch as he ambled past the corral toward the barn. He said, "What do you think about that piece of ground over yonder for a garden?"

"You must be feeling lots better, thinking about gardening. Looks good, close to the faucet, and you said your well is strong." She walked to the space he'd pointed to. "I think the sun here would be right for the plants in the mornings and when summer comes, the barn will make some shade in the hottest part of the day." She hoped he would be strong enough by May to do some gardening.

With the three of them at the table, eating, Ryder said, "I never did hear that story before, about the wildcatter. How did it end up?"

He watched his uncle push back from the table and raise a finger in Speck's direction. When the dog trotted to the table, Butch tossed him a small bit of crust from the last of his sandwich. He dusted his hands together, then leaned forward and put both elbows on the table. "I'll tell you, it was the best gamble I ever took. That old boy drilled four wells and every one of them struck. Doubled my money, first off, so I turned around and dickered down the price of that land and bought it. The royalty checks came in real regular for quite a few years. Now I see one every three or six months, depends. But I don't require much, neither. Nice little cushion to go with my Social Security."

Ryder sat back, shaking his head. "I knew you were lucky, but I never knew how lucky. You made a couple of mighty good bargains back then." He watched Cheryl taking it all in, not saying a word. He asked her, "We saving that pie for a different day?"

She said, "I'll make coffee and clear this away. You two relax a few minutes."

When she called them back to the table for coffee and pie, Butch cut the triangular tip off his piece and speared it with his fork, held it above his plate. He cleared his throat and said, "Now that you know I'm good at making bargains, I have a proposition for y'all to think about."

Here it comes, Ryder thought, his plan to convince them he should move back here. Cheryl would be even more disappointed than he would. He didn't say anything, just put his fork on his plate. Cheryl held her coffee cup part way to the saucer.

Butch looked directly at Ryder. "I suppose you know you're as close to a son as I could have. A long time ago, I made a will and put you as my heir for this place. That's why I wanted you to see all of it before I brought this up."

Ryder took a deep breath. He'd never allowed himself to think of Butch dying, even when he saw him in the hospital, much less thinking about what would happen to his property.

Butch ate the point of his pie slice. "Now that you and Cheryl are married, and I know her, I'd tell anyone I met that if I chose a daughter, she'd be the one." He ate another small piece of pie, then took a sip of coffee. "So here's the proposition. I'll stay at your place as long as you want me to if you'll figure out how all of us can live out here together. Since this is going to be yours someday, you might as well have it to work now instead of later."

He held up a finger. "Before you say anything, I know it'd take a while to figure out—changing jobs, selling your place, things like that. Speaking of which, how much equity do you have there?"

Ryder held his left thumb and forefinger a half inch apart and said, "About that much." He saw Cheryl studying his reaction, wondered what showed. He knew what he'd say if he was single. But they were a pair and this was a decision for both of them to make. "If it sold for what it's appraised at, what I'm, we're, paying taxes on, we might come out about even."

Butch nodded. "Another thing to think about—you need your privacy. This house could be built onto, or a little one for me put out back." He smiled like he had a secret. "That's easy enough to take care of. That oil company's been better to me than I needed for many a year. Like I said, I don't spend much."

Ryder watched Cheryl's face. She said to Butch, "You've been thinking about this for a long time, haven't you?"

"A while."

"All that time, I thought you were watching the bull riding."

"Most of that's reruns. I know who wins." He laughed at his own joke. "You don't need to give me an answer now. Just promise me you'll think about it." He took a deep breath. "Well, it's getting dark. About time for us to head back, I guess."

While they loaded the cooler in the pickup, Speck pestered Ryder, skittering around his legs, nipping at his pants. Then he sped off toward the corrals, chasing something only he could see. Butch watched like an indulgent parent. He said, "He's a good pup. Be good for a kid to grow up with." He whistled and the dog immediately raced back and hopped in the truck.

Ryder drove toward the front gate. As the tires bumped over the cattle guard, Butch said, "I sure did enjoy this day. Thanks, you two." Before they'd gone five miles, he was snoring quietly, the dog asleep in his lap.

Cheryl reached to Ryder and put her left hand in his right. He lifted it and kissed it, and kept holding on. He said, "It could work, maybe." After a few more miles, he said, "We have a lot to talk about. Living arrangements, work, selling the other place."

"There's something else, too."

"Like what?"

"We'll get to it." She smiled and leaned forward to adjust the heater control.

They passed through the double curve and entered a long, straight stretch of highway. Ryder leaned back in the seat, pushed his hat off his forehead.

"You thinking about something in particular?" she asked.

He nodded, leaned forward like the empty road required concentration. "I've been thinking about when your friend Karla asked for advice about being married." He glanced Cheryl's direction. His voice soft, his words coming slowly, he said, "People need to consider how cattle are, what they do when a storm comes up. Cattle turn away from the wind and put their heads down, like getting away is the only way to stay safe, move ahead of the wind and just keep moving. They'll break down fences to keep going away. That's why they have to be tended to every day, reminded where home is. Otherwise, when a storm comes they end up drifting—ordinarily they stay herded up, but in a storm they'll drift, end up lost, far apart, hurt. I think that can happen to people when they're married, if they don't tend to each other.

Cattle don't know any better. People should."

Cheryl didn't speak for several miles. Then she said, "That's good advice. I'll tell her." A few minutes passed with the only sounds in the vehicle the low hum of the heater and Butch's occasional snores. She said, "I wish it hadn't taken me so long to learn that."

"Me, too." He raised an eyebrow like he sometimes did when he joked, but his voice sounded serious. He said, "Seems like we figured it out together. About the same time."

They passed through Muleshoe and into open country, moving steadily toward home. He sighed in a way she thought sounded satisfied. He said, "This has been a good day."

She reached to hold his right hand again. "I can't remember a better one."

CONNECT WITH THE AUTHOR

For more information about the author or to contact her about presentations and book signing events, please visit www.tjoneswrites.com and http://facebook.com/welltended."